Minds That Hate

Minds That Hate

Author's Presentation Copy,

Bill Kitson

For Carol & Ed,
With thanks for your continued support &
encouragement. Who'd have thought when
you lent me that "steam-driven" computer
it would have led to this!
Love to you both,
Bill Kitson

JULY 2010

ROBERT HALE · LONDON

ISBN 978-0-7090-9049-6

Robert Hale Limited
Clerkenwell House
Clerkenwell Green
London EC1R 0HT

www.halebooks.com

2 4 6 8 10 9 7 5 3 1

Typeset in 10/13pt Palatino
Printed in Great Britain by the MPG Books Group,
Bodmin and King's Lynn

For Val

Wife, lover, best friend, critic and editor.

acknowledgements

A lot of people helped to turn my error-strewn manuscript into the finished volume you are holding. For their input, however great or small, I am truly grateful.

I'd like to thank Pat Almond and Cath Brockhill, for reading the original, unedited work and giving their opinion.

To my wife Val, for her patient reading, proof-reading, continuity and copy-editing.

To Derek Colligan, whose awesome artistic talent has provided stunning jacket images for all three of the Mike Nash books.

To John Hale and his staff whose professionalism and patience I must test on an almost daily basis. How they must enjoy their weekends.

To Zoe Sharp, for her timely advice on copyright.

chapter one

The moorland road was little used. Grass had encroached onto the middle of the tarmac as it meandered between scrubby banks of heather and gorse. Sheep strayed across, unfettered by walls, unthreatened by vehicles. The scenery was spectacular, savage and untamed. The only sign of human influence was a stationary car. Inside the vehicle, the encounter was over. The couple struggled to dress. As they wrestled with recalcitrant clothing, they talked.

'I've had news from Felling.'

She didn't need to ask who or what Felling was. She knew, only too well. 'And?'

'Three months from now.'

'God, that's soon. Why isn't it longer?'

'That's how it works.'

'It doesn't give us much time.'

'There's worse. He's coming here.'

She stared, disbelieving. 'I thought that wasn't allowed?'

'They can't stop him.'

'Aren't there rules?'

'They can't enforce them. He still owns the house.'

'There'll be trouble.'

The man drew a sharp breath. 'If not, we're going to have to cause some.'

'That won't be difficult.'

'We should start immediately.'

Her eyes were cold as she stated flatly, 'He ought to be dead.'

'He soon will be. He'll be easier to get at outside.'

'Will this interfere with your plans?'

'On the contrary. We can kill two birds with one stone, so to speak.'

She shivered, but it was a shiver neither of cold nor fear. It was the thrill she got from the power he exuded. She wriggled closer. 'Tell me what you have in mind.'

DI Mike Nash woke early. Last night had been a hell of a party. Maria had wanted Gino's birthday celebrated properly. Not a problem for the owners of a restaurant.

Nash had drunk too much. Discomfort in his bladder told him so. That he could deal with; the hangover wouldn't be as simple.

He tried to recall how the evening had ended. Gino had introduced him to someone; he'd been talking to them. Who was it?

This thought disturbed him. He moved his leg. It brushed against something. Flesh! Nash panicked momentarily. As if alarm was contagious, the person alongside him moved slightly. Again he felt their skin against his leg.

He eased himself out of bed and groped his way to the shower room, switched the light on and looked back.

She was lying face down. The sheet did little to cover her. Nash admired her figure, the warm tones of her skin, her lustrous long dark hair across the pillow. He fought against his rising excitement.

She was undoubtedly young; appeared to be good-looking. She'd obviously come home with him. Equally obviously, they'd gone to bed together. The next question was far trickier. Who was she?

He returned to the bedroom. His earlier guess had been inaccurate. She wasn't good-looking. She was stunning. An image flashed through his brain. She'd been standing next to the bar, tall, elegantly dressed, laughing at some remark of Gino's. As she turned, she'd made eye contact with Nash.

He stretched out alongside her. The touch of her skin completed his arousal.

'Hello, Michael,' her voice, heavy with drowsiness, was husky with passion.

He put his hand on her waist and began to caress her. Even as they made love, one problem remained. He couldn't remember her name.

It was late when he woke again. There was a note on the pillow. 'Michael, had to go to work. Thanks for a wonderful night. Will call you. X.'

He appreciated the note, but her name would have been helpful. His glance strayed to the clock. 9.05. Nash groaned: he'd a meeting at ten. Where was Clara? As if in answer, the doorbell rang. He staggered out of bed and stubbed his toe. Swearing loudly, he struggled into his dressing gown and hobbled to the door.

'Christ, Mike! You alright? You look like death warmed up.'

'Thank you, Sergeant Mironova, and good morning to you. Come in. You make coffee whilst I grab a shower.'

'I'd better make it black, to match your eyes.'

'Don't be bloody cheeky,' he snapped.

Minutes later, Clara was seated at the kitchen table. Nash had showered, but still looked terrible. 'I hope you haven't been having nightmares again,' she asked.

'No, thank God. The doctor reckoned they were caused by mixing my medication with alcohol. One of the two had to go.'

'It's obvious which you chose.' Mironova glanced at the clock. 'We'd better go or we'll be late. Any idea why we're wanted?'

'None, but Tom implied it might be serious.'

Clara drove them to Netherdale, where Superintendent Tom Pratt was based. During the journey she continued her interrogation.

'What was it? A late session at The Horse and Jockey or have you been on the nest? If I'd to guess, I'd say you've been at it all night. You look shagged out.'

'I like the delicate, polite way you express yourself.'

Clara grinned. 'Who is it? Anyone I know?'

'I'm not sure.'

'You're not sure whether I know her, or you're not sure who she is?' There was a long silence. She laughed. 'You're the last of the great romantics. You mean to tell me you picked a girl up, took her home, and you don't even know her name?'

'I'm not aware that I told you anything,' Nash muttered. 'Anyway, it wasn't like that.'

Clara bit her lip. 'Go on, Mike, tell me what it was like.'

Despite severe provocation, Nash remained silent for the rest of the journey.

'Morning, Mike. You look a bit rough. Are you OK?'

'Tom, don't! I'd enough problems with Clara. Any more lip from her and I'll be tempted to send her back to Belarus.'

Mironova grinned unrepentantly.

'What's the panic about?' Nash asked.

'I had a call from the governor of Felling Prison. They've a prisoner coming up for release and it could mean trouble.'

'Who is he?'

'His name's Vickers. I've read the case notes: very nasty.'

'What's he in for?'

'He raped and murdered the daughter of his live-in lover. He got life, but he'll be out in three months.'

'Was it round here?'

'Yes, they lived in Helmsdale. Her body was found in the woods by the banks of the Helm.'

'They'll not let him come back here, surely?' Mironova interjected.

'He insists on coming back.'

'I thought they could block that?'

'The trouble is, Vickers isn't dependant on housing or social services. He's got money and he owns a house.' Pratt paused before adding, 'On Grove Road.'

'Grove Road? That's on the edge of the Westlea.'

Nash knew there was more. 'You'd better tell us the rest,' he prompted.

'The girl Vickers murdered....' Pratt cleared his throat. 'She was Jake and Ronnie Fletcher's niece.'

'Oh hell, they'll fillet the bastard!' Mironova muttered.

'There've already been death threats. The governor told me they're all postmarked from round here. He was attacked several times. The worst was a stabbing that nearly finished him off. The governor suspects someone might have bribed inmates to have a go. Strangely, they stopped after a few months.'

'I wonder why he insists on returning? If he'd any sense, he'd stay well clear,' Nash said.

'We've got three months to dream up a strategy to keep him alive. Vickers always maintained he didn't kill the girl. Complete nonsense of course, the forensic evidence puts it beyond doubt. He didn't defend himself at his trial; in fact, he didn't say anything. I want you to study the file. Maybe go to Felling as well.' He looked across at Nash. 'Persuade Vickers to think again. Suggest he goes elsewhere. Tell him if he returns to Helmsdale we don't give much for his chance of survival.'

The Wagon and Horses was built during the 1960s. It was ugly, and looked dated before the paint dried. Time frequently softens the harsh lines of a building: here, time failed miserably. Not that the regulars cared. Had the beer been sour or the lager flat, that would have been different. The room was busy, as befitted a Friday night. The atmosphere was heavy with cigarette smoke and other more exotic aromas, despite the government ban on smoking.

The corner seat was occupied by a well-known trio. Well-known and feared. There were a few hard men in the bar, yet Jake and Ronnie Fletcher were of a different calibre. If Gemma Fletcher wasn't feared like her brothers, she was equally respected.

Gemma outlined her problem. Ronnie was all for direct action. That was typical. His rash nature had landed him in trouble several times, one resulting in a custodial sentence. Gemma wasn't prepared to risk that. 'You can't, Ronnie,' she objected. 'I'm not having you sent down over that pillock.'

Jake represented a more chilling threat. Hatred quivered through his voice. 'No, Gem, we've got to finish him. If the law won't, it's up to us. We'll make him suffer. When I think of our Stacey—'

'Leave me alone with the twat,' Ronnie growled. 'I'll deliver his bollocks on a platter.'

'Listen,' Gemma insisted, 'I'm not risking either of you going inside. We need another way. And I think I know one.'

'It'd better be good, Gem,' Jake muttered angrily.

'We're all agreed as to what we want, right?'

The brothers nodded.

'Anything happens to him, they'll automatically suspect us.' She didn't have to explain who 'they' were. 'Here's what I suggest.'

Jake and Ronnie listened with admiration. There was no doubt it would work. But then, Gemma had always been the brightest. That's why she'd made a successful career in advertising, whilst they sweated and toiled as jobbing builders.

'That's brilliant, Gem, but who's going to do it?' Ronnie was keen to know.

'I thought Danny and the Juniors might be up for it.'

Jake whistled. 'Christ, Gem, that's genius. With Danny on our side, think what his brother Billy might do.'

Ronnie agreed. 'Given half a chance, Billy'd have the whole town in ashes.'

'I'll buy him the petrol and matches,' Jake agreed. 'When do you want to start?'

'Straightaway.'

'But you said he wasn't due out for three months.'

'If we start now, there's a chance our incident will be passed over as part of it. *"Oh dear, what a bleeding shame. Not to worry, he won't be missed".'*

'If Danny and the Juniors get going, there'll be bloody riots.'

'Don't you see? That's what we're after.'

When Gemma left, she was satisfied her brothers would already be implementing the plan. She climbed into her car, and reached for her mobile.

'It's me,' she said. 'Can you talk?'

'Yes. How did it go?'

'Fine. I told you it would. What about your end?'

'I've a meeting tomorrow. I'll know better after that. I'll ring you when I'm sure.'

chapter two

JT Tucker's work was read wider than the circulation of the *Netherdale Gazette*: syndication took it throughout the north of England. Tucker was in the graveyard, the basement where old copies were stored. Computerization hadn't reached the repository of the newspaper. Researchers still had to wade through files of back numbers.

Although Tucker churned out weekly articles of general interest, he occasionally produced excellent pieces of investigative journalism. He'd a keen nose for impropriety. This, combined with his contacts, a good memory, and hours of research, led him to uncover misdeeds which many would have preferred to remain unearthed.

His articles had caused ripples within local politics, business and even the church. Tucker was on the scent of another such scandal. So far the aroma was faint but to Tucker, unmistakable. Time and patient probing could cause the stench to ripen.

On the desk were back numbers of the *Gazette*, folded to reveal two articles on the same topic.

Thursday 12 August 1993

Police confirmed today that the body discovered in remote woodland was that of missing photography student, Stacey Fletcher. Forensic examination would be needed to establish how she died.

Tuesday 8 March 1994

A jury at Netherdale Crown Court today convicted Gary Vickers, a twenty-five-year-old graphic artist, of the rape and murder of his lover's daughter. The body of twenty-year-old Stacey Fletcher was found in Helm Woods last August. She had been sexually assaulted and strangled. Traces of Vickers' DNA were found on the dead girl's clothing and body. The judge, approving the verdict, warned Vickers that he would be facing the maximum sentence for this crime. Sentencing will take place next week.

Tucker was unaware that the official version of these events was being studied a few miles away.

Clara was examining a photograph of Vickers when she heard Nash muttering. 'Sorry, what was that, Mike?'

'There's something odd here. The evidence is overwhelming. Vickers' semen was removed from inside the dead girl's vagina and on her pubic hair. And from the sheets on her bed as well. Considerable quantities, not just traces. They also recovered his pubic hair. If that's not the clearest possible proof, I don't know what is. So why has Vickers consistently denied raping her? He'd have to be stupid to go against that evidence, and from what we know about Vickers, he isn't stupid.'

'Maybe he thought by admitting to rape, he'd be confessing to murder as well?'

'What mileage was there in not pleading guilty? He might have caught the judge in a lenient mood. He could have claimed provocation, suggest the girl seduced him or something. Plenty of others have tried that. Some have got away with it.'

'You've just read the evidence out loud. There's no way Vickers isn't guilty.'

'You're probably right, Clara, but the more I read this file, the more questions it throws up.'

Clara sighed. She knew Nash well enough to realize if he got his teeth into something he wouldn't let go. She'd also enough experience of his insight to be cautious about contradicting him. He'd been proved right too often. 'OK, what don't you understand?'

'Imagine you're Vickers, and, for the sake of argument, pretend you didn't rape or kill the girl. Beyond entering a plea of not guilty, he didn't say anything in his defence. All his counsel did was question the arresting officers and the forensic experts. He didn't call any witnesses or put forward an alternative story. So, why not plead guilty? If Vickers truly was innocent, why not say so? Why wait until after he'd been tried and sentenced? And why kick up such a fuss later?'

'Perhaps he was bored. He was banged up alone in a cell for twenty-three hours a day.'

'As a reason for the campaign he waged, I find that a bit thin.'

'The evidence is overwhelming, Mike. Have you anything to suggest he might not be guilty?'

'Nothing. All I can see is a lack of evidence.'

'From what you've said, I thought there was too much rather than too little?'

'There is and there isn't. There's plenty of evidence of sexual activity. But if Vickers raped Stacey, where's the other evidence?'

'What other evidence?'

'Why does the PM report fail to mention bruising? Rape victims almost invariably have bruises to their arms, their body, their legs. They often have gag marks or bruising from a hand across their mouth. There's no mention of any defensive injuries. Why not? If he'd drugged her first, I could understand it. I checked the toxicology. There's no evidence of drugs in her system.'

'Perhaps he didn't need to keep her quiet. Maybe the rape took place somewhere he knew they wouldn't be disturbed.'

Nash shook his head. 'The rape took place in her room. We know that from forensics. That's another fact that doesn't add up. If he raped her in her bedroom, why take her to Helm Woods before he killed her?'

'He could have killed her at the house, then transported the body afterwards.'

'No, he couldn't. Vickers didn't own a car. Besides, there were no bloodstains at the house but plenty in Helm Woods. Incidentally, there's also nothing to suggest there were bloodstains on any of Vickers' clothing.'

'Anything else?'

'In the vast majority of rape cases, the killer strangles his victims with his bare hands or an item of their own clothing. According to the evidence, Vickers garrotted the girl with piano wire, hence the blood.'

'So, he wanted to be different.'

'You've missed the point, Clara. Not that I blame you. You haven't seen this.'

Nash passed her a sheet of paper, an inventory of the furniture at Vickers' house. 'There's no mention of him owning a piano. What's more, the prosecution couldn't produce proof of Vickers buying any wire. The arresting officer made a note of it alongside the inventory. It reads: "Where did the wire come from?" I guess that got deliberately overlooked by the prosecution, and his counsel didn't pick up on it.'

Clara conceded the point reluctantly. 'It's intriguing, I grant you, but it still doesn't amount to much.'

'There's another thing about the wire. If Vickers did buy piano wire, that argues premeditation, as does taking her into Helm Woods to kill her. So, how did he persuade her to go with him? The prosecution case is that Vickers got overcome with lust, raped her and then got scared she'd tell her mother. Knowing that, he panicked and strangled her. There's a huge contradiction in that argument.'

'I see what you mean, although it isn't conclusive. What do you intend to do?'

'Nothing until we've spoken to Vickers. I want to look him in the eye before I form a judgement.'

There was another curious fact Nash had noticed about the case but he decided to keep it to himself.

Nash's mobile chirped to signal an incoming message. He read the text slowly and groaned.

'Bad news?'

'Not really. At least, I don't think so.' He read aloud, '"Michael, going to France on business. Back Friday. What about weekend? X".'

Clara fought to restrain her laughter. 'That sounds like good news.'

'It would be, if I could remember the girl's name.'

'Where did you meet her?'

'Gino's fortieth birthday party. You know, from La Giaconda.'

'The answer's simple. Go to La Giaconda and ask Gino.'

'I can't do that! Most of the guests were either his or Maria's family.'

'Oh sorry, I didn't realize. That could be difficult. I don't suppose it's etiquette in Italian society to say, "I had a great time at your party. Afterwards, I gave your cousin a good shagging. Would you tell me her name"?'

'Not if you want to stay healthy it isn't.'

'First time you've visited Felling?' the prison officer asked Nash and Mironova.

Nash nodded. 'My job usually finishes when the judge passes sentence.'

'That happened to Vickers a long time ago.'

'What's he been like?'

'A pain in the arse. Nobody likes Category 43s even when they're quiet, and Vickers certainly hasn't been quiet. Forever writing letters and trying to stir up a campaign to prove his innocence. He pestered anyone he thought might show an interest, not that it did any good.'

'The others gave him a hard time, I understand?'

'Funny you should say that. There was a load of aggro in the early days – usual treatment. His food was doctored regularly – not the usual stuff though. Three times he'd to be pumped out; been poisoned. He was beaten up half a dozen times, knifed twice. In the worst incident he nearly died; he was on life support for three days. After that he was watched pretty carefully. Then suddenly the trouble stopped, almost as if someone had ordered it. I mentioned it to Vickers and he laughed. He said, "Oh, it won't happen again. I've arranged it," and you know what? He was right. As you say, they go out of their way to make life unpleasant for sex offenders but I can't explain why Vickers escaped the treatment. It's almost as if they thought he got a rough deal. Why they should think that, God knows.'

'That's interesting.'

'They're not usually far wrong; that's what intrigues me. Even now I have doubts.'

'Why?'

'About six months back, I read the story in one of those true crime magazines. It carried a photo of the girl – Stacey, wasn't it? I got a hell of a shock when I saw it.'

'Why?'

'Because I'd seen that photo. Vickers keeps it in his cell. He has a stand-up photo wallet; photo of his parents on one side, the girl on the other. I know all sex killers are perverts but I've never heard of one keeping a photo of his victim. Maybe a porno type, but this is more like a photo you'd keep of your wife or girlfriend. I reckon it'd take a really sick mind to keep a photo like that. However hard I try, I can't make it fit with the Vickers I know. Anyway, you'll meet him in a few minutes; judge for yourselves.'

Nash waited until they were on the return journey before asking Clara, 'What do you make of Vickers now?'

'I don't know. I came away wondering if we'd achieved anything, or if our visit was a waste of time. I keep wondering if we've actually met the real Gary Vickers.'

'You mean because he was so quiet?'

'Quiet! Mike, I've known deaf mutes make more noise. He never volunteered a statement, made a spontaneous remark or contradicted us. Where was the trouble-maker who continuously made a nuisance of himself? Where was the man who pestered the press, the radio and TV? Where was the angry man who wrote screeds of letters asking to be cleared? Above all, why did he sit quietly in front of us and fail to protest his innocence? All he did was stare at us and answer in monosyllables.'

'Yes, I found that intriguing. He was obviously not scared of us. But then, why should he be? The law's already punished him. As to why he didn't proclaim his innocence, he probably reckons he'd be wasting his breath, seeing who we are. But I agree, I reckon we're a long way from having met the real Gary Vickers, let alone finding out what makes him tick. There's one question I'd have liked to have asked, but it'll wait until Vickers feels able to talk freely.'

'What was that?'

'I want to know why Vickers made all that fuss. You just listed the people he canvassed to get his case looked at. There's one glaring omission, and frankly I'm at a loss to explain it.'

'I don't follow you.'

'We know Vickers is well off. The file says he got a big insurance payout after his parents were killed. Plus his father had life cover on the mortgage, so that got redeemed. Vickers has paid for a property maintenance company to look after the house whilst he's been inside. That won't have been cheap. In other words, he has ample resources at his disposal. So why has he never appealed against his conviction? If he's as innocent as he makes out, that would be the first thing he'd want to do.'

'Does that mean you think he is guilty?'

'No, that's not what I'm saying. On balance I believe he probably is, but there's a whole raft of unanswered questions. And that's making me uncomfortable. If he isn't guilty, why not appeal? Why court the publicity when he knows it won't lead anywhere?' Nash thought for a moment. 'Unless he was sending a message. You heard what the prison officer said about the attacks stopping suddenly. Perhaps there was an order given for them to be discontinued. Maybe Vickers did all that protesting to let people know he was on their case.'

'Why on earth would he do that?'

'One reason would be to stop the punishment he'd been getting. If that was so, it worked. And it would explain why Vickers was so confident he wouldn't be attacked again. Apart from that, I'd only be guessing. Perhaps he kept quiet during his trial and didn't go for a formal appeal because that would have required him to give evidence. If he remained silent because he was shielding someone, that might explain his actions. I checked the file after we talked to the warder and, guess what? All the fuss Vickers made began after he was attacked.'

'Sorry, I don't see how that's significant?'

'Suppose Vickers was protecting somebody and found out that the person he was shielding had paid someone to top him. He had death threats, remember. That might have been the spark that set him off on his campaign.'

'But his campaign fell short of an appeal.'

'That ties in with him sending a message. An appeal needs solid evidence. Vickers isn't stupid. He'd know he didn't stand a chance of clearing his name. So he doesn't appeal, he just makes a nuisance of himself. If I'm right, that also explains his insistence in returning to Helmsdale.'

'You think he has an agenda?'

'Yes, and I've an idea what it is. I think Vickers wants to settle matters with whoever ordered him to be killed. I think he believes they're responsible for the girl's death.'

'You really have serious doubts about his guilt don't you?'

'In some ways I do. What the prison officer told us about the photo worries me too. That's not the action of a guilty man. There's one thought that scares the pants off me, though.'

'What's that?'

'You remember I asked him why he wants to come back to Helmsdale? Although he didn't reply, he was looking at me as I said it. There was an expression in his eyes I found frightening. It was the closest I came to getting a reaction from him.'

'What sort of expression?'

'It was like a boxer before he steps into the ring or a soldier going into action. Psyched up for the battle ahead. Unless I read him wrong, Vickers is going back expecting there to be trouble. In fact, I believe he'll provoke it. Maybe he no longer cares what happens? Or maybe he sees it as the only way the truth will come out. Either way, I'm sure of one thing. We're in for one hell of a summer.'

chapter three

'Councillor Appleyard?'

'Speaking.'

'Carl Rathmell here. I thought you might like to join me for lunch at my place. I'm inviting one or two friends. I believe our discussion might prove mutually beneficial. What do you say?'

'That's very kind. When do you suggest?'

'Are you free tomorrow?'

When Appleyard arrived, the gravel sweep in front of Rathmell's house was almost full. Alongside several luxury cars were some run-of-the-mill vehicles, including a worse-for-wear Toyota pick-up.

Rathmell opened the door. 'Good afternoon, Councillor. We're in the drawing room. Follow me.'

Appleyard glanced round the wide hall. Everything suggested wealth, status and power. He'd heard that Carlton Rathmell, Member of European Parliament, had married into one of the richest families in the county. Seemingly, the report wasn't exaggerated.

Heads turned as they entered. Appleyard recognized several guests at a glance. His host performed introductions.

As Appleyard joined in the social chit-chat, he speculated on those present. Rathmell's agent seemed the most obvious. The two businessmen, heads of local electronics and plastics firms, were no surprise. Slightly more obscure was the presence of a trade union convenor, a man well known for his outspoken views.

Two others seemed totally out of place. Jake Fletcher, a building contractor with a reputation for toughness, who'd worked on several of Appleyard's properties. Their business relationship had been more than satisfactory. Appleyard couldn't imagine how Rathmell was acquainted with the builder, whose upbringing on the Westlea council estate was a world away from these surroundings.

The last guest caused Appleyard to give up speculating. Why Rathmell would need an alliance with a senior police officer, he couldn't imagine.

The conversation over lunch was more small talk, although here and there politics entered via questions from one or other of the diners. Rathmell and Appleyard were naturally expected to reply to these. Both took their part, but the whole business was managed so skilfully that Appleyard didn't suspect an ulterior motive.

It was only when they were having coffee that Rathmell provided an explanation. 'Gentlemen,' the MEP began. 'With one exception,' Rathmell smiled apologetically at Appleyard, 'you all know the reason for this gathering, and most of you know Councillor Appleyard. Before I go further, I need everyone's reassurance that we're of the same mind.'

Rathmell's remarks were greeted with a chorus of approval. He turned his attention to Appleyard. 'It's time to put our cards on the table, Frank.' Rathmell sipped his coffee. 'We propose to create a new political entity. A break from the traditional parties involved in that sham at Westminster. We intend to create a social force that will attract people disaffected by politics. We mean to step outside the existing structure. It will cause disapproval and condemnation. That won't bother us. If it didn't, I'd be worried we weren't doing it right. We believe our radical policies will appeal to voters. They'll bring us to the forefront of British politics and sweep the others into the wilderness.' He gestured to his agent. As the man filled Rathmell's cup, the MEP continued. 'The average Englishman feels trapped and powerless. What happens on their own doorstep is beyond their control.'

Appleyard listened intently. He'd attempted to put across similar fears in council, but met only hostility. It felt good to hear someone voicing the same concerns.

'I agree,' Appleyard told his host approvingly. 'I've longed to find someone prepared to take a lead in such matters.'

Appleyard's words were greeted with smiles of satisfaction. They'd definitely made the right choice.

Rathmell continued. 'Local people see politicians toadying to incomers and resent it. They see council officials bending over backwards to give immigrants the assistance they need. They see foreigners getting benefits locals aren't entitled to. Crime on the Westlea and similar estates is out of control. Ask Jake. Ten years ago he wouldn't have needed a sign on his vans that there were no tools left inside overnight. Now, it's dangerous for a woman to walk along the street at night because foreigners have the wrong impression as to what that signifies. The police have neither the manpower nor the willpower to combat crime on the estates.'

Rathmell turned to the police officer. 'I'm sorry if that sounds like criticism, Martin. I have great admiration for your officers, but they lack the necessary support. They need a judicial system that doesn't protect the guilty and a sentencing policy that doesn't make them a laughing stock. They've lost control of the streets.'

The policeman threw up his hands despairingly. 'Once, I'd have argued with you. If any of you have any doubts about what Carl has just said, my presence here should cast them aside.'

Appleyard leaned forward in his chair, his face animated. 'You're dead right. I know from constituents how bad things are. But what's to be done? Nobody has come close to identifying the problem, let alone suggesting a solution.'

'The only way is by forcing the issue. Bad has to become worse before anyone will act. Look at the symptoms. Those who get the best treatment are the immigrants, legal or otherwise, the asylum seekers and those who are already a drain on society.

'We've just paid millions for that smart new facility for travelling people to the east of Helmsdale. Do the gypsies use it? No way. Instead you see them camped on every bit of grass verge. Their caravans are unsightly; they leave litter and God knows what other unpleasantness behind.

'Go into the Good Buys convenience store on the Westlea and listen to the conversation. You'd struggle to hear a Yorkshire accent. You'd be more likely to hear Latvian, Polish or some Baltic tongue. Even the shopkeeper's an immigrant. If we don't see action soon, there'll be trouble on a big scale.'

'How can it be prevented?' As Appleyard spoke, he wondered how Rathmell knew so much about the Westlea.

'It may already be too late. But I'm not sure it should be stopped. Not completely. We need direct action to focus on the problem, to highlight how serious the situation's become.'

'Direct action?' There was concern, but no alarm in Appleyard's voice. 'What do you mean by that?'

'If folk can't communicate their fears by orthodox methods, they'll use other means. It's the only way left open to them. Let the authorities know how deep their resentment goes and send a message to the parasites that they're no longer welcome.'

'It sounds like a recipe for trouble,' Appleyard commented.

'Sometimes the cure's as painful as the complaint. Our task would be to co-ordinate and guide the local population so they can act without fear of reprisal.'

'How do we go about it?'

Rathmell leaned forward. 'We,' he gestured round the group, 'need someone on the inside. Somebody who's trusted, maybe even feared. If you and I control the policy, a man like that would plan the actions and ensure they were carried out successfully.'

'He's talking about me, Frank,' Jake grinned.

Two hours later Rathmell watched the cars leaving. As the lead vehicle turned onto the main road, he picked up his mobile. 'It's me,' he said. 'It went like a dream. Appleyard and Jake will start work tomorrow. Speaking of tomorrow, are you going to be free?' He listened. 'You don't have to worry about that. My beloved wife has taken her money to London on a shopping spree. Usual time and place?'

Billy was excited. The younger of the Floyd brothers and unarguably volatile, Billy had suffered as a child. That changed when he was twelve. He'd been watching TV at home. He wasn't supposed to be alone. Billy's parents had gone to the pub. Billy's sister was baby-sitting.

She'd interpreted her duties freely. She'd made Billy a sandwich and disappeared upstairs with her boyfriend. After they'd been gone half an hour, Billy decided to see what they were doing. He forgot that the bedroom door creaked. Confronted by his sister's angry boyfriend, Billy stared in wonder at the huge thing sticking from between his legs. He failed to see the punch. The pain in his gut underlined the message as clearly as the accompanying words. 'Get back downstairs, you pervert, or I'll stick this up your arse.'

Billy crept back downstairs. A film had started on TV during his absence. As he watched a couple on the screen doing what his sister and her boyfriend had been doing, Billy's interest grew. As the tower block they were in caught fire, his interest turned to excitement. Billy discovered that his thing was getting bigger too. Thereafter Billy's confused mind linked the conflagration of fire with the passion of lovemaking. A year later he put this to the test. He took a girl from his class across the fields to a barn. He told her he'd seen some newly born calves. When they were inside, Billy forced himself on the girl. He'd grown and filled out in the last year and the girl was no match for him. Despite her muffled screams and writhing protest, he managed to achieve what he'd seen his sister enjoy. Just before his climax, Billy paused and withdrew. The girl was quiet now, barely breathing.

He walked over to a corner and took a lighter from his pocket. He set fire to the edge of a straw bale and watched the flames grow and flicker. As the polythene covering the bales took hold, the fire began to roar and Billy's arousal became unbearable. He went back and stood for a second, looking down at the girl's naked form, before flinging himself on her. He began to thrust, harder and harder, deeper and faster.

The smoke was all round them now, writhing, curling and choking. The roaring in Billy's ears was part excitement and part the engulfing sound of the barn crumbling to destruction. Barely a minute later, Billy ejaculated. As he lay panting, something hot and heavy dropped close by. He staggered to his feet and stumbled outside, before collapsing on the ground. He turned to look back. A huge display of sparks flew up, as the roof timbers collapsed on the unconscious girl.

Despite exhaustive enquiries, the cause of the blaze and the reason for her presence in the barn were never discovered. Billy realized he'd been lucky. After that he became more careful.

Now Billy could pay girls to pretend to enjoy doing it with him. He also learned to be more selective about where and when to practise his love of fire.

Today he was excited, because he'd been asked to indulge his second passion. What was even better, he was going to be paid for it. That would mean he'd be able to afford Trudy. She was his favourite, but she cost more than the others. He'd been promised enough money to be able to visit her a few times. The job wasn't even difficult. A caravan's an easy target. The confined space, the single exit and the gas cylinders would make it easy. After all, he was an expert.

The caravan and its occupants shouldn't be there. Danny told him that. They didn't belong there. They didn't belong anywhere. 'They're not like us, Billy,' Danny explained. 'They're gippos and we don't want gippos round here. They don't contribute anything. They cost us money. They don't pay tax, they don't work. All they do is steal and beg. They're sub-human parasites living in filthy squalor just like rats.'

Billy had no idea what sub-human parasites meant. But he did know rats. Knew them and detested them. 'They need driving out, Billy. They're just like rats.' Danny was Billy's hero. Although he was only three years Billy's senior, Danny was like a god to the impressionable youth. Danny had a gun. Billy knew that. He'd seen it. What's more, Danny had used it. Billy knew that too. More than once, Billy reckoned. If Danny said something was right, Billy would never argue.

Billy might have rushed the job, but that wasn't the way it had to be. Danny had left him in no doubt. 'You must make sure nobody suspects us, Billy.'

Billy took his brother's words for gospel. 'Plan it carefully. Take your time. We need to scare the lot of them off for good, just like rats.'

As Billy watched the caravan, making his plans, he had no doubt he was doing the right thing; a good thing. He muttered the mantra over and over. 'Just like rats. Just like rats. Just like rats.'

chapter four

Drugs had been a problem on the Westlea for years. Getting hold of them, that is. Recently this had changed. The improvement was due to Ricky Smart. Ricky ensured they got what they needed. All he demanded in return was prompt payment. For some, this presented a problem, usually solved with a little opportunist crime. Nobody argued with Ricky. He'd been shrewd enough to seek protection. Smart had approached Danny Floyd. The move was a tactical triumph. His predecessors had gone it alone. Offering Danny a cut of the proceeds made Smart the dealer of choice. Competitors got a rough ride. Smart's trade flourished as did Danny's share.

Now they'd a unique proposition to consider. When Danny put the idea forward he believed it originated from Jake Fletcher. He couldn't have guessed the true origin.

Smart was initially appalled. 'Free gear for your lot this summer?'

'Free to them,' Danny reassured him. 'But the stuff will be paid for.'

'It'll cost an arm and a leg. Who's going to shell out?'

'Some geezer wants the Juniors to do some stuff. Quite heavy stuff too.'

'Must be real heavy if he's stumping up that sort of cash.'

'You're better off not knowing. Believe me. Make sure you've plenty of gear when it's needed. I don't mean next week promises. I mean there and then. The Juniors won't be happy if they're kept waiting. Not when they've been promised. And you know what they're capable of.'

'Will it be cash up front? That's a heavy layout.'

'It'll be cash on delivery. Just you see you've plenty of stock.'

'That won't be a problem.'

'I've a meeting this afternoon,' Nash told Clara.

'What is it this time?'

'The new deputy chief constable's discussing staffing levels.'

'Sounds like fun.'

'You've a weird notion of enjoyment.'

'What's he like? Being from the lower ranks, I haven't met him.'

'You've not missed much. DCC King is a career policeman. He won't have noticed the likes of you. His eyes are fixed on higher things. I'm sure he regards this posting as a backward step.'

'Sounds a real berk. Mind you, he should get on with Creepy.'

'DS Mironova, you shouldn't speak of your superiors in that way. Inspector Crawley is one of our most respected and able officers – in his opinion, at least.'

'That's the only opinion Creepy values.'

Nash sighed. 'Whatever happened to good old-fashioned values, like catching criminals and protecting the public?'

'They got buried under red tape.'

'The job's turning you into a cynic.'

Clara grinned. 'Talking of old-fashioned values, have you remembered your girlfriend's name yet?'

Nash winced. 'What made you bring that up? Was there a specific reason or was it sadism pure and simple?'

'Being from the lower ranks, I have to get my pleasure where I can.'

'For your cheek you can make the coffee. And bring some salt and vinegar.'

'What for?'

'The chip on your shoulder.'

'I'll be glad when Viv's back off leave.'

'So will I. Not only does Pearce make better coffee, he's far more respectful.'

Tom Pratt managed a word with Nash before the meeting. 'Try not to antagonize King. We know it'll be bad news.'

'I'll let Creepy do the talking.'

Pratt laughed. 'Much good that'll do.'

Nash remained calm whilst the DCC outlined his plans. It was an effort.

'I intend to initiate a review that will point the way to the most effective and cost-efficient service.' King looked hard at Nash. 'I shall be paying close attention to the smaller units and asking some pertinent questions regarding their viability.'

'I'd have thought recent events might have shown that Helmsdale can't be policed effectively from Netherdale,' Nash objected mildly.

'I shall approach this review with an open mind,' King told him sharply. 'However, I remain to be convinced that the community wouldn't be better served by concentrating our resources where we can make an effective difference, rather than squandering them on small units covering areas with low levels of unsolved crime. I see a strong case for centring operations at Netherdale. That can be achieved either with the existing personnel' – King's stare grew colder – 'or by replacing officers who don't fit in with the new order.'

Nash ignored the implicit threat. 'Could the low level of unsolved crime be because of an effective presence?' he suggested.

King shook his head. 'I'll examine the logistics of ensuring an equally effective service from Netherdale. Given the will, and the right officers, it can be done. Nothing will be decided until I've completed my review.'

'And that will be conducted with a completely open mind?' Nash suggested, putting a little stress on the word 'open'.

As they were leaving, King detained Crawley. 'I'd like a word.'

'What do you think that's about?' Pratt jerked a thumb backwards as he and Nash walked down the corridor.

'Probably asking Creepy to do his dirty work. They're two of a kind. I'm just glad one of them isn't female.'

'Why?'

'The thought of an offspring from that union is too horrible. I wonder what God makes of King. Do you know?'

'God hasn't confided in me. Anyway, you should know. You're her blue-eyed boy. I reckon she looks on you as the son she never had.'

Their chief constable's nickname was obvious, not only from her rank but her initials. Gloria O'Donnell did indeed have a soft spot for Nash. 'I wouldn't have thought any mother would refer to her son as she speaks about me,' Nash objected.

'Alright,' Pratt confessed, 'so she calls you "that randy bastard at Helmsdale". You can't tell me that isn't a term of affection?'

'Hardly matronly.'

'Whatever, I think you're right about Creepy.'

Had they remained in the meeting room, Pratt would have been able to congratulate Mike on the accuracy of his guess.

'I've been reading the files of the officers under my command and I believe you're the ideal candidate to assist me. I intend to build a team that's second to none. There will be a considerable number of changes, in strategy, working practices and personnel.

'There will be no room for lone-wolf operators. Procedures will not be ignored or bypassed. The chain of command will operate at all levels, with strict attention to correct reporting.

'Every officer will have a clearly defined role. They will know exactly what's expected. I intend to ensure this area is free from old, bad practices. There will be no prima donnas.'

'I'll do whatever I can to assist.' Crawley's eagerness was pathetic.

'We'll go into detail when I've established the parameters. In the meantime, tell me about Nash. I understand he has an active social life?'

'He's never short of female company,' Crawley agreed.

'I'm no prude, but I prefer my officers to have settled domestic arrangements.'

'There have certainly been a lot of women.' Crawley leaned forward confidentially. 'There was even a rumour concerning Nash and DS Mironova, although that's unconfirmed.'

'That's something I won't tolerate. Romantic entanglements between officers inevitably cause problems. It impairs the efficiency of those concerned and others who work alongside them. There's only one way of ending such an unsatisfactory situation and that's by separating the parties. We must pay close attention to this.'

Nash's mobile bleeped during his drive to Helmsdale. On reaching his flat, he checked the inbox. 'Michael. Have to go to New York. Will call you. X.' He groaned. Why didn't the wretched girl sign her text? If he couldn't remember her name, he'd be in real bother.

He noticed the message alert flashing on his landline. He'd to replay the message before the significance struck home. 'Michael,' a man's voice said. 'We need to talk about my sister.'

Nash stared down at the phone in helpless frustration. A fault had developed, which rendered every voice, male or female, totally unrecognizable. It was as if all messages were being delivered by a ten-year-old Jimmy Osmond. Now her brother wanted to see him. He couldn't identify the brother's voice any more than he could remember the girl's name. As if things weren't bad enough.

Reporters often have to wait a long time for a story. Tucker sat outside Gemma Fletcher's flat each evening until he was sure she'd gone to bed. The following morning he was there before she left. He watched her as many hours as he could, given that he'd his weekly column to write.

He'd submitted this to his editor on Wednesday lunchtime and that afternoon had his first slice of luck. Gemma left work early. Tucker followed her as she drove west out of Helmsdale and headed deep into the countryside. His curiosity was roused: Gemma didn't strike him as a nature lover. So where was she bound?

When she reached a remote moorland road, Tucker eased off the accelerator and maintained a discreet distance. Had he been fifty yards further back he'd have missed her turn off. He drove past the end of the rutted, unmade lane until he reached the brow of a hill and parked on the grass verge. It was an excellent vantage point. Tucker reached into the glove compartment for his binoculars.

Twenty minutes later, he saw another vehicle turn onto the track. As it pulled to a stop, Tucker saw Gemma leap from her car and dash to meet the other driver.

He saw their passionate embrace before the couple dived hurriedly into the man's vehicle. What Tucker was anxious to discover was the identity of Gemma's lover. Any doubt as to the status of the relationship was dispelled by the gentle rocking of the vehicle and the steamed-up windows.

'Way to go, Gemma,' Tucker murmured approvingly as he noted the car's registration number. 'Where would reporters be without a bit of good old-fashioned adultery?'

'What news have you got?' Appleyard began.

Jake Fletcher stared across the desk. 'Everything's ready. You don't want to know the details. You should hear something today or tomorrow. With the right incentives, other incidents will follow.'

Appleyard passed him an envelope. 'The first instalment; I hope the results will be worth it.'

'You needn't worry. When will you start?'

'There's a meeting next Friday. Normally they're only attended by three men and a dog, but I want to ensure there's a full house.'

'What's the meeting?'

'Westlea Residents' Association.'

Jake nodded approval. 'You'll be preaching to the converted there. How can I help?'

'Make sure we get a good attendance.'

'It could be tricky getting folk from in front of their TVs. Those that aren't in the pub, that is. I'll ask Ronnie to try a little persuasion. Anything else?'

'I might arouse some strong emotions. It would be sensible to have a few people about.'

'Danny and the Juniors will do that. I'll be on hand with Ronnie to supervise them.' Jake grinned. 'Most of them have suffered at the hands of bouncers. It'll appeal to them to act the part.'

At one end of the Westlea, planners had included a set of lock-up garages. Most had been unused from the date of their completion. Many had fallen or been pushed into disrepair. Neglect and vandalism had reduced many to doorless shells. Not that they were unused. During the daytime they formed goalmouths for children playing football. When the weather intervened, the interior provided a welcome refuge. Detritus littered the crumbling concrete floors in the form of lager cans, cider bottles, cigarette ends and other smoking products even less healthy.

More sinister was the presence of used needles and syringes, aerosols and plastic bags for those who needed extra stimulation. After dark the garages were in regular use by a wide variety of occupants. Amorous encounters, between mixed-sex and same-sex couples. Many a girl from the estate enjoyed her first experience of true love in the garages.

One of the garages had long been the meeting place for teenagers from the Westlea. The gang had certain membership criteria. One of the most rigid was ethnicity. It probably hadn't been a group member who daubed the racial slogans on one of the walls, but the sentiment met with their wholehearted approval.

Not that they were racist. They hated everyone with equal ferocity. Age was another qualification for joining the group. This rule was less tightly applied but it was generally held that anyone over the age of eighteen or under the age of twelve was excluded. Danny Floyd and his brother were exceptions, but then they had other excellent credentials. These took the form of one of the core values, a capacity for violence, preferably with a proven track record.

'Shut it!' Glazed eyes turned in the general direction of the voice. As they attempted to focus on the speaker, one or two mutters continued. 'I said, shut it.' The half-light made it difficult to focus. The fact that they were stoned didn't help.

'We all know there's too many Immigrunts on the Westlea.'

A growl of anger emphasized their agreement.

'Now we've chance to get shut of them.'

'How we gunna do that, Dan? There's hundreds of 'em.'

'Shut up and listen. Then you'll find out, won't you? Here's the job. We make life so fucking miserable for them they'll be queuing up to get the first bus out.'

'How, Dan?'

'Never mind how. Are you up for it?'

'Too right.'

'The best bit is, there's others think like us. We'll even get re-fucking-warded.'

'What you mean?'

'We're going to get free gear. Good shit too. All we've to do is earn it.'

'What! By getting shut of the Immigrunts?'

'You got it.'

'I'd do it for nowt.'

'I'm in if there's free stuff.'

'Me too.'

'And me.'

'I'm in.' A dozen voices chimed their agreement.

'When's this going down?'

'We wait for a sign. Billy's going to torch a gippovan. We start after that.'

chapter five

Billy waited patiently. He was ready. As soon as the caravan was in darkness and quiet, that was his cue.

His hold on reality had always been precarious. A good psychiatrist might have saved him. But Billy had never been treated. That wasn't the way things happened. No one realized how close he was to being psychotic; the thin dividing line between normality and a psychopath. It needed only a small push to send Billy over the edge. Setting the caravan fire took Billy to the brink. As he lay in the hedgeback watching it burn, watching the gas bottles exploding high into the night sky, he teetered on that edge.

Then, as he masturbated towards a climax, the caravan door burst open. For a second Billy froze, unable to comprehend what he was watching. A burning ball fell to the ground and rolled over, before coming to rest in a pyre of smoke and flame. As recognition came, Billy knew beyond doubt that what he'd watched had been a human being. Now a human torch that burned even brighter than the blazing caravan beyond.

As Billy lay spent and gasping, his mind plunged into an abyss of darkness. There could be no return. The last vestige of his sanity was destroyed in that instant, gutted as completely as the caravan.

Nash's sleep was disturbed by the wailing of sirens. He stirred, but as their clamour faded, he dropped back to sleep.

Later, his mobile rang. 'Nash,' he growled.

'Mike, it's Clara. I'm on Netherdale Road. There's been a caravan fire; completely gutted. I'm with Doug Curran. He reckons it's arson.' Clara's voice quivered with distress. 'There's at least one dead. We found a body outside the van; burned to a crisp, completely unrecognizable. There may be more inside, but we can't get near. Mike, the bloody thing's just melted.'

'I'll be as fast as I can. Whereabouts exactly?'

Nash wondered how a crowd of onlookers could have gathered at such an early hour. Did they lie awake, waiting for the sound of sirens?

He ducked under the incident tape and paused for a brief word with Sergeant Binns.

'Clara's over there, with Curran.'

Binns pointed towards the first of three fire engines. 'She's pretty shaken.' Binns paused. 'She's not the only one.'

Nash had to pass the caravan to get to Clara. The van was a hot, smoking shell of twisted metal and melted fibreglass, testimony to the ferocity of the blaze. Alongside it a dark tarpaulin sheet covered a shapeless bundle he knew would be a body. His nose wrinkled in revulsion as he recognized the sickly, cloying smell of burnt flesh.

He nodded to his sergeant and the chief fire officer. 'Any more news?'

They shook their heads.

'Clara, go to the travellers' amenity site. Find the local headman. Get him out here ASAP. We need to know whose van this is. Was,' he corrected himself. 'And how many were inside.'

He turned to Curran. 'Clara said you think it was arson?'

'Yes,' Curran answered heavily. 'Caravan fires are very rare. The odds against one going up are long.'

Nash looked across to where Curran's men were playing hoses over the wreckage. 'Anything more positive?'

'We'll have to wait on forensics, but come and have a look at this.'

Nash followed Curran. Closer to the caravan, he could feel the heat from the smouldering wreck. Curran pointed to the ground. Nash could see a broad streak of scorched grass leading to where the gas bottles had been stored.

Curran looked at him and was about to speak when he saw the faraway expression on Nash's face. He'd never seen that look before, but had heard Mironova describe it. What was it she called it? 'Thinking, do not disturb', that was it. He waited in patient silence.

For Nash's mind's eye, the darkness intensified. He crouched in the bank of bushes, waiting. He would have to wait, to avoid detection. As soon as the caravan's occupants had switched the lights out, as soon as they were settled for a good night's sleep; then he could move. He'd ensure their sleep was eternal. At last, the lights went out; his signal for action. 'This is it,' Nash murmured to himself. 'You've waited; now you can do what you came here for. They've gone to bed. Now you must creep ever so quietly, closer and closer. Now for the tricky bit. You've to disconnect the fuel lines and open the valves on the cylinders, all without making enough noise to disturb those inside; your target, your victims. You've done that, now the rest should be easy. Sprinkle the petrol you've brought onto the ground. When you're far enough back, simply strike a match and toss it onto the ground. Whoosh! Instant inferno! What now? Did you wait and watch? Enjoying the tragedy you've created? Glorying in it? Why? What had they done to hurt you? Was it a grudge? A dispute? Had they crossed you in some way? Or worse.' Nash chilled at the thought. 'Are you a psychopath? In which case, nobody's safe.'

Nash was closer to guessing the motive than he realized. Which, given the confused state of Billy's mind, was quite an achievement. Not that it helped.

Back at Helmsdale, Clara sat opposite Nash as he phoned Tom Pratt. They could still smell smoke from their clothing. 'The van belonged to a family named Druze. The leader of the local tribe reckons we're looking for three bodies. Druze, his woman and a girl; six years old.'

'What's Curran say?'

'He says it's arson. Mexican Pete and the brigade forensic team are on site. We'll have to wait for their reports.'

'Nothing we can do in the meantime?'

'Appeal for witnesses, but that's probably useless.'

'I'd better tell our new DCC.'

'You might ask him how he thinks closing Helmsdale would have prevented it.'

'I would if I thought it'd do any good. How's Clara?'

'Pretty shaken. She was first on the scene.'

'She'll cope. She's tough and professional.'

Nash put the phone down. 'Tom thinks you're a tough old boot,' he told her. 'Reckons you're like an old pro.'

Mironova glared at him, distress in abeyance. 'I bet he didn't say anything of the sort,' she snapped.

Nash smiled. 'Not exactly.' He repeated Pratt's actual words. 'Now, would the tough old boot like a coffee?'

*

37

Rathmell was watching the local TV news when his phone rang. 'Carl, it's Frank Appleyard. Have you seen the report about the incident at Helmsdale?'

'I was watching it on TV when you rang; terrible tragedy. One I'm sure would never have happened if the family had stayed in the travellers' site.'

'My thoughts exactly. However, that wasn't why I rang. I have everything set up for our campaign. I've handed over the first part. We need to make arrangements for the remainder.'

'When?'

'As and when they carry out each assignment, a sort of productivity bonus.'

Rathmell laughed. 'That sounds appropriate. Give me twenty-four hours to make the arrangements. We also need to talk about next week's meeting.'

'Whereabouts? At your house?'

'That would be inconvenient. My wife is in residence, and the less she knows about what's going on the better.'

'Where, then?'

'I know the ideal spot. For the moment it would be better if we avoid being seen together until after next Friday.'

Gemma's mobile rang. She glanced at the display. If it had been anyone else she wouldn't have answered. 'I'm about to go into a meeting. What is it?'

'Not on the phone. We need to meet ASAP. When are you free?'

'After work. Usual place. I can get there by six?'

'I'll be waiting.'

This time Tucker was prepared. As soon as he saw Gemma's car turn onto the moor road he stopped and reversed onto the verge. He got out of the car and balanced his binoculars on the wall. He lit a cigarette, wondering how many he'd get through before the end of his vigil.

Nash had the radio on. He heard the news announcer read a statement from the Home Secretary on the subject of the prison service.

'In view of the current level of overcrowding, all inmates whose sentence is due to end within the next three months will be released immediately. This will apply whatever their offence or the original length of sentence. The Shadow Home Secretary and spokesmen from other opposition parties condemned the move as an indictment of government policy. Calls for an emergency debate are expected to be tabled during Prime Minister's question time.'

Nash paused, razor in hand. One effect would concern him directly. Vickers would be out within days. He was still pondering when he reached Helmsdale.

Clara looked up from the report she was reading. 'There's been another arson attack. Or an attempted one.'

'Not another caravan? Anyone hurt?'

Clara shook her head. 'No, this time it was a house, fortunately unoccupied. A woman feeding her baby during the night raised the alarm. Only superficial damage.'

'Where was this?'

Clara glanced down. 'Number thirty-two, Grove Road.'

'Isn't that—'

'Gary Vickers' house.'

They were still considering this development when the phone rang. It was Pratt. 'Did you hear this morning's news, Mike?'

'You mean about prisoners being released early?'

'Yes. Well, I've just had word. Vickers will be out on Friday next.'

'That's the last thing we want. He's going to need round-the-clock protection, Tom.'

'I don't see that. He chose to come back to Helmsdale.'

'Maybe, Tom, but that was before last night.' He explained about the fire. 'This situation's impossible. We can't leave Vickers unguarded. King's attitude means we can't draft anyone in. Given Vickers' record, leaving Clara to guard him is out of the question.'

Pratt agreed. 'It's a bloody shame Pearce is on leave. All I can suggest is I lend you a DC from Netherdale.'

'It would help if you can supply someone to baby-sit during the day. I'll do the night shift until Viv comes back.'

'I could always go over King's head and ask the chief.'

'That would prove King's point. It'd set his back up even more. Besides, we can't prove the fire was directed at Vickers. It could be a random act of vandalism.'

They were unaware of a conversation taking place elsewhere.

'Jake, how did it go?'

'Danny sent Billy. Somebody must have spotted him. He'd to scarper when the fire brigade rolled up.'

'Shit! I wanted that place destroyed.'

'Don't worry, Gem. I'll get him to try again.'

'You don't understand, Jake. He'll be out in a few days.'

'Even better: next time we'll torch the house with him in it.'

'Tucker speaking.'

'I've got the information you asked for.'

'Fire away.'

'The vehicle is registered to Mrs Vanessa Rathmell, of Houlston Lodge, Helmsdale.' Tucker whistled. Sometimes a journalist has to pay a lot for information. Sometimes the information is worth the outlay. Tucker knew this was worth every penny.

Now he'd a decision to make. Should he follow Rathmell and the adultery angle, or continue to follow Gemma for more background on the Vickers case? He'd been tipped off by a contact at Felling that Vickers was due out. What intrigued him was the planned return to his home, almost unheard of for a convicted sex offender. There was a human interest angle in Vickers' tale.

On the other hand, there was Gemma Fletcher's adultery with the local MEP. Elected as an Independent, Rathmell had shown little inclination to either wing of the political spectrum. Despite that, there were rumours that Rathmell held strong views on immigration and race. Tucker thought there'd be more mileage in pursuing Rathmell. It was no secret that Rathmell relied on his wife's money. It was also known that Vanessa Rathmell's family were staunch Catholics, certainly where divorce was concerned. They were also intensely private and wouldn't take kindly to their name being splashed across the tabloids. First he'd research the man. This involved scanning newspaper files and reading his speeches and press announcements. Not a task Tucker looked forward to with enthusiasm.

chapter six

Juris was content. Homesick, but content. When his father died, the future looked bleak for him, his mother and his younger brothers. At eighteen, Juris was unable to support the family. Mechanization had reduced the need for agricultural workers dramatically. Unskilled in anything else, Juris had to compete with other, more experienced applicants.

A welcome solution arrived. The rumour flashed round the village that a stranger was offering work. True, it was many hundreds of miles away, but the pay was good and the stranger was prepared to loan the fare. It was agricultural work too. He met the stranger, a Lithuanian called Zydrumas, and the deal was struck. That had been two years ago.

When he arrived in North Yorkshire, Juris was billeted in a camp for migrant workers. After three months, more suitable accommodation was found, close to the farm where he worked. Juris wrote to tell his mother he was sharing a house on an estate called Westlea. He wrote home often with his news, and to send money. She received the letters and money with equal pleasure and wrote back to thank him. She expressed her pride and love. Her only sadness was that she missed him.

The work was seasonal, but by limiting expenditure, Juris could support his family throughout the year. Although there was opportunity to return home once the season was over, Juris declined this. That would mean extra fares. He would rather save that money and remain in England. He might even find work during the winter.

He'd no success the first year and to alleviate his boredom Juris began improving his limited English. Although his education had been basic, he'd a quick brain and soon mastered a few simple words and phrases. Listening carefully and copying those around him accelerated the process and by winter Juris felt confident enough to enrol for night classes.

During the second winter he found casual work in the kitchens of a local hotel. It was only at weekends, except during December and January when this extended to most nights of the week. Juris didn't mind that it was tedious, repetitive work. He didn't even mind being sworn at, or blamed for everything that went wrong. Although his English was improving rapidly, the college courses didn't give him the fluency a few nights in the hotel kitchen provided.

Later, his teachers explained the difference between English and Anglo Saxon. He learned that a snappy response delivered by a chef isn't always polite. Juris discovered that calling somebody 'a lazy twat', or 'an ignorant dickhead', was no way to win friends.

The farm where Juris worked was visible from the migrants' house. To get there by road would mean a walk of three miles, but there was a footpath that cut this to less than half a mile. When Zydrumas had to speak to the farmer about the forthcoming harvest, he took Juris along.

The first part of the meeting concerned the labour needed. When the discussion turned to rates of pay, Juris set off home. Zydrumas said he'd follow.

The day had been overcast and cool. The track led through a small wood before it bisected a series of miniature farms, dedicated to the growing of vegetables and other produce. Juris had learned these were called allotments. His teacher had explained the reason for their existence. The woods were a dark impenetrable mass of foliage, tangled briar and brambles. As Juris walked, he heard the rustle and creak as the wind stirred the trees around him. Suddenly he felt very alone, very far from home and, for no logical reason, very afraid. It was only when he'd passed the woods and come to the edge of the Westlea that the irrational fear subsided.

Billy sat in his room. His hand moved lazily to and fro as he passed the long bright blade of his knife across a sharpening stone. His movements were accurate, with precision born of practice. His eyes appeared to be fixed on the wall opposite. In fact they were unfocused, far away.

Danny led by example. Billy remembered when Danny returned home with the gun, remembered with equal clarity when Danny used it. He hadn't been allowed to see the weapon, but the look on Danny's face told Billy more than his elder brother suspected.

Before Ricky moved in, the Juniors had been having a lot of trouble with their drug dealer. Poor-quality gear and lack of regular supplies were only part of the problem. More critical was the exorbitant price charged by the Turkish Cypriot who controlled distribution.

When Danny returned after being absent all day and half the night, Billy knew something must have happened. Danny didn't stray from Helmsdale and the estate often. He certainly didn't vanish for such a long time without a convincing explanation.

Next day, Billy saw the news report on TV. Telling of the discovery of a man's body in a house on the outskirts of Leeds, the item went on, 'The man is believed to be of Turkish Cypriot origin. Police investigating the shooting are looking into a possible drugs connection.'

Danny had pointed the way. Billy knew exactly who Danny was referring to when he mentioned 'the Immigrunts'.

He wasn't quite as clear as to how the Immigrunts had made their lives so miserable, but Danny had said so, and Billy wasn't prepared to argue. Billy knew what to do. He had to kill one. It didn't much matter which one. That wasn't the point. He'd a target in mind. Not a person but a location. He remembered them working on the farm close to the Westlea. They were starting to arrive back now. He'd seen two in the street, bold as you like, strolling along. It stood to reason they'd be working at the farm again. That meant they'd be walking through the woods. It'd be exciting. Not like the fire of course, but good nevertheless.

His decision made, Billy put the stone away. He fingered the blade, then wiped it with a soft cloth. He replaced the weapon in the sheath on his belt and put his jacket on, left the bedroom, left the house and headed for the woods.

Tucker had followed Rathmell for three days without anything to show for his efforts. Many journalists might have abandoned the story, but Tucker was made of sterner stuff. On day four he followed Rathmell out of Helmsdale. Within minutes of leaving the town Tucker thought he could guess who Rathmell was going to meet. His guess was wildly inaccurate.

When Rathmell turned onto the moor road, Tucker allowed his car to coast to a stop and got out.

As Appleyard headed towards the meeting place, he was so deep in thought he almost missed the turning. He swung off the main road, slowing to avoid missing the next landmark. He noticed a car parked alongside the dry-stone wall. He saw that the driver had left his vehicle, apparently to relieve himself. Appleyard hoped he hadn't startled the man.

Tucker was surprised, although not as Appleyard imagined. He heard the sound of the approaching vehicle before it came into view. He expected Gemma Fletcher's flashy red convertible. To avoid suspicion Tucker adopted the stance of a man in the act of urinating. It was natural to glance over one's shoulder at the intrusion on so private a function; Tucker was glad he was only simulating the act or his surprise might have provoked an accident. It wasn't Gemma Fletcher's car. Nor was it a female behind the wheel. Was this coincidence, or was the driver on his way to meet Rathmell? If so, to what purpose? It was understandable to want a secluded spot for an illicit romantic assignation, but this was obviously not the case. So why the secrecy? A meeting neither party wanted witnessed, that was obvious. Tucker's journalistic instinct told him there might be more to this rendezvous than the adultery he'd set out to expose. Back to watching and waiting. But at least there was the possibility of something worth waiting for.

Tucker waited almost an hour. The sun was hidden by low cloud and the wind blew cold. He was about to get back into his car when he heard the sound of approaching vehicles. As the first of them came into view, Tucker recognized it as Rathmell's. He watched it speed past, noting that Rathmell was alone. Although his quest centred on Rathmell, the man he'd been meeting in such secrecy interested Tucker more.

The car was travelling faster than on the outward leg. Despite this Tucker was confident he'd be able to read the number plate. The ground on the opposite side of the wall rose steeply, so his eyes were almost at road level.

Tucker raised his binoculars and adjusted the focus. As he concentrated on the number plate, his vision was filled with a solid wall of white. Before Tucker realized what had happened, the car sped past and receded into the distance. The fading light had caused the car's automatic headlamps to switch on. Tucker swore virulently at the trio of sheep grazing peacefully on the verge. They stared back curiously, before returning to their afternoon tea.

The meeting had been a great success. Zydrumas emerged from the farmhouse, shook hands with the farmer and wandered to the end of the yard. He paused and lit a cigarette. His client was an ambitious man. He'd outlined plans for the development of the business. These would involve Zydrumas and his workforce. Part of the farm was on heavy clay. This made production difficult. The farmer intended to install tunnel greenhouses to enable a range of produce to be grown all year round. He was also planning to acquire two other farms, one in Lincolnshire and another in Scotland.

Extra labour would be required. 'What I need is a reliable workforce at reasonable cost. That's where you come in. I want you to start straightaway. Leave Juris to run things here. He's capable of controlling the other workers and reliable enough to take charge when I'm not about. That's going to be increasingly often.'

Zydrumas stubbed his cigarette out and opened the gate. The farmer had just made his day. He was about to do the same for Juris.

Billy reached the allotments. The Immigrunts would have to stop work soon. Then they'd walk back along this track. Back from the work they'd stolen from people like Billy, towards the houses they'd stolen from people like Billy.

This was what he'd been told. Billy had never applied for a job in his life. He wouldn't have wanted a job if he'd been offered one. The Floyd family already had a house, provided free of charge courtesy of the local authority and any number of social security benefits. Billy didn't think of this. All he knew was he hated Immigrunts. He'd torched a gippovan. Now he was going to go one better.

He reached the place he'd picked, hid behind an elm tree and eased the knife from its sheath. A quarter of an hour passed. Then he heard footsteps. Billy strained his eyes. He peered through the foliage. Someone was walking on the path. Billy edged forward. The footsteps approached, slowly. The man on the path wasn't hurrying. Billy moved further forward. A twig snapped under his foot.

Silence. Then the man called out, 'What is it? Who is there?'

The accent was enough. Billy launched himself forward. He raised his arm. The blade gleamed as he brought the knife down. He struck again. This time there was no reflection from the blade. Or the next time, or the next.

chapter seven

'What are you doing this weekend?'

Clara looked up from the paperwork. 'David's home on leave – we're going rock climbing. He's picking me up. I'll need gallons of coffee to stay awake on Monday. What about you?'

'Not much. I'll probably go for a pint. I was going to La Giaconda, but I'll give it a miss this week.'

Clara burst out laughing. 'Still frightened of the Mafia?'

'Too right. I'd a message on my voicemail from her brother.'

'What did he say?'

'Just, "Hello Michael, we need to talk about my sister".'

'No name?'

Nash shook his head.

'Well, that's easy enough. Dial 1471 and it'll give you his number.'

'Damn! I never thought of that. No good now – I've had a load of calls since.'

'You didn't recognize his voice?'

'No chance. My answer machine's got a fault. Everyone sounds like Frankie Valli on helium.'

'Where will you go for a drink?'

'The Horse and Jockey. It's a good pint, and I want to find out how your other boyfriend's getting on with his new dog.'

Clara looked at him suspiciously. 'My other boyfriend?'

'Jonas Turner. The one who calls you Sergeant Miniver. He asks about you whenever I go in.'

'Oh, him. What's this about a dog?'

'He bought a Jack Russell to keep rats off his allotment. Apparently he was conned into it by one of his cronies. He was asking for advice and his mate sold him a Jack. Told Jonas they were "ferocious little buggers, one man dogs and it took a bite out of his missus's leg". Jonas was sold on the idea, much to his wife's annoyance. She's trying to make its life as miserable as Jonas's. I want to find out how the training's going.'

'What training?'

'He's trying to teach it to bite his wife.'

'That's cruel.'

'I'll tell him you're threatening to call the RSPCA, shall I?'

'I didn't mean that.'

It was almost midnight when Nash left the pub. The door to his flat was in deep shadow. He located the lock, but couldn't get the key in. After three attempts, he worked out that the key was upside-down. He was about to open the door when a voice behind him whispered, 'Hello, Michael.'

The key fell onto the pavement with a clatter. 'Oh bugger!' Nash exclaimed. He squinted. 'I didn't expect you,' he said weakly.

'I said I'd be back. Didn't you get my texts?'

'Er, yes,' he mumbled. 'I've been busy though.'

'I can see that. Are you going to invite me in?'

'Oh yes, sorry. I'll just find my keys.'

She bent down and scooped the ring off the pavement. 'Let me.' She opened the door, then guided him through the hall and into the lounge.

He smiled at her. 'God, you're lovely.'

'And you, Michael, are drunk. I hope you're not too drunk. I've been travelling for fifteen hours. I don't want the journey to be wasted.' She began to unfasten his shirt. Gently she fingered the puckered edges of the healed scar on his chest. 'What's this?'

Nash looked down and shrugged. 'Perils of the job. I was shot by a madman who objected when I tried to arrest him.'

'A bit of an extreme reaction. Does it cause you any problems?'

He grinned. 'I hope not. You can judge if it affects my performance.'

Later, Nash said, 'I've a confession to make.'

'What is it?'

The beer had removed his inhibitions. 'I've forgotten your name.'

Her rich peal of laughter rang around the bedroom. 'But, Michael,' she told him reproachfully, 'how could you forget my name?'

'I don't know,' he confessed miserably. 'I realize it's unforgivable.'

'That's not what I meant. How could you forget my name when I've never told you it?'

Nash sat bolt upright. 'You mean that? I've been racking my brains to remember, and all the time you never told me? I don't believe you. Are you pulling my leg?'

Her reply was another outburst of laughter, smothered by Nash.

As dawn was breaking, their sleep was interrupted by the phone ringing.

Nash listened. 'I'll be right there.'

He looked at her. 'Sorry, I've got to go.'

'What's happened?'

'A body's been found. It sounds like murder.'

'When will you be back?'

'I've no idea. I can't tell whether I'll be four hours or forty-eight.'

She pulled the covers round her. As he began to get up she reached across. 'I think you need an incentive.' She kissed him, her tongue exploring his mouth, her hand gently massaging him. Eventually she released him.

'I'll be as quick as I can,' he gasped.

He was halfway through ringing Mironova's number when he remembered she was off duty. With Pearce on holiday, Helmsdale had no one available. He cancelled the call and dialled Netherdale. 'Who've you got in CID?'

Nash waited a few moments. 'DC Andrews is on call.'

Nash dialled her home phone number. A few minutes later a drowsy voice answered.

'Sorry to disturb you, Lisa. It's Mike Nash. I've got a stiff on my hands.'

'I don't want to know your personal problems.'

Nash grinned. 'I mean a body; a murder victim.'

'You pick your time, don't you?'

'I didn't pick it, any more than the corpse did.'

'It's a good job I wasn't up to no good.'

'Aren't you the lucky one.' Nash looked down. 'You should hear the complaints I got.'

A sleepy voice from Nash's bed muttered, 'You haven't heard anything yet.'

Lisa said, 'I'll be on my way as soon as I've got dressed and had a coffee.'

'A coffee! I wish somebody here would get out of bed and make coffee.'

'You want coffee, try Starbucks,' came from the bed.

Lisa continued, 'Where shall I meet you?'

'Can you pick me up? I had a few last night, so I don't want to drive.'

'Give me half an hour.'

The call to Andrews had been easy. Nash still had to ring the pathologist. He winced at the thought of what Ramirez would say. He hoped it would be in Spanish.

Nash had just finished his coffee when Lisa's car pulled up.

'Where are we going?' she asked.

'Head for the allotments on the edge of the Westlea. A bloke walking his dog found a body. The victim is male; has multiple stab wounds to his chest and stomach.'

'Any ID?'

'Not yet.'

The flashing lights pointed them to the crime scene. The constable keeping onlookers at bay acknowledged Nash and Andrews. 'The guy who found the body's over there talking to one of our men,' he told them.

'Did you check the body?'

'No, we thought it better not to disturb anything.'

'Good man.' Nash nodded his approval. A tarpaulin sheet hid the body from view. As they got closer Nash stopped dead.

'What's matter, Mike?'

He pointed. 'The man who found the body. I was drinking with him in The Horse and Jockey last night.'

'Ayup, Mr Nash.'

'Now then, Jonas. This is a surprise.'

'Surprise! It were hell of a shock, I can tell you.'

Nash looked down to where the terrier was scrabbling for attention. 'Now then, Pip.' Nash bent and stroked the dog. 'Did you find the body? We'll make a police dog of you yet. You're out and about early, Jonas.'

'This is one of my busiest days. Greengrocer calls on his way back from market. I've to be 'ere to load him up. Then I let Pip have a run before I go back home for t' toast the wife's cremated.' Jonas's gaze strayed to Lisa. His eyes sparkled pleasurably.

'Who's this then?' He nodded towards Andrews. 'What have you done with Sergeant Miniver? Don't tell me she's been transferred?'

Nash smiled. 'Don't worry, Jonas. She's off duty, that's all. This is Detective Constable Andrews.'

Turner surveyed the replacement. 'By gum, Mr Nash, they've got it right when they call it a bobby's job. You surround yourself with some smashers, don't you? Pleased to meet you, Miss Andrews. You'd better watch yourself with Mr Nash. He's allus got one girl or another on his arm.' Jonas winked conspiratorially at Lisa. 'Aye, I reckon he's a bad lad, is our Mr Nash.'

'Don't worry,' Lisa told him cheerfully, 'we all know that. Anyway, I'm spoken for.'

Turner's face fell. 'Damn. And there I was, thinking my luck had changed.'

Nash reverted to business. 'What time did you find the body?'

Turner scratched his head thoughtfully – no mean feat for one wearing a flat cap. 'It were just gone five o'clock when I left home. Takes me quarter of an hour to get here, so I'd be at t' allotment by about quarter past, twenty past at latest.'

'Was there anybody about?'

'Not a soul. I'd have noticed, specially at that time.'

'How long did it take you to load the produce?'

'I'd to cut it, or dig it up. Then wash t' mud off. Say half an hour, three quarters at most. We'd been walking about ten minutes afore we found t' poor chap.' Turner gestured to the tarpaulin.

'So we're talking about six o'clock to half past,' Nash suggested.

'Aye, that'd be about right. Then I'd to bike it into town to phone your lot. I tried t' boxes over there' – Turner jerked a thumb towards the Westlea – 'but they'd all been vandalized. If you work back from t' time I called in, say a quarter of an hour afore that.'

'Did you look at the body?' Nash asked.

'I saw enough.' Jonas shuddered.

'Did you recognize him?'

Turner scratched his head again. 'I did and I didn't.'

'What does that mean?'

'I don't know who he is … was. But I've seen him about. Never spoken to him, but I noticed him round here a time or two.'

'When you say "round here" where do you mean?'

'I've seen him a few times on this path. Enough for me to think, there's that chap again, if you get me.'

'OK, that'll do. We'll need a statement later, but we'll let you get off for your breakfast. We don't want your wife worrying.'

'That'll be the day.' Turner sniffed. 'It'll be cinders by now.'

They watched Turner walk towards the allotments. 'That doesn't sound like a marriage made in heaven,' Lisa suggested. 'What makes a man so bitter about his wife?'

'You haven't met her.'

They were interrupted by the uniformed officer. 'The pathologist's here.'

'This should be fun,' Nash said, as they approached Ramirez. 'Good morning, Professor.'

'It was,' the pathologist said sourly. 'Can't you save your necrophilia until normal hours?'

'I didn't choose the time,' Nash protested. 'You know DC Andrews, do you?'

Ramirez nodded. 'Don't get hooked up with Nash,' he told her. 'Not unless you share his passion for cadavers.'

'We'll let you get on with your examination,' Nash told him. 'Check the body for identification, will you? We'll be over by the road when you've finished.'

The SOCO team were stringing their incident tape in a wide circle round the area when Ramirez reported back. 'There's nothing to identify the victim. A couple of the coat pockets were inside out. There are several stab wounds to the chest and abdomen. Any of them would have caused death. The deceased has been deceased for between ten and fifteen hours. That's as much as I can tell you until the post-mortem.' Ramirez nodded to Andrews and walked briskly to his car.

'What's the significance of the pockets?'

Nash looked at Lisa. 'Removal of identification, I guess. Whether that was to make our job harder, or whether there's a deeper significance, I'm not sure. We need to ask Turner if he was at the allotment late yesterday and whether he saw anything then. Let's give him chance to digest his cremated toast. Then we can take him with us to Helmsdale station and get his statement. I'll have a word with the SOCO leader, then we'll get something to eat.'

'There were nobody about yesterday afternoon.'

'Have you noticed anyone hanging about there recently, Jonas?'

'I don't know if it's worth owt, but I noticed a car there a couple of days ago.'

'You don't happen to know the make or model?'

Nash was surprised when Turner said, 'Aye, I do.'

Nash looked up.

'It were a Superdo.'

'A what?'

'A Superdo. One of them sporty things. A Superdo Impressor, I think they call 'em.'

The fog in Nash's brain cleared. 'You mean a Subaru Impreza?'

'Aye, that's reet.'

'How do you know that?'

'Next-door neighbour's son; spoiled rotten. Soon as he got a licence they bought him one of them Superdos. He super-did it up.' Jonas chuckled at his own joke. 'It made a hell of a racket. All hours of t' day and night. He had it a year; then wrote t' bugger off. We all slept better after that – until t' little sod bought a motorbike.'

'I can see how that might stick in your memory,' Nash agreed. 'Can you tell us anything more about the Subaru near the allotments? Colour, for example?'

'It were a sort of mucky green,' Turner told him. 'And it were ought four red chester.'

Nash glanced at Lisa, who looked completely nonplussed.

'Sorry, I don't follow you,' Nash was forced to admit.

'Superdo near t' allotments. It were an ought four red chester.'

This time Nash caught on. 'You mean a nought four registration?' Turner nodded. '2004. You can't remember the number, can you?'

'No, sorry.'

'If you remember anything else, let me know. Or DC Andrews,' he added. He saw the sparkle in Turner's eyes and threw in a further incentive. 'If it's after the weekend you can tell Sergeant Mironova.'

'I'll do what I can for 'er, Mr Nash,' Turner promised with a salacious leer.

chapter eight

The murder kept Nash busy throughout Saturday. When he returned home, he found a note on the breakfast bar. 'Got to go to Milan tonight. See you soon, x.'

Nash smiled. She was teasing him, and he couldn't do anything about it. He settled down for the evening. He'd reports to read, but decided they could wait. He flicked the television on to watch *Match of the Day*. The theme music hadn't finished before he was sound asleep. He slept through two hours of TV before dragging himself to bed.

Next morning he felt refreshed and was up and about before 7 a.m. He brewed coffee and sat at the table. He pulled the folders out of his briefcase and began studying them. The report on the caravan fire confirmed Curran's suspicions. Nash's face was grim as he read the cold facts.

He turned his attention to the Vickers file. There were only a few days before the prisoner would be released. He picked up his phone. Fifteen minutes later, he set off for Felling Prison.

'I want you to reconsider your decision. If you come back, there's going to be trouble. It's already started. Your house was broken into a couple of nights ago. You nearly didn't have a home to go to.'

Vickers lifted his head. 'What do you mean?'

'The intruders set a fire. The fire brigade managed to put it out before it did much harm.'

'What was the damage?'

'The fire was contained in the lounge.'

'And that's all it was? The fire, I mean? There wasn't anything stolen?'

'Not that I'm aware.' Nash saw the prisoner relax.

'So, it's started already.' Vickers didn't seem particularly upset or shocked. He'd been concerned about something, though.

'You were expecting this.'

Vickers nodded. 'I knew something would happen.'

'Because of what you've done?'

Vickers' laugh was devoid of humour. 'Because of what I represent.'

'I don't follow.'

'Some people regard me as a threat. But I can't expect you to understand.'

'Why don't you try me? In a few days' time you'll be out of here. That doesn't mean you'll be free. You'll be watched by us; your movements will be restricted. There are people who won't be happy until you're dead. And yet you still insist on returning to Helmsdale? You must be crazy.'

If Vickers was alarmed, it didn't show. 'The ones who fear me; they're the reason I must return.'

'Then tell me what you know; what you suspect. Give me some idea how to protect you.'

When Vickers replied, his voice was barely above a whisper. 'My life doesn't matter. Other things are more important. I'll tell you when I'm back in Helmsdale. Not before.'

Monday morning found Tom Pratt in Helmsdale along with Clara, listening to Nash. 'That was it. I tried to make him change his mind. I suggested he put the house up for sale and move elsewhere. He wouldn't hear of it. I told him how much the house is worth. He wasn't interested. He reckons people are after him because he represents some sort of threat. About what, and who they are, he wouldn't say.'

'You don't think this is an act?' Clara asked.

'It could be. Or it may be Vickers doesn't know anything.'

'Do you still think he might be innocent?'

Pratt looked surprised by her question. 'You're not serious? Mike, you've read the evidence. There can't be any doubt.'

Nash explained his reservations. Pratt shook his head. 'I don't agree,' he muttered.

'Let's see what Vickers has to say when he's in Helmsdale. In the meantime, we've more pressing problems.'

Nash explained about the body found near the allotments. 'We need a description circulating to the media. I want a description of the dead man in tonight's paper,' Nash told Clara. 'Call the *Gazette*. Ask them to send someone over. The sooner we get identification, the sooner we can start looking for a motive. At present we're just sitting on our hands singing psalms.'

'That's an interesting concept,' Clara commented.

'Any clues from the crime scene?' Pratt asked.

Nash shook his head. 'SOCO reported this morning. It didn't amount to much. There are some footprints in the undergrowth close to where the body was found. Apart from that we've a sighting of a car. But they could be coincidence.'

'Hardly conclusive. Anything more on the caravan deaths?'

'Only to confirm it was arson.'

'No clues on that either?'

'Forensics picked up a substance from the undergrowth close to the caravan. It was semen. They've gone for DNA profiling on it. It's probably nothing to do with the fire. On the other hand, we've to look at every scrap of evidence.'

'If that's all, I'm off back to Netherdale. I'm seeing your friend King this afternoon. He'll want a detailed report. Shall I give him your love?' Pratt saw Nash's expression. 'Very well,' he laughed. 'I won't bother.'

Clara watched the superintendent leave. 'He's in a genial mood today. Surprising when you think what's going on.'

'He's not got long to go to his pension, that's probably got a lot to do with it. How was your weekend? Did you get high with the galloping major?'

'That man's got far too much energy.' Clara saw Nash's raised eyebrows and blushed. 'That's not what I meant. He had me dashing up and down mountains all day Saturday and yesterday. I've come to work for a rest. How was your weekend?'

'Nothing special, except I found out I don't have amnesia.' Nash explained about the practical joke.

'Good for her,' Clara approved. 'It's time somebody took you down a peg or two.'

'For that you can make the coffee.' Nash scowled.

When Clara returned, Nash handed her some paperwork. 'These are the notes I made after I'd seen Vickers.'

Clara's coffee had gone cold by the time she finished reading. 'Your doubts about Vickers are stronger than ever.'

'Yes. Either he's bluffing or there's something wrong about the whole case. One thing's certain. He doesn't care what happens. Nothing's going to stop him coming back to Helmsdale.'

'Are you visiting him again?'

'I said I'd pick him up on Friday.'

'Then we'd better start planning.'

They were interrupted by the phone. Nash answered, and after a few seconds he began to smile. 'I thought you were going to be longer. What do you want to do? That's fine. I need all the help I can get. No, she's not much help. All she does is sit here, making snide remarks about my love life and being generally insubordinate. And her coffee's lousy. Give me chance to clear it with HR. Call me later today.'

'Pearce?' Clara guessed, as Nash replaced the receiver.

'Yes, the second leg of his holiday was cancelled. Something to do with an airline strike. He wants to come back to work.'

'And the crack about me being insubordinate? What did Viv say about that?'

'He said, "Nothing's changed then".'

Appleyard was in his study. After a few minutes' thought, he picked up his pen and started to write. He set down a few sentences, paused and read them aloud.

He gathered his thoughts and began scribbling again. Eventually he put his pen down and read through the speech, altering a word here, a phrase there.

Appleyard would need to show it to Rathmell before the residents' meeting on Friday. He made a note to print off a press release. No point in making the speech if nobody read or heard it.

He picked up the phone to call Rathmell. He felt a glow of pride: he was about to announce a new political philosophy. 'Where do you want to meet?' he asked eagerly.

Rathmell frowned. 'I'm a bit pushed for time. Better make it in Helm Woods. If you drive along the road by the river, you'll come to a picnic area opposite the bridge over the Helm. Take the path through the woods. After about a mile it crosses the path for Kirk Bolton. Turn right and you'll see a clearing. I'll be waiting for you there, seven o'clock tonight.'

Rathmell finished the call and dialled another number. 'Are you free this evening? I've to meet the councillor at 7 p.m. in the clearing. I'll get rid of him as quickly as I can. I'll see you straight after. I'll bring a rug so we can be comfortable. I'm getting a bit tired of the confines of the car, even the Merc.' Rathmell cast a swift glance round before continuing, 'She's talking about a two-week trip to America, which means I'll have this place to myself.'

chapter nine

Netherdale Gazette was not blessed with limitless resources or the backing of a large conglomerate. The paper was owned by the Pollard family. They took an active part in the running of the daily. The founder had been involved until he was into his eighties. His two sons divided their responsibilities: the elder brother ran the newspaper whilst his sibling managed the other family enterprises. When they retired, the editorial duties were handed to the eldest grandson. Nor did the family's involvement rest purely with the male side: Helen Pollard had been features and women's editor for many years. Now nearing retirement, she was grooming her niece Becky to succeed her.

Becky, a good-looking and popular girl in her early thirties, was responsible for overseeing such technological advances as the paper could afford. She also acted as staff photographer and relief reporter.

It was in the photography role that Tucker sought her out. He hoped Becky could provide the equipment he needed and teach him how to use it. Becky stared at him in disbelief. 'You must be joking. Have you any idea how much they cost?'

Tucker shook his head.

'You'd get no change out of £4,000. And you're asking me to lend you equipment like that, when you don't have any idea how to use it?'

'I'll take care of it,' Tucker muttered defensively.

'Why do you want it?'

'I'm on a story. It might lead nowhere, but I don't think so.'

'I can't let you go gallivanting off with a highly sophisticated digital camera,' Becky objected.

'Haven't you got a spare?'

'The *Gazette*'s not made of money. We've only got two. One that I use and the other as backup. If mine developed a fault and you're off somewhere with the reserve, I'd get a right shafting. Sorry, JT, I can't risk it.'

'I thought you'd enjoy getting shafted,' Tucker murmured. 'So there's nothing you can do?'

'There's an old one you could use. It's a good enough camera. It's just not digital.'

Tucker looked baffled. 'What's that mean?'

Becky explained. 'The drawback is you can't view the images; you have to get them developed. I can lend you the analogue version. Give me half an hour and I'll get it out and give you a quick tutorial.'

'That's great, Becky. But there's another favour.' Tucker hesitated.

'Go on. Spit it out.'

She listened in growing astonishment. 'Hell's bells, JT! You don't want much, do you? What makes you think I'd have that sort of gear?'

Tucker shrugged. 'I thought you might know someone.'

Becky thought it over. 'There is a bloke I could ask. But it won't be cheap.'

'That's alright.' Tucker grinned. 'I can put it on my expenses.'

Becky gave him a long, cold stare. 'That's supposed to be an incentive, is it? Oh, very well, but I'm not promising anything.'

Juris had been worried since Zydrumas failed to return, and had spent a dreadful weekend. He'd decided to go to the farmer but as he set out for the farmhouse, he'd seen the flashing lights. His courage failed him. He'd retreated to the house and locked and bolted the doors behind him. It was only later that he thought that the police activity might have something to do with Zydrumas. That intensified his fear. By Monday morning, when Zydrumas was still absent, he went to seek out his employer, and told him of the Latvian's disappearance.

The farmer told him of the stabbing and asked, 'Do you think the dead man might be Zydrumas?'

'I do not know. I am very much afraid.'

'We'd better go to the police.' The farmer saw the look of anxiety on his employee's face. 'You've nothing to worry about. Your papers are in order?'

Juris nodded. 'Well then, don't fret,' the farmer continued. 'The police in this country aren't to be scared of, unless,' he added with the bitterness of experience, 'they've got a bloody radar gun in their hand.'

*

Clara was giving the *Gazette* reporter a description of the victim. She'd barely left Nash's office when his mobile bleeped. At the same time the phone in the outer office rang. He glanced at the text – 'Michael darling. Leaving Milan tomorrow a.m. Dinner? X.' He turned his attention to the phone. 'Mike, there's a couple of blokes in reception reckon they know the dead man. Shall I get them up there, or do you want them in an interview room?'

'Bring them here. Whilst you're at it, get Clara on one side and explain what's going on.'

Nash eyed the two men. The older looked confident and relaxed. The younger man looked nervous. The farmer gave his name, and introduced his companion. He explained what Juris had told him, and the conclusion they'd drawn.

Nash turned to the younger man. 'When was the last time you saw your friend?'

Juris spoke slowly and clearly. His English, though accented, was good. 'I left farm. It was Friday afternoon. We had been making meeting. Zydrumas was to follow. He did not come. I waited at house all of Friday night. On Saturday I had shopping, but was only gone one hour. Still Zydrumas did not come. On Sunday I was at house all day. No one came. So I told to our employer' – he glanced at the farmer – 'this morning. That was first I heard of dead man.'

Nash looked at the older man. The farmer nodded. 'Zydrumas left me about twenty-five minutes after Juris.'

'This meeting. What was it about?'

'Zydrumas is in charge of my labour force. We employ workers from Eastern Europe, Lithuania, Latvia and Poland principally. The meeting was to arrange for Juris to take charge at Helmsdale Farm. That would leave Zydrumas free to concentrate on recruitment. I've just bought two more farms. That's going to mean a lot more staff.'

'The name Zydrumas.' Nash turned back to Juris. 'Where's that hail from?'

'Zydrumas is from Lithuania,' Juris replied simply.

'Are you also Lithuanian?'

'No, I am of Latvia.'

'First off, we'd better see we're not panicking over nothing. I'm going to get someone to take you to view the body. Not very pleasant,

I'm afraid. If the dead man is Zydrumas I'll need you both to give official statements.'

He picked up the phone. 'Is DS Mironova still with that reporter? Ask her to pop back here.'

Juris had never been in such a place. He looked at the drab grey walls and shivered. The furniture was purely functional. A small table with a plastic top and matching chairs. No pictures broke up the monotony of the walls; no magazines softened the harsh lines of the table.

A man dressed in a loose-fitting olive-green shirt with matching trousers entered. His costume was as drab as the room. He beckoned them to follow.

Juris looked at the long table covered with a sheet. He swallowed; he knew what was beneath. The pathologist drew back the sheet. Juris stared at the corpse.

'Well?'

The pathologist's single word was like a thunderclap. Juris nodded bleakly. 'This is Zydrumas.' He turned away, the horror overwhelming him.

Outside the building, the young Latvian leant against the wall to quell the nausea in his stomach and try to stop his knees from shaking.

What would this mean? Now that Zydrumas was dead would Juris's job go with it? He looked up as the door opened, and the detective ushered the farmer out. Juris's employer looked equally shocked. 'We've to go make a statement,' he explained.

The first half of the journey was spent in silence. Eventually, the farmer spoke. 'I don't know, lad.' His employer shook his head. 'This is a hell of a mess.'

'What will happen now?' Juris asked, fearful of the reply.

The farmer had obviously given the matter some consideration. 'I've a farm to run,' he told the younger man. 'Three farms,' he corrected himself. 'I was relying on Zydrumas to get me the men. Where I'm going to find enough labour, I haven't the foggiest idea.'

'Is there no one who can find the workers?'

'Nobody I know of,' his employer stated flatly. He paused and looked searchingly at the young Latvian. 'At least, not until a few seconds ago. I need to think about this.' They were on the outskirts of Helmsdale before he broke silence. 'As things stand, I've only a handful of workers coming back from last year. At best I've only enough to man one farm. I need workers quickly. Do you reckon you could do the job?'

Juris looked up in surprise. 'You want me to do the work of Zydrumas?'

'Why not? You know my methods. What do you reckon?'

'How do you know I could do this?'

'I don't,' the farmer admitted bluntly. 'Right now you're my only choice.'

Juris remained unconvinced. 'I would not know how.'

'Begin by finding people and offering them money. That usually works. You've done the job, you talk their lingo. Is it a deal?'

Nash looked up as Clara entered. Her nod was sufficient. 'Get their statements typed up and signed, then join me back here,' he told her. 'We've only four days until Vickers is released. I hope nothing else happens in the meantime.'

Clara shook her head. 'And you're always telling me not to tempt fate!'

Becky showed Tucker how to work the camera and to load and unload a film. She watched him shoot a variety of subjects using the zoom and wide-angle facilities. When he finished the reel and unloaded it, she said, 'Come back tomorrow and I'll show you the results. As to the other, you're in luck. I can get what you wanted, but it'll take a few days. It's going to cost you an arm and a leg.'

Tucker picked up the camera bag. As he left the *Gazette* offices he'd only one more decision to make. Which of his targets should he follow? He opted to follow Rathmell and parked a discreet distance from the Euro MP's house, Houlston Grange. It was 6.30 p.m. when the Mercedes glided out of the gateway. He followed.

When Rathmell turned onto the lane that ran alongside the river, Tucker dropped further back. Passing the bridge, he thought he'd lost him until he spotted the picnic area to his left. He glanced into the car park. Barely visible through the trees was Rathmell's Mercedes; the only vehicle.

Further along, Tucker located a track where his car was well nigh invisible. He picked up the camera and was about to set off when he heard a vehicle approaching. He stepped behind a bank of silver birches and waited. Only when he heard the clunk of the car door did he move.

He walked slowly down the road and into the car park. Tucker could see the vague outline of someone moving along the path leading through the woods.He inspected the other vehicle. It looked like the one he'd seen on the moor. This time he wasn't going to be thwarted. He made a note of the make, model and registration number, stuffed his notebook away and followed the new arrival.

More at home in towns, Tucker was far from confident in his ability to follow someone through open country. Fortunately, the man he was tracking was even less of the outdoor type. Tucker stumbled from one patch of cover to the next, suffering painful scratches from briar and brambles. When the man in front paused at a junction, he panicked and sought refuge behind a pain-free laurel bush. After the man stepped into a large clearing, Tucker edged closer until his quarry came into view. The location seemed vaguely familiar, but he couldn't think why. Before he'd chance to dwell on this, his attention was occupied with what was happening.

Carlton Rathmell emerged from behind a clump of shrubs. Tucker watched the men converge and begin talking, wishing he could get close enough to hear their conversation. He sighed in frustration. If he'd only got the equipment Becky had promised. He strapped the camera round his neck and attached the telephoto lens. Then he paused, remembering where the buttons were located before he adjusted the focus. As the image sharpened, he lowered the camera again in surprise. Councillor Frank Appleyard! What was he doing, meeting Rathmell in secret?

Tucker eased his finger onto the shutter release and was about to depress it when Appleyard moved. Tucker waited. He watched the councillor take a sheet of paper from his pocket and unfold it. Tucker pressed the button as Rathmell began to study the document. The click of the shutter and the whirring of the auto-wind sounded like gunfire. Tucker held his breath and prepared to take flight. In the clearing, neither man had moved. The trees formed a natural amphitheatre. There had been plenty of rain in recent weeks, the River Helm plunged enthusiastically over one of the weirs that marked its progress down the dale. The noise of the cascading water masked the sound of the camera. The noise was a mixed blessing. It shielded the reporter, but made it impossible for him to eavesdrop. Although he'd have preferred the riskier option, Tucker relaxed and raised the camera. He'd used almost a whole reel of film before Rathmell folded the paper and handed it back. Then Appleyard turned to leave.

Tucker saw Rathmell hadn't followed. He decided to wait. As he eased his aching limbs, he heard the sound of someone approaching, their footsteps light but definite. He shrank back into the painful concealment of the gorse. The footsteps came closer and Tucker schooled himself to breathe silently. A minute later the newcomer passed: Gemma Fletcher.

It was an hour before the couple left the clearing. It came as something of a shock when Tucker glanced at his watch. When he heard the sound of their departing cars, the pressman emerged from his hiding place. He was cold, stiff, scratched and sore. He'd been dined on by a colony of midges and had to remove over a dozen spines donated by the gorse bush.

However, he'd some salacious photographs, such as were rare outside the confines of a hard porn film. The politician and his mistress had stopped at little in slaking their lust. Tucker had the pictures to prove it and was already devising captions. 'European Member Exposed!' was his favourite.

Shortly after Rathmell turned into the main road, the evening sun struck metal, sending a shaft of light into his eyes. He glanced sideways, to see a car tucked away in what was little more than a cart track. Rathmell braked hard. Why was the car hidden? He discounted the obvious reason. For one thing there was no movement. For another the windows weren't steamed up. It was probably nothing, but to be on the safe side he scribbled the car registration number down.

'JT? It's Becky Pollard. Those rolls of film you left me? I've developed them.'

'What are they like?'

'The ones you shot with the lens cap on didn't come out at all. After you took it off, the quality got better.'

'No need to rub it in.' Tucker could almost picture Becky's grin.

'As for your second roll, there's certainly no doubt what's behind that relationship.'

'It didn't take rocket science to work that out.'

'I thought you'd branched out into hard porn before I recognized Rathmell. Who's the woman? I take it she isn't Mrs Rathmell?'

'Certainly not.' As he spoke, the relevance of the location came to him. He gasped aloud.

'JT, are you there?'

He realized Becky was speaking. 'Sorry, something distracted me. I'll tell you later about the woman. Let's just say her identity could be highly significant. There may be another angle to this story I hadn't grasped until now.'

'Sorry, JT, you've lost me completely.'

'I'll tell you when I've figured it out for myself.'

'I'll try to control my impatience. What do you want me to do with these photos?'

'Stick them in an envelope and post it to my flat. I'm not sure when I'll be back in the office.'

'What about that gear?'

'Leave it with reception. I'll pick it up when I can.'

'I'll call you when I've got it.'

chapter ten

Rathmell was discussing progress with his agent, who was explaining, 'I've put the word out through the local press regarding Friday's meeting and suggested they get their stringers along. I warned them, if they miss out it will cost them. I've spoken to local radio and TV and they'll have crews there. I've concentrated on Appleyard's involvement. I haven't gone any further than that.'

'Get back and tell them I'll also be speaking.'

The agent was surprised. 'I thought you were leaving it to Appleyard? Wouldn't that look as if you're jumping on his band-wagon?'

'Not at all. I'll get Frank to put forward his ideas. After he's finished, I'll announce our plans.'

'That's brilliant; it'll ensure bigger and better coverage.'

'I want you to liaise with Jake Fletcher to make sure the attendance is as strong as he promised. And that security is water-tight.' Rathmell smiled. 'Not too water-tight, though. It would be a good idea to organize some heckling. Maybe a few mildly violent protests too.'

'You want trouble?'

'As long as it's contained. The more unreasonable the "protestors", the better we'll look. It'll also give us the sympathy vote.'

'As long as no one suspects the trouble's of our own making.'

'I'll leave that to you and Jake. I'll call Appleyard and explain the change.'

'Before I go, Carl, I've got the details of that car.' He passed a piece ·of paper to Rathmell. He saw the MEP's expression change. 'Is that bad?'

Rathmell looked up. 'I can deal with it.'

The agent saw the look in his employer's eyes and shivered.

*

Nash had been in bed less than fifteen minutes when he was disturbed. He fumbled for the phone and grunted into the receiver, a sound that by use of some imagination might have been 'Hello'.

'Michael, it's Leonie.'

'What? Who?' he was totally confused.

'It's Leonie. Gino's sister?'

Nash was beginning to wake up. 'Forgive me for not recognizing the name.'

The sarcasm was ignored. 'Michael, I'm calling from New York. I have something to tell you.'

Nash struggled to guess. Pregnant? He doubted it. What then? Found someone else? He played for time. 'That's why you're ringing in the middle of the night. I thought you were in Milan?'

'Sorry. I forgot about time zones and yes, I was. But, Michael, I've been offered a new job. One that's too good to miss. I start next Monday.'

'Good for you.' Was it worth waking him up to tell him this?

'The problem is it's here, in New York. I've been appointed fashion editor for one of the big American glossies. It's the chance of a lifetime. But it means I won't be back in England for a long time. I wanted you to be first to know. I haven't even told Gino yet. I didn't want you finding out from him. I'm sorry, Michael. Sorry for waking you up too.'

'Leonie, don't worry. Maybe we'll get together sometime.' They talked for a while before he wished her well and said goodbye. After he replaced the receiver, Nash lay for a while in the darkness pondering this turn of events. Perhaps Clara was right. He seemed unable to maintain a relationship.

Nash met with Mironova and Viv Pearce next morning for an update. 'We need to get to grips with things before they get out of hand. Even more out of hand,' Nash corrected himself. 'So far we've had an arson attack that killed three people, plus a fatal stabbing. It's possible these are racially motivated.'

'Mike, you're forgetting the other arson attack. On Vickers' house,' Clara reminded him.

'That blows the racial theory out of the water.'

'There could still be a link,' Clara hesitated. 'The attacks might have been timed to coincide with Vickers' release.'

'What's the point of that?' Viv was still trying to grasp all that had happened.

Clara looked at him. 'I'm not sure. Perhaps they're intended to mask Vickers being the real target. But no, that's too far-fetched.'

'I don't think we should dismiss anything out of hand until we uncover the motive,' Nash pointed out.

'That could be tricky if it's a psychopath.'

Billy was restless. The knifing had been alright. He'd loved it when the blood spurted, even when it went all over him. But it wasn't nearly as good as a fire. He wanted lots more fires. Then he could get rid of hundreds, if he picked the right place. Club Wolfgang would be good. He'd seen it on Friday nights. He'd thought of it before. Now he knew some of the migrant workers went there, he'd do it. One Friday: soon.

He tried to calm himself. He'd got another target from Danny. He'd do them tonight. He wondered if any of them would come running out, all on fire. Like the bloke from the gippovan. That would be something.

Billy had been watching them for days. He knew their routine; when to do it and how. He was getting good at this. If he'd worked it out before, he wouldn't have failed at the pervert's house. But Danny promised he could have another go, when the pervert was there. Billy liked that. It was alright doing an empty house: he'd done one before. Well, three to be exact, plus a few barns and outbuildings. But it wasn't the same. He had to be patient. Danny had said it would only be a few days. The bloke had been inside for rape and murder. So it was going to be justice. But for the moment, all that mattered was tonight. Tonight it was their turn. Their turn to burn. Billy felt the rhyme in his head. It made him smile. Their turn to burn. Their turn to burn. Their turn to burn.

The flat above the paper shop had been home to the Hassan family since Khalid and Zayna married. Their younger son, Hafiz, woke up. The tightness in his chest was the first symptom; a feeling all too familiar. He groped on the bedside table for his inhaler. Then he remembered. He'd left it in the lounge. He waited, hoping the asthma attack would go away. The tightness got worse. He was beginning to gasp. Hafiz thrust back the duvet, stood up and swayed slightly. His head felt muzzy. This was different. This wasn't like his previous attacks. It was then he noticed the smell. Something was on fire. He opened his bedroom door. The smell got worse. He went to his parents' room and hammered on the door. 'Mama!' half shout, half scream. 'Papa!' more scream than shout; all terror. 'Wake up! Wake up! Fire! Wake up!'

Khalid opened the door, eyes drugged with sleep. Thought the boy was dreaming but this nightmare was real. He caught the smell. 'Zayna! Zayna, come quick. The house is on fire.'

Khalid went to the next door, shouting, 'Jalila!' He ran in and shook his daughter. 'Jalila, get up! Now! Fire! Now, girl! Now!'

He ran to Adil's room. The boy was already up. Khalid went to the flat door. He reached for the handle: too hot. He pointed to the other end of the corridor. The smoke was getting worse; choking. Hafiz could barely breathe. 'Adil, take care of your brother.'

Khalid opened the French door onto the balcony, their one addition to the property. The family stumbled outside and clustered together; breathed the clean, fresh, night air. Behind them the smoke was thicker, accompanied by a roaring sound. Khalid looked back. Yellow flames, licking round the flat door. If he'd opened that ... They needed to get away. The balcony was a respite, not a haven. The drop was too far. Sheets, they needed sheets. Khalid signalled Adil, explained tersely.

'Hafiz's bedroom, it's nearest.' Adil stepped towards the corridor.

Khalid shook his head. 'No, single bed – sheets not big enough. Our room's better.'

'No, Khalid!' Zayna yelled. 'Airing cupboard – it's closer.'

It took less than two minutes. It felt like two hours. Back on the balcony, both of them were coughing. Khalid closed the doors behind them as Adil looped a sheet round the rail. He paused. 'Listen!'

In the distance they could hear the faint sound of sirens. 'Fire engine,' Adil said. 'Shall we wait?'

Khalid glanced back. 'No.' He pointed. Through the glass, flames glowed and flickered evilly. 'No time.'

Jalila went first. They tied her in a sheet and told her to cling on. She reached the ground, and unfastened the sheet. Hafiz was next. The boy was almost passing out. He reached the ground, but was too weak to unfasten the knots. Jalila helped him. On the balcony Zayna was arguing with her eldest son. Adil was tying his mother into a sheet whilst she was still protesting. As they gently lowered her to the ground, Adil could feel warmth on his back. Knew the fire was getting nearer. It seemed an age before the knots were undone. 'You next, Papa.'

Khalid blinked. His son was ordering him! 'No,' he protested. 'You must go.'

Adil shook his head. 'They need their father. Go!'

As Khalid disappeared over the rail, Adil heard the glass in the door shatter. Felt a wave of heat. Desperately, he pulled the sheet up. He could feel his hair singeing. No time for knots. He grabbed the end of the sheet, put one foot on the rail, then jumped.

Nash's mobile chirped. It was Clara. 'More trouble,' she began tersely. 'Fire on the Westlea, an immigrant family's shop and flat. Nobody badly hurt, thank God. But the fire brigade's been attacked by a mob. I'm on my way.'

'I'll meet you there.'

The fire was all but out when Nash arrived. Clara greeted him. 'Doug's over there.' She pointed to one of the trio of appliances that were parked, lights flashing. They stepped carefully over the snaking hoses.

'Busy night, Doug?'

Chief Fire Officer Doug Curran looked harassed. 'I'm thinking of getting a transfer to your mob. Our work's dangerous enough. But when we get attacked by a gang throwing stones and Molotov cocktails, it makes you wonder if it's worthwhile. Damned good job your uniformed men arrived.' Curran gestured to a small group of officers climbing into a Transit minibus.

Nash frowned. 'What happened?'

'It could have been worse. The family escaped via a balcony and some makeshift ropes. Sheets to be exact. It was arson again. Oldest trick in the book – petrol poured through a letterbox and a match tossed in. The flat's gutted. Fortunately the shop's barely damaged; separate entrance. Two minor casualties besides smoke inhalation. One of the children had an asthma attack. He's been taken to hospital along with his brother, who sprained his ankle. The mother's gone with them and the daughter too. The little girl's just suffering mild shock. Father's over there.' He pointed to a blanket-draped figure, wearing an oxygen mask, sitting in the back of an ambulance.

'What about the attack on your officers?'

'A couple of grazes from stones, nothing worse. Some bastard sliced through one of our hoses with a knife. Your lot turned up and charged them. They all scarpered and haven't been seen since. It was bloody hairy for a few minutes though.'

'I'd better have a word with our guys. Then I'll talk to the victim.'

'His name's Mr Hassan. Family's been here for ages. Well known and well liked. Or so everybody thought.'

'Thanks, Doug.' Nash gestured to Clara to follow him. Before they reached the Transit, it pulled away.

'That's odd. Who ordered our men here?'

'I thought you'd done it.'

'I didn't have time. Besides, there were half a dozen of them. We don't have that many. Maybe somebody at Netherdale used their initiative.'

'They did right. It could have turned nasty if that mob hadn't been scared off.'

'Let's see what Mr Hassan can tell us.'

They paused for a word with the paramedic before speaking to the newsagent. Hassan was able to add little to their knowledge. After a few minutes the ambulance took him to join his family.

As Nash was leaving, his mobile rang. He listened for a moment before replying. 'Right, Mironova's with me. We'll be straight round.'

He turned to Clara. 'That was Viv. Our stone throwers didn't disperse. They merely moved on. They've been attacking another house. Care to guess where?'

Clara looked baffled.

'Thirty-two Grove Road.'

Nash pulled in behind the police car. Pearce and a couple of uniformed men were standing outside Vickers' front gate, surrounded by a small group of interested bystanders. Neighbours or stone throwers? Nash wondered.

'What's the story?'

'I was about to set off to join you when a treble nine came in. I got hold of these two and we came straight round. The mob had scarpered by the time we arrived so we've been talking to the residents. They reckon there were about a dozen, all in their late teens. Nobody saw them clearly.'

'No descriptions?'

'All I got was "they looked like all teenagers", which doesn't help.'

'Have you checked the house?'

'All the front windows have been smashed. They've done a couple at the back as well.'

'Any other properties damaged?'

'Not that I can see.'

'Have you been inside?'

'No, I waited for you.'

'OK, Clara, you try and get statements. I want all the names and addresses. We'll have a look round inside. Scrounge a rug or something to put over the broken glass. I don't fancy doing myself an injury climbing through the window.'

As far as they could tell, nothing inside had been touched. Nash left Clara with instructions for a guard to remain overnight. 'Ring an emergency glazier and then go home. We can't do anything else tonight. I'm going to Netherdale first thing tomorrow to talk to Tom. The situation's getting unmanageable.'

When Nash returned next morning, he went straight into his office. One look at his face forbade them asking him how the meeting had gone. 'Toss you for it.' Viv stared at Nash's closed door. 'See who asks him if he wants a coffee.'

Clara smiled. 'One of the penalties of rank. Go put the kettle on.'

Nash was studying reports on the latest violence. 'Coffee?' she asked.

Nash grunted.

'Viv's making some.' She sat down. 'Go on.'

Nash raised his head. 'Go on what?'

'Spit it out. It obviously isn't good. You're back in Helmsdale, remember? We're all in it together.'

'Tom wasn't alone. He had King with him. King already knew about the fire and the trouble at Vickers' place. Where he got that info, I've no idea. I asked for more officers and a higher level of backup. Tom supported me all the way, but King would have nothing to do with it.'

'He turned it down?'

'Yes, and made it clear I was wasting my time asking.'

'Not even extra backup for the Westlea problems and Vickers?'

'He told me we should ignore Vickers. We should concentrate on the arsonist and the knife attack. He added a threat for good measure. "If you can't cope, we'll replace you with officers who can. I suggest you pay more attention to your duties as an officer of the crown and spend less time on your hyperactive social life".'

Clara whistled. 'He doesn't pull his punches, does he? Was that all?'

'I've no idea. I left at that point.'

'You walked out?'

'It was either that or throw him through the window. I don't reckon that'd look too good on my CV, do you?'

'Probably not. What was Tom doing?'

'Trying to pretend he wasn't there. He saw there was no point trying to stick up for me.'

'What are you going to do?'

'Carry on as before. We'll have to manage. I'm going to ask Tom for a memo confirming the details of this morning's fiasco. When every-thing goes pear-shaped I'll produce it in my defence. King's a great one for doing everything by the book. I'll just have to make sure I've covered my arse.'

'I don't reckon King's acting alone. I had a call from Creepy whilst you were out. He's been asked to come here next week. A fact-finding visit regarding DCC King's restructuring plans. I told him I'd check with you.'

'Let the bugger come. With luck our pyromaniac will have the Westlea ablaze by then. I'll send Creepy to piss on the fire.'

Clara winced. 'Don't say that, not even as a joke.'

Nash was about to reply when the phone rang. He listened. 'That's good news. I wish it could have been longer. Thanks for letting me know.' He turned to Clara. 'That was the governor of Felling Prison. Apparently there's been a mistake on the paperwork for Vickers' release. Somebody filled the wrong date in. He doesn't get out until Sunday.'

'I suppose we should be thankful for small mercies.'

'True. Two days extra isn't much of a breathing space, though. Let's hope we can make the most of it.'

chapter eleven

Westlea Community Centre was a two-storey redbrick building. It boasted an auditorium capable of seating 300, and a stage of which Helmsdale Amateur Dramatic Society availed themselves for their shows. Two nights a week, the more athletic residents played badminton on the two courts. Senior citizens' groups hosted socials and coffee mornings. The WI held weekly meetings and the local Scout group met there, as did the girls in the Brownies.

The Residents' Association usually met in one of the smaller side rooms on the upper floor, convenient for the tea-making facilities. For this event, however, nothing less than the main hall was suitable. On Friday evening, as Rathmell's agent looked out from the wings, he could see the hall was full. There were no spaces in the press seats, which was even more satisfying. He spotted two TV cameras in the side aisles. Obviously the press releases had worked.

There were three gatherings of young men and women standing in watchful groups around the hall. They would be the stewards Jake Fletcher had promised would be present 'in case of trouble'. As he watched, Fletcher joined him. 'Everything set?'

Fletcher nodded. 'We've got the security in place.' He pointed towards the youngsters. 'They may not look much, but they're capable of sorting anything that might happen here.'

'What about the trouble-makers?'

'They're all close to where the stewards are standing. Makes it easier to get them outside.'

'What happens outside?'

'They'll be taken to the pub and bought drinks all night.' Fletcher grinned. 'Cheap enough, even the amount they can sup. Where's Carl? We're due to start in ten minutes.'

'Relax. He's been here a while. He said he was going into the dressing room to have a chat with Frank. Thought it would be better if he waited until the house lights are down before he took his seat. That way, attention will be on Appleyard.'

Rathmell hadn't reached the dressing room. As Fletcher was speaking with the agent, the MEP was inside one of the cubicles in the Ladies' with Gemma Fletcher. Their conversation was a whispered one. 'You know what we're going to do tonight, don't you?'

'Of course. I'll be cheering with the rest. That's all I can do for the present. In public at least.'

'It won't always be that way. When our movement takes off I'll be free of the financial shackles. Then we can be together properly.'

'You're sure?'

'Absolutely. But there's still the other problem.'

'You mean Vick—'

'Shhh, don't mention that name. Don't worry, he'll soon be history. I promised he'd be dealt with as soon as he became available. I tried to scare him off. But this will be a more permanent solution.'

'Carl, promise one thing?'

'What's that?'

'Whatever you arrange, it won't involve Jake and Ronnie. You know what they're like. If they get near him, they'll lose it. I don't want them to finish up inside.'

'I'll do my best.'

'Can I tell them what you're planning?'

'Better not. Leave it to me. Now, as of Tuesday, I'll have the house to myself for a couple of weeks. Would you like to visit for a few days?'

'I have to go to work. I'm away Monday and Tuesday setting up a sales demonstration.'

'Can't you call in sick?'

Gemma felt her resolve weakening.'I shouldn't.'

'OK then, how about you come over on Tuesday when you've finished work?'

'I'll think about it,' she told him. As if she hadn't already made up her mind.

'There's bound to be a fair amount of media interest after tonight, so I'm afraid you'll have to stay out of sight at the house.'

Gemma began to caress him. 'Have you anywhere in mind?'

'I know the ideal place. My bedroom.'

*

Appleyard started with a degree of nervousness he hadn't antici-
pated. He was used to addressing public meetings, some of them
hostile, but tonight's speech was the most contentious he'd ever
delivered.

'Thank you for coming,' he began. 'The attendance reflects a
strong community spirit. It's that spirit I wish to appeal to, the
pride in one's neighbourhood and a desire to retain the values that
make it so special. I'm also speaking of the wider community that
is Great Britain. Are we content with Britain? Or do we want it to be
Great Britain? Are we to be British? Or should we stick with being
"Brits"?

'This is not an attack on any ethnic group. Rather it is a defence of
the most ignored, vilified and abused section of our community. I
refer to the ordinary working people, whose parents and grandparents laid down their lives for this nation in two world wars, in the
belief that their sacrifice would keep Britain sacrosanct. Our ancestors
toiled unceasingly in mill and factory, farm or pit, to maintain a way
of life that is uniquely British. Now we must ask some hard questions.
Questions like, why am I passed over for job after job? Or why am I
at the end of a housing list when asylum seekers go straight to the
head? And why don't I get furniture, fixtures and fittings at the
expense of the state? Or how come these newcomers have access to
social services and benefits that are denied my family?

'When such inequalities occur throughout the land it's no wonder
that same indigenous lower ' – Appleyard corrected himself swiftly
– 'hard-working sector feels let down by the representatives they
elected. Their optimism has long since turned to cynicism. It has
been destroyed by the systematic attack on their traditional way of
life. Instead of rewarding their voters, politicians dump extra
burdens of tax on them. Their traditional pleasures, alcohol and
tobacco, have been taxed out of sight. If they can afford a car they
have to pay more and more for their petrol. They find themselves
beset from all sides.

'What started as a whisper of discontent has grown to a rumble of
anger. If the position continues unchecked, it will become a shout of
defiance, and violence will spill over onto the streets. Politicians must
act now before it is too late. They must meet the people who elected
them, the people they have so callously abandoned. Only when they
address the inequalities that discriminate against the indigenous
population can they hope to avoid the consequences of their years of

active neglect. Only then will there be any chance of Britain reverting to its former status of Great Britain.'

Appleyard paused. To the audience, it was a pause designed to increase the impact of his words. To a few, however, it was a signal. The pause, following the phrase 'Britain reverting to its former status of Great Britain', was the cue for the first disturbance.

Four hecklers rose from the second row and began chanting 'Fascist pig', 'Racist bastard', 'Nazi swine', in a confused yet curiously well-orchestrated series of taunts. They were swiftly surrounded and bundled, with minimal resistance, from the hall.

Appleyard smiled, unruffled by the interruption. 'I was prepared for some opposition to what I had to say,' he told the audience. 'I didn't expect it to be delivered with such wit.'

His words were greeted with laughter. Those who had been primed laughed because it was expected. But that was what they were there for. The others followed suit. Appleyard allowed the audience to settle.

'Turning to local issues, the disquiet is apparent. Last week saw a tragic waste of life when a caravan belonging to a family of travelling people was attacked. Possibly they should have been on the site provided. That's not the point. The attack was a symptom of fear; distrust of those whose lifestyle and values are different to our own. Then a migrant worker was stabbed to death. Although the motive is as yet unclear, it may well be a symptom of rising discontent.'

Again he paused. It seemed as natural as the previous one. The press seats were too far from the stage to allow the use of recorders or mobile phones, so reporters were busy scribbling and didn't notice anything amiss, until the prolonged silence made them look up.

Becky Pollard had positioned herself in the lighting gallery, at the rear of the upper floor, overlooking the hall. It was the ideal position to get shots of the stage, the speaker and the audience. It also gave her an unrivalled view. She watched a further group of protesters begin to object. This time they weren't content with hurling abuse at the councillor. They threw tomatoes and eggs. These fell short, some disastrously so. One, to Becky's delight, hit the reporter from a local TV news programme.

Becky was almost sure the protesters had begun rising from their seats as Appleyard was still speaking. Had it been chance that he'd paused? Or were they prepared? How could they know the councillor would stop just then? Curiously, Becky watched as stewards wrestled with the objectors. From her vantage point, even that seemed staged. She hurried downstairs, across the large vestibule, into the car park; then dodged round the corner of the building and waited.

The small knot of protesters emerged, surrounded by stewards. Once outside, the struggles ceased and the group united in smiles and pats on the back. Two stewards joined the protesters as they left. Becky continued shooting, grateful for the silent operation of her camera. She waited until the remaining stewards re-entered the building before returning. For the first time in her career with the *Gazette*, Becky felt afraid.

The incident had lasted a few minutes. As Becky reached the gallery, she heard Appleyard coming to the end of his diatribe.

'The choices are stark. If we don't see action in the near future, I tremble to think of the consequences. If the people of this country can't obtain justice, they might form themselves into action groups. If that happens, if the rule of law becomes the rule of the vigilante, who knows where it will lead? The country could dissolve into two camps. One occupied by those for whom the rule of law isn't acceptable, set against them the decent people who won't tolerate lawlessness. At that point society will be close to terminal meltdown.'

Appleyard held his hands out wide, as if embracing his audience. They rose to cheer him. Again, Becky had the feeling everything was being carefully choreographed. She got a couple of shots of the stage surrounding the councillor. She captured images of three men standing in the wings. One, she knew. It was Carlton Rathmell's agent. The other two were familiar, although Becky couldn't name them.

Her attention reverted to centre-stage as she realized the action wasn't over. Appleyard was extending his right hand towards someone in the front row. A figure emerged from the dark and as he reached the brightness of the footlights, Becky gasped in surprise. Her training to the fore, she concentrated her lens on the newcomer.

Appleyard performed the introduction. 'For those few who don't recognize him, I'm pleased and proud to introduce Carlton Rathmell, who has represented this region's interest in the European Parliament so vigorously.'

The applause broke out again as the two men shook hands. The pressmen scribbled, cameras flashed, a few camera phones blinked, the TV cameras swivelled from MEP to councillor and back, then to the ecstatically applauding crowd. Eventually Appleyard stepped back a pace. Rathmell stood at the podium, one hand resting lightly on the surface, at ease, smiling. He waited until the noise in the hall decreased and the audience regained their seats. Then he began.

'Councillor Appleyard, ladies and gentlemen, when I found out that Frank was speaking, I knew what he had to say would be worth listening to. Hearing his words of deep wisdom, let me say I am in complete agreement. I am pleased to endorse his statements completely. I believe the actions of those few malcontents we have witnessed tonight underline the validity of his remarks better than anything I can say. As he was speaking, I believe what we witnessed here tonight should mark a starting point. It takes a brave man to attempt to forge a new beginning in British politics. I believe that two brave men stand a better chance than one. What we have to say is too important, too vital to the future of this country to be wasted on the night air. Therefore I am pleased to announce that we will work towards forming an alliance that will make those views heard by the people. We will represent the needs, wishes, dreams and aspirations of the indigenous British population.

'Let no one here in this hall underestimate what they have witnessed. In years to come Helmsdale will be known as the birth-place of a radical new force in British politics. It will represent a fresh start, and enable us to put the Great back in Great Britain.'

Rathmell signalled the end of his speech with outstretched hands, just as Appleyard had. The audience rose again. Becky took one last photo. She lowered her camera, suddenly aware of her position. Up there alone; exposed. Again she felt afraid. Suppose she'd been spotted outside? Suppose they were waiting for her in the car park, or already on their way up? She grabbed her camera bag, put her equipment in and zipped it up. Even the sound of the zip seemed loud.

When the audience began spilling out of the hall, she tiptoed swiftly downstairs and joined the throng of chattering, excited residents as they jostled their way through the vestibule. She reached the open air in the middle of a group. Before walking quickly towards her car, she glanced about, resisting the temptation to break into a run, resisting the temptation to look back; to glance nervously left and right. To do anything that might draw attention to her. As she walked, she fumbled, first in one coat pocket, then another, then in her jeans pockets, before she found her car keys.

She got into the car and turned the ignition. For a heart-stopping moment it refused to fire, then again. Becky fought down the rising tide of panic; took a deep breath and tried a third time. The engine spluttered before bursting into life. She heaved a sigh of relief and gunned the accelerator gently, aware of the danger of stalling the engine, of having to wait for it to start; of flattening the battery. She engaged first gear and let the clutch out. The car lurched but didn't move. 'Handbrake, you idiot.' Becky cursed her stupidity.

A loud bleeping sound brought back the panic until she realized the cause. She slowed to the kerb and put her seatbelt on. Twenty minutes later she was back in her flat, where she double-locked the door and slid the bolt across. In the kitchen she poured a large whisky, her hands trembling. She took a hefty slug. Only then, as she felt the warmth of the scotch, did she begin to relax. Only then did she wonder if she was being irrational. Despite her best efforts, Becky was unable to convince herself that she'd panicked needlessly.

chapter twelve

It had been a quiet Friday night. Nash ate dinner, drank a couple of glasses of red wine and was in bed early. Next morning, he was shaving when the phone rang. 'Mike? Tom Pratt. Have you heard the local news?'

'No, I haven't had the radio on. Why?'

'There was a meeting of the Westlea Residents' Association last night. I suggest you tune in to Helm Radio. They're running the story non-stop. Councillor Appleyard addressed them. It was about as inflammatory a speech as he could have dreamed up. What the blazes he was thinking of, I can't imagine. It more or less gives the green light for attacks on migrants. All about "Britain for the British". Not content with that, Carlton Rathmell joined in. Said Appleyard was the best thing since sliced bread, and they'd be looking to form a new political alliance. God save us from ruddy politicians. Sometimes I think Guy Fawkes had the right idea. It was little short of incitement to racial hatred. I dread to think what might happen on the Westlea after this. And it's all going to be dumped on you.'

'Thanks a bunch, Tom. They'd love us, wouldn't they?'

'Sorry, I'm not with you.'

'Our little force at Helmsdale, I mean. With Clara originally from Belarus and Viv's Antiguan ancestry, we must seem like their worst-case scenario. We're only a little sub-station. Heaven only knows what they'd think of a police force from one of the big cities with all the ethnic mix they've got. Any more good news?'

'Not really. I'm just sorry King's put a block on reinforcements. I reckon you'll need them.'

'Make sure I get that memo about the meeting. If needs be, I'll show it to God. I'm tempted to have a word with her anyway. I can't stand by and let things slide.'

'You stand more chance of persuading her than anyone.'

'I'll see how things develop. I don't want to jump in too soon and waste my ammunition.'

'Keep me informed. I'll let you have that memo on Monday.'

Becky Pollard was also up early, but it wasn't because she'd had an early night or a restful sleep. Her flat was in a Victorian house on the outskirts of Helmsdale. Like most old buildings, it had developed its share of creaks and groans. Each one kept Becky awake. Each one had her wondering. She lost count of the times she told herself her fears were unfounded. She lost count of the times she failed to convince herself. It was with considerable relief she reached Netherdale, and the offices of the *Gazette*. She opened the door into reception at almost the exact time Nash reached Helmsdale CID office.

The receptionist greeted her. 'Becky, you asked me to keep an eye out for a parcel. I'm afraid nothing's arrived. I thought you'd want to know, in case it's gone astray.'

'Thanks, I'd better check with the guy who sent it.' She decided to leave it until mid-morning. First, she wanted to upload the previous night's photos onto her computer.

By the time she'd finished, it was nearly lunchtime. Becky dialled Tucker's mobile. As she waited for the call to connect, she wondered why he hadn't been at the meeting. Then Becky remembered the photos of Rathmell. Perhaps Tucker's interest was restricted to the MEP's misconduct. As she was pondering, she got through to Tucker's voice-mail. Becky muttered something unprintable. 'JT? It's Becky again. The package hasn't landed. Hope you don't need it over the weekend.'

Had she been five minutes earlier, Becky would have been able to speak to Tucker in person. He'd checked his mobile before switching it off. He didn't want his surveillance of Rathmell to be blown by his phone bleeping. By the time he got Becky's message, it was far too late to call her.

Mironova and Pearce reached the CID suite in Helmsdale at the same time. Although they weren't late, it was obvious their boss had been in for some time. The large table in the outer office had half a dozen morning papers on it, each open at an article on the subject of the meeting.

'I take it you know about this?' Nash gestured to the papers. They nodded. 'I heard the gist of Appleyard and Rathmell's speeches on Helm Radio,' Nash told them. 'Tom rang to warn me.'

'I heard it as well,' Mironova confirmed.

'It was on Shire FM too,' Pearce added.

'It's like throwing dynamite into a bonfire,' Nash growled. 'The problem is we'll have to deal with the explosion. We've already a knife-wielding maniac and an arsonist at large; this sort of rhetoric gives them licence to run riot. Now, let's get on with some work. We need to get to grips with paperwork today.

'I've had the go-ahead for two firearms trained officers to carry. As Clara and I are the only ones who qualify, that leaves you out, Viv. I don't want you attending any incidents, however trivial, without one or other of us. That applies across the board, but more particularly in the Westlea area. The only exception is when you're baby-sitting Vickers.'

'Are you still going ahead with that?' Mironova was surprised.

'I am. Vickers' house has been targeted twice already. When he's released, I feel sure that activity will increase. Viv and I will alternate on the nightshift. I'll take the first one tomorrow night. It means you'll have to bear the brunt here, Clara. Now, let's get started.'

Tucker listened to the message from Becky. Now he knew what the two men had been discussing, the need for surveillance equipment wasn't as urgent. As he was about to put the phone back in his pocket it bleeped to signal an incoming text. The message read: 'V. Sun. 9 a.m.'

Not much for £50, Tucker thought, but it was enough. Vickers would be released at nine o'clock the following morning. Tucker knew there would be little point in watching Rathmell on Sunday. He could go to Felling and meet Vickers. Even give him a lift back to Helmsdale. Tucker was determined to get an interview. He felt sure Vickers would want to talk.

When Nash reached Felling Prison, the visitors' car park was deserted apart from one other vehicle. Inside it, the driver was sheltering from the squally rain. With the wipers off, the occupant was unidentifiable. Nash hurried towards the side entrance and was admitted immediately.

After the screening procedure, he waited in the holding area. Fifteen minutes elapsed before Vickers emerged. He was ushered in by an officer, who said, 'Wait there until I get the release papers and your other gear.'

Vickers was carrying a small holdall. He smiled ruefully. 'I was expecting you.'

'You'd better get used to me. I'm going to be with you for a while.'

'I know my windows have been smashed. Has there been more trouble?' Nash thought he detected a trace of eagerness in Vickers' voice.

'Not aimed at you exclusively. There's been a spate of violence in the town. It seems to be mainly targeting migrant workers and immigrants.'

'That lets me out.'

Was Vickers disappointed? 'Maybe that's because you weren't about. We need to get you installed without attracting attention. Fortunately there doesn't seem to be any media activity.'

Vickers stared at Nash. 'Why would I want to avoid attention?'

'Because it'll be more dangerous.'

Vickers shook his head. 'You don't get it, do you? The minute I step through that door, I'll be in danger, whether the media put anything out or not. The people who pose a threat know I'm due out. Probably know it'll be happening today. Right now even.'

'Who are you talking about?'

Vickers laughed. 'You've read the file. Don't you know?'

'Who, specifically?'

'Come on, Nash. Use your brains. They tell me in here' – Vickers jerked his thumb over his shoulder – 'that you're one of the best detectives around. Work it out. Ask yourself who has a vested interest in seeing me dead. Compile a list of the leading candidates. Amongst them you'll probably find the name of Stacey's killer.'

'You still insist you're innocent?'

Vickers' reply was slightly oblique. 'When I walk through that door, the crime will have been paid for, in the eyes of the law. There's no need for me to pretend to be innocent. The justice system' – there was no disguising the contempt in Vickers' voice – 'can't touch me. So what's the point of me continuing to protest my innocence? Unless I didn't kill her.'

Nash was still pondering this when the prison officer reappeared. He was carrying a large cardboard box. Nash looked at Vickers questioningly.

'They allowed me a CD player,' the prisoner explained. 'I wasn't going to leave it.'

'At least we'll get some peace now,' the officer chimed in. 'A blessed release from Beatle-mania. He plays nothing else.'

'I like The Beatles,' Vickers protested.

'That doesn't mean we've to endure them 24/7.'

As they stepped into the car park, the driver's door of the other car opened. Nash tensed; he saw someone emerge. He was carrying something. Gun? The driver held up a hand. 'Vickers? Gary Vickers? My name's Tucker. I'm a reporter.'

Nash relaxed slightly. Not a gun, only a camera. The shutter clicked several times in rapid succession.

'Mr Vickers has nothing to say,' Nash called out.

Tucker approached. 'I'm sure Gary can speak for himself.'

'He's got nothing to say. If you've any questions, address them to me.'

'Who are you? His solicitor?'

Nash took out his warrant card. Tucker glanced at it before turning his attention to Vickers. 'Haven't you had a bellyful of policemen, Gary? Hop into my car, I'll drive you to Helmsdale. You can tell me your side of the story. The side the courts never got to hear.'

Vickers hesitated, uncertain. 'Sorry,' Nash said. 'Mr Vickers is under police protection. He goes nowhere without my say-so. Certainly not into a reporter's car.'

'Come and see me in Helmsdale,' Vickers told Tucker. 'Wednesday, say. I'll talk to you then.'

Tucker turned to Nash. 'Better keep him hale and hearty till then.'

The journey to Helmsdale was conducted mostly in silence. As they neared the outskirts of the town, however, Vickers stirred in his seat. 'I'll need some food. It's Sunday. Will there be somewhere open?'

Nash laughed. 'You have been out of circulation a long time. There's a branch of Good Buys supermarket in the Market Place. They're open until four o'clock.'

The shopping took half an hour or so. Some of the time was down to Vickers examining packets of food he'd never seen before. 'You're right,' he told Nash after staring at a shelf displaying Thai cuisine. 'I'm definitely out of touch.'

The checkout operator glanced at them before focusing on Vickers. Nash saw her slightly puzzled expression. She looked up, without pausing from passing items over the scanner. 'Don't I know you?'

Vickers smiled. 'Possibly. I've been away for a long time. Fifteen years to be exact.'

The cashier checked the last item and announced the total. 'Been working abroad?'

'No. I've been in prison,' Vickers replied as he passed the cash across, then paused for a second before adding, 'For murder. My name's Vickers. Gary Vickers.'

They crossed the cobbles to Nash's car in silence. After loading the shopping, Nash sat behind the wheel and looked at his passenger. 'Why did you do that? The news will be all over Helmsdale within the hour.'

Vickers smiled, his expression one of triumphant satisfaction. And something else: a touch of malice.

'You realize it's going to make our job doubly difficult? It'll be virtually impossible to guarantee your safety now.'

'I'm not interested in my own safety.' Vickers statement was bald, the rider even more uncompromising. 'Nor am I interested in making life easy for the police. I owe you nothing. I owe this town nothing. I owe society nothing. On the contrary, I'm owed fifteen years, and more.'

Rain was falling heavily when Nash pulled up at Grove Road. At least that would keep the neighbours indoors. Not that it mattered now. Vickers had seen to that. He was looking for trouble.

Vickers stared at the front of the house. 'The outside looks alright,' he said more to himself than Nash.

'Why wouldn't it be?'

'I paid a lot of money for maintenance and cleaning,' Vickers told him. 'From the photos the agents sent, I couldn't be sure I was getting value for money. But they've repainted the outside as I asked. That's a good start. Let's see what the inside is like.'

'It might be a bit of a mess. The glaziers have replaced the window panes but I'm not sure how well they'll have cleaned up.'

'It'd better be pristine, the amount it cost to get the cleaners in yesterday.'

Nash stared at him. 'You organized the cleaners already?'

'Of course, as soon as I heard about the damage.'

'You weren't wasting time, were you?'

Vickers smiled mirthlessly. 'I'd nothing else to do.'

The house appeared clean and tidy. 'Good for them,' Vickers muttered. They went through to the kitchen and dumped the shopping on the large table. Nash noticed something different. 'Is that fridge-freezer new?'

'Yes. I had it delivered yesterday. I instructed them to switch it on so it would be ready to use. You don't think I bought all that frozen stuff on chance?' Vickers put the shopping away whilst Nash watched him. His curiosity was heightened by Vickers' actions. Everything he did seemed part of a preconceived plan.

'You've worked all this out, haven't you?'

Vickers paused, a carton of milk in his hand. 'Tea or coffee? Seeing we're going to be housemates we might as well try to get along.'

'Coffee, please.'

Vickers filled the kettle and switched it on. 'Of course I worked it out. In the last year I've thought of little else. I wanted to be sure I left nothing to chance. You make the coffee, will you? White, no sugar for me.'

Vickers went out of the kitchen and Nash watched him walk down the hall, opening first the dining-room door, then the lounge, pausing in each doorway as if taking mental stock of the contents. After a few moments he heard Vickers climb the stairs. Nash brewed the coffee and walked to the front of the house. 'Coffee's ready,' he called upstairs. There was no reply.

Nash climbed the staircase, glancing at the many framed photographs lining the walls, to find Vickers standing in the doorway of one of the bedrooms. 'This was Stacey's room,' he said softly. He turned and looked at Nash, his expression as bleak as a midwinter day. 'She was full of life and laughter. Just being near her was a delight.' It was as if a mask had slipped, allowing Vickers to reveal some of his emotions. In an instant the mask was back. 'Coffee's ready, you said?'

Nash followed him downstairs thoughtfully. As they drank, he tried to get the mask to slip again. 'Are you happy with the way they've looked after the house?'

Vickers nodded. 'They've done everything I asked.'

'What's next?'

'They're coming to reconnect the phone tomorrow. The amount they charge for reconnection is scandalous.'

'That's not what I meant. Tell me something. Why didn't you sell this house?'

'Why should I? To invest the money maybe? I couldn't have earned as much in interest as this house has increased in value. Besides, what would I have done with money? Gone on a cruise?'

It was like a fencing match. Thrust and parry. Nash probing for information, Vickers determined not to give him any. 'You always intended to return here?'

'Why not? It's my house. It was my parents' and grandparents' house.'

'Even though everybody knows you're a rapist and murderer?'

'A convicted rapist and murderer,' Vickers stated, without expression.

Nash shrugged. 'What's the difference?'

'I was convicted of those crimes. That doesn't mean I committed them.'

'Why not go for a fresh start, under a new name? Somewhere you don't have to look over your shoulder?'

'If I'd done that, everyone would assume I killed Stacey.'

'You're saying coming back is a statement of innocence?'

'Partly, but more besides.'

'Such as?'

'Unfinished business. You may have drawn a line under her murder, but I haven't. If you won't bring her killer to justice, I'll do it myself.' Vickers paused and, without a flicker of emotion, added, 'It'll be my kind of justice, not yours. So it won't be me that'll be looking over my shoulder.'

'Do you know who the killer is?'

Vickers stared at the detective, as if the question was stupid. 'Not yet. But I soon will.'

That evening, after they shared a pizza from Vickers' new freezer, Nash checked the front and back doors and ensured the bolts were securely closed. He wandered into the lounge and stared at the TV, undecided whether to switch it on. The sound of movement came from upstairs. He turned and went to find Vickers. He was inside the room he'd been looking in earlier, opening and closing wardrobe doors, sliding drawers from the bedside cabinets and dressing table in and out. 'Lost something?'

Vickers looked round. Nash was aware of that same wintry expression he'd seen earlier. In a second it was gone. The mask was securely in place. 'Not exactly.'

'What are you doing then? Searching for something?'

'Sort of.'

'If you tell me what you're looking for, I'll give you a hand.'

'I can't do that.'

'Why not?'

'Because I don't know what it is. Not yet at any rate.'

'Now you've lost me.'

'I'm looking for something. But I won't know what it is until I find it. And I'm not sure where it'll be.'

'Hang on a bit. If you don't know what or where it is, how can you be sure this mysterious "something" actually exists?'

Vickers' smile was as cryptic as his reply. 'That's the one thing I do know.'

'Yes, but remember the house was broken into only a week ago. How can you be sure what you're looking for wasn't taken?'

'That wasn't the first time the house has been broken into. Five times over the last two years, to be exact. The maintenance company reported each incident. The break-ins are the reason I know it exists. And the attempted arson proves it hasn't been found.'

'I'm confused. What do you think this mysterious object might be? And how can you be certain it ever existed?'

'I know it exists, because I was told it did. I've no idea what it is, but I know what it represents.'

'What's that?'

'Proof.'

'Proof? Proof of what?'

'Like I said, you're the detective. You figure it out.'

Nash thought for a moment or two. 'You said there'd been a few burglaries, yet you're certain what they were looking for hadn't been removed?'

Vickers nodded.

'Then how can you be sure what they were looking for was in the house?'

'It must have been in the house, it couldn't have …' Vickers' voice trailed off into silence. He stared at Nash, but it was obvious his thoughts were elsewhere.

'Well?' Nash prompted.

'Nothing,' Vickers said unconvincingly.

Nash declined Vickers' offer of a bed. 'My job's to keep you safe. I can't do that if I'm asleep. I'll settle for a dining chair and freedom to drink your coffee. I take it you'll be in the front bedroom? I assume that was yours.'

Nash was watching Vickers. The expression on the released man's face was curious. It took Nash a few moments to identify it. It was one of distaste. 'No, I'll be in the middle room, where you saw me earlier.'

'That was Stacey's room. People might consider that perverted.'

'I don't care what people think.'

'Will you be able to sleep in that room? Knowing what happened to Stacey?'

Vickers' laugh was completely devoid of mirth. 'You think I'll have nightmares? You think I'll spend the night tossing and turning, because of where I am? No, that room is the one place I can be assured of a good night's sleep.'

Nash watched him walk upstairs. He was convinced Vickers was after revenge. That made Nash's job doubly difficult. They had to make sure Vickers didn't come to harm. They also had to prevent him attacking the person he believed had killed Stacey. That wouldn't be easy. The fact that they didn't know the identity of Vickers' intended victim made it impossible.

chapter thirteen

Overnight, boredom made time drag. Nash needed something to while away the hours. He was relieved when he heard Vickers moving about. It was 6.30. The sun was streaming through the window. Within minutes Vickers joined him. He looked refreshed, alert and eager. 'How did you sleep?' Nash asked.

Vickers smiled. 'It was the best night I've had for fifteen years. If the sun hadn't been so strong, I'd have been asleep still.'

'Is that because you're free? Or because you were sleeping in Stacey's room?'

'Probably because I wasn't disturbed by other prisoners. How was the security patrol?'

'Bloody boring. I tried TV. That didn't help. I thought daytime telly was bad enough. What they put on in the early hours is absolute dross. The most exciting event of the night was two cats shagging in your back yard.'

Vickers shook his head sadly. 'You've a perverted sense of fun,' he mocked. 'Care for toast and coffee?'

'Toast will be handy. I'll pass on the drink. I've been supping coffee all night.'

Shortly after 8 a.m. Nash's relief arrived. Pratt had opted to use Bishopton's small squad as backup. Nash briefed the man before he left. 'DC Pearce will be here at 6 p.m. to take over.' He turned to Vickers, who was watching in quiet amusement. 'Behave yourself. Do what the officer tells you and keep out of sight. I'll see you tomorrow evening. In the meantime, give some thought to letting me into your confidence.' Vickers raised an enquiring eyebrow as Nash continued, 'If you want to convince me, you'll have to trust me. If you think I'm going to stand by whilst you wage some private vendetta, think again. I'll put as much effort into stopping you as I will in preventing Jake and Ronnie Fletcher slitting your throat. Is that clear?'

Nash called at his flat for a shower and shave, and was in the Helmsdale CID office little later than usual. Mironova was already there. 'How did the child-minding go?'

'It worries me,' Nash confessed.

'You've been through the evidence again?'

'Yes. I couldn't find anything worth bidding for on the Shopping Channel, so I read the case notes. There's no other motive. There were no jilted boyfriends, no love triangle. There was nothing about Stacey's life that presents even a whiff of suspicion against anyone but Vickers. She was a photography student at Netherdale College. The staff and other students spoke of her as a popular girl, friendly but with little involvement in anything but her coursework. She hadn't had time to make enemies. Nor was she involved in drugs, gangs or criminal activity. Nothing about her murder makes sense, apart from the fact that Vickers got overcome with lust and raped her. Knowing what the consequences would be, he killed the girl to stop her going to her mother or the police. In fact, he'd probably have been more scared of her mother. Because Gemma Fletcher would have gone straight to Jake and Ronnie, and we all know what would have happened then. It's a cast-iron, logical case any jury would convict on.'

Mironova knew there was more to come. 'Except?' she prompted.

'Except those two huge holes in the evidence. What happened to the piano wire? And, if he killed her at the house, how did he get her to the dump site? Apart from that, I thought Vickers was scared of Jake and Ronnie Fletcher. But he never has been. If he'd been frightened of them, he'd never have returned here. He'd have sold that house years ago. The fact that he went to so much trouble and expense shows he always intended to come back. All his thoughts and actions were bent on coming back to Helmsdale. And I know why. Vickers intends to find Stacey's killer and take revenge. He doesn't trust us to do it.'

Clara sighed. 'It's a nightmare. Accepting that he didn't, do you think he knows who killed Stacey?'

'I don't think so. In fact, I'd say he only knows one thing we don't.'

'What's that?'

'Only he knows if he's innocent. But he's sure there's something that will tell him what he needs.'

'I don't follow you.'

'Last night he was searching the house. He said he was looking for something.'

'Did he say what?'

'He just said it was "proof". Proof of what, he wouldn't explain.'

'What do you intend to do?'

'There's nothing we can do, except wait on developments. One thing's certain. As soon as word gets round that he's back, there will be developments.'

The weekend had been busy. The media had descended on Houlston Grange en masse. Rathmell was courteous, welcoming, and bore even the most hostile interrogations with calm good humour. Monday marked no lessening in the feeding frenzy, and it was late afternoon before the pack of scribes and TV crews departed.

On Tuesday morning, Rathmell spent several hours running through schedules of interviews and public appearances with his agent. Following that, a prominent TV political correspondent quizzed the MEP about his intentions for the fledgling movement. After the pundit left, Rathmell reviewed the meeting before bidding the agent farewell. When he was alone, he turned his attention to thoughts of the no less exciting events that were to come later that day. He was excited by the thought of having Gemma here. Of having her to himself. Of being able to do all the things they wanted with all the time they needed, without the constant fear of discovery. As he sat in his study, his eyes flicked occasionally to the CCTV monitor covering the various entrances to the estate. This was a reflex action. He knew she wasn't due for several hours yet.

The cameras had been installed at the insistence of his insurers. Rathmell's eye was attracted by a movement on the screen covering the main gate. He picked up the remote control and panned the camera. He operated the zoom and the object came into sharper focus. Rathmell's eyes narrowed as he identified it. He stared at the screen for several minutes before he picked up his mobile.

'It's me,' he began. 'Slight change of plan. I've some business to attend to.'

'My meeting's finished early – I was about to leave.'

'Even better. Meet me in the woods in an hour. I'll be in the Land Rover.'

Rathmell disconnected and put the phone back on his desk. His gaze returned to the CCTV monitor. He stared at it for a long time. Eventually, as if he'd come to a decision, he turned and walked briskly from the room.

Becky Pollard had been one of the visitors to Houlston Grange. Her photos were too late to make the Monday evening edition but they would form a good background to the profile the *Gazette* was running the following day. By mid-morning on Tuesday, she'd sent them for printing and was working on other weekend events. She was interrupted by a call from reception. 'There's a parcel arrived. It's to sign for,' the receptionist told her.

'At last,' Becky said. 'I'll be down in a minute.'

'Where's this been?' she greeted the courier. 'Did you send it via the North Pole?'

The man looked faintly embarrassed. 'Sorry about the delay. It got sent to our Northampton depot. How anyone mistakes Northampton for Netherdale, I've no idea. If you want to make a claim, the details are on the back of the form. We don't get many go astray,' he added defensively.

Becky signed for the parcel. 'I don't suppose it matters.' She turned to the receptionist. 'I'll leave this with you. Stick a post-it on, will you? JT will be in to collect it. I'll give him a call.'

She was about to return to her office when the receptionist's phone rang. She answered it and held up a detaining hand. 'Yes, she's here,' the woman said. 'OK, I'll tell her.'

She turned to Becky. 'There's a meeting. From what Helen said, you can forget lunch; report to the boardroom straightaway.'

'Damn. Do me a favour. Give JT a bell. Let him know that parcel's here.'

Pearce reported a trouble-free night, so the team was able to give their attention to the various unsolved crimes they had on their plate. Top of the list were the murders of the Druze family, along with the stabbing of Zydrumas. The arson attacks had left them with few clues, although a whisper from one informant had provided Mironova with a name.

'He's got form. Mostly juvenile, although there are suspicions he might have graduated into more serious stuff,' she told Nash.

'Who is he?'

'Name's Billy Floyd. His brother Danny has been linked with the main supplier of drugs in the area. Danny Floyd heads up a teenage gang known as Danny and the Juniors. They more or less run the Westlea. And rumour has it Jake and Ronnie Fletcher keep a parental eye on them.'

'Tell me about Billy.'

'I'm only going on hearsay, but whereas Danny's rumoured to carry a gun, Billy's said to be more than a bit handy with a knife. However, his favourite pastime is setting fires.'

'And we've got three arson victims and someone killed with a knife.'

'Nobody's credited Billy Floyd with them. In fact the Westlea's remarkably tight-lipped. The only person I could get to talk says everyone's a bit nervous. Well, more than a bit. "Scared shitless" was the expression they used.'

'Any particular reason?'

'Billy Floyd's the reason. He's just plain monstrous, reckoned to be a psychopath or damned close. Hobbies: rough sex and setting fires. It's only rumour that puts him in the frame for the knifing and the Druze and Hassan attacks, but I think we should pull him.'

'We can't do that without justification.'

Mironova allowed her frustration to boil over. 'Bloody stupid regulations! They make our job twice as hard.'

'Maybe, but that's the law. Go back to your informant and see if you can persuade them to part with anything more. Might be worth mentioning that the sooner we get these murders cleared up, the sooner we'll leave the Westlea in peace.'

'I'll try, but I'm not promising anything. Last Friday's meeting has put everyone in a strange frame of mind. There seems to be a body of opinion that lays the blame with the victims. Something along the lines of "wouldn't have happened if they'd stayed in their own country". You know the sort of thing.'

'Bloody interfering politicians.' It was Nash's turn to get annoyed. 'If they'd only keep their trap shut, we'd all be better off.'

Nash was studying reports when he was interrupted by the phone. He answered, his face darkening with annoyance. 'Take it slowly,' he told the caller. 'I'll be with you in ten minutes.' He slammed the phone down. 'Clara, Viv!' he shouted.

Mironova and Pearce appeared in the open doorway. Nash was already moving round the desk. 'Come on, both of you. We've got another problem.'

The hall at Grove Road was quite large but with four officers in it, there was little room. 'Tell me again,' Nash said patiently.

'Everything was fine. I'd checked round a few times, looked out the back, made sure everything was locked.'

Nash nodded. 'OK, then what happened?'

'Vickers said he'd arranged to buy a DVD player, something to pass the time. I heard him on the phone. He'd asked the shop to send someone round to demonstrate a couple. When the doorbell rang I thought it was the man from the electronics shop. I answered the door. Vickers was in the kitchen making coffee. He even called out for me to ask the salesman if he wanted some. But it was a taxi driver. He said he'd had a call to the address to pick up a fare. Even then I didn't suspect anything,' the officer said miserably, 'until he told me the passenger's name was Nash.'

'What happened next?' Nash frowned at Mironova and Pearce, who were trying not to laugh. 'I dashed back into the kitchen. Vickers had scarpered out the back. I went into the alley but he'd long gone.'

'You're certain he went of his own accord?'

'He must have. The back door had been locked and bolted. Chain across too.'

'That's bloody brilliant.' Nash was exasperated. 'Now we've got Vickers on the loose in a neighbourhood where most of the residents would slit his throat for a fiver.'

It was that dead hour in the middle of the afternoon when traffic is at its lightest and pedestrians are few and far between. The Market Place had only a scattering of cars parked on its cobbles. Vickers passed only half a dozen people on his way through town. None of them gave him more than a glance.

He made his way down a narrow, twisting alley. There were a series of these running towards the Helm. Known as wynds, they were barely wide enough to take a car, and were surrounded on both sides by pretty mews cottages. Vickers didn't pause to admire them. He neither glanced to left nor right. After a hundred yards the wynd opened onto the road that ran alongside the river. Vickers crossed it and took a footpath signposted for Helm Woods.

He increased his pace. Vickers could hear the river now, the water roaring as it tumbled over the weirs. His objective was close. The path split, the left fork leading to Kirk Bolton. Vickers didn't need the sign. He knew only too well where he was. A couple of hundred yards along the track he stepped into the clearing and walked slowly across the uneven surface. He reached the trees by the river and looked around. It was not as he remembered it. It took him a moment to realize why. The trees were taller. Fifteen years of growth had changed them greatly.

He stood alongside an ancient oak tree. This, at least, was unchanged. It was in precisely this spot that Stacey's naked body had been found, her beauty disfigured by the bloated effects of the strangulation. Vickers thought fleetingly of Nash. He remembered the phrase about a murderer returning to the scene of his crime. Was that what Nash would think?

He shook his head to clear his brain. Thinking of the past, repining for his actions was something he'd taught himself to avoid. Now was no time to start. Not even here, when the reminders were most potent. He had to start searching.

Gasping slightly from the unfamiliar exertion, he straightened his back; heard someone approaching. Indecision gripped him momentarily. Should he hide and hope they failed to spot him? He couldn't afford to be found here, of all places. Better to leave. He set off walking, glancing nervously over his shoulder, and rejoined the path. Fear of discovery prevented him lingering. Only when he was well clear of this spot would he feel any degree of safety.

Tucker was almost taken by surprise. The vehicle was not the one he'd been expecting. He'd been looking for the sleek lines of a Mercedes, not the squat functionality of a Land Rover. It was only when the vehicle slowed that he caught a glimpse of the driver. The Land Rover was almost out of sight when he set off in pursuit.

Long before they reached the destination, Tucker guessed where they were heading. 'So it's the woods not the moors today, is it?' He glanced at the dashboard clock. 4.30 p.m. Well, why not, he thought. A spot of afternoon delight. Can't beat it. On the other hand, it might not be Gemma that Rathmell was going to meet. Tucker cursed. He wished he'd got the eavesdropping equipment. If the meeting was political, not sexual, he'd have given a fortune to overhear what Rathmell was discussing.

He saw Rathmell swing into the car park. This time Tucker wasn't going to be caught napping and pulled off the road onto the farm track. He reckoned he could make his way along the river bank and come on the clearing from the opposite side.

The plan worked. Tucker reached the edge of the clearing before Rathmell came in sight. He took up position and waited. Five minutes later he heard the sound of someone approaching. The reporter lifted his camera and held it ready. He focused on the narrow path as the footsteps drew nearer. When he saw who it was, Tucker stared in amazement, realizing the significance of the man and his presence there. He recovered quickly and squeezed off a couple of shots. This time his subject was much nearer, but so was the river; hopefully drowning out the noise from the camera motor. The man stopped, raised his head and turned, as if alerted by the sound. Tucker dived behind the undergrowth.

Becky Pollard emerged from the unofficial board meeting shortly after 5 p.m. She'd all but forgotten JT's parcel until the receptionist stopped her. 'I tried to get hold of JT on both his mobile and his home number. No luck on either. Did you want me to leave a message?'

'It's alright, I'll do it.' She found JT in her mobile contacts as she crossed the car park. Predictably, the phone went straight to voice-mail. 'JT, Becky again. That parcel's in reception at the *Gazette*. Pick it up when you can. Cheers.'

She was surprised JT hadn't replied to her earlier messages. She knew he was following up on a story he felt was likely to be a big one. Even so, she thought he'd have been in touch by now, if only to chase the kit he wanted.

Nash sent patrol cars out hunting for Vickers but without success. Although they scoured the town from end to end, they reported no sighting of the missing man. 'Where the hell's he got to? He can't have gone unseen. Helmsdale's not big enough for that. Not with the cars we've had whizzing around.'

'He might have gone shopping, or gone to the pub.' Mironova attempted to calm him.

'He went shopping on Sunday. And I don't think he's the type to go on a pub crawl. No, he's either indoors, and who would he visit, or...?'

'Or what?'

'Or he's left Helmsdale altogether.'

'That means catching a bus. Our men checked the bus station a couple of times. I don't think there's a train stops at Helmsdale until the evening ones, from about 5.15.'

'He might have taken a taxi,' Pearce interjected.

'I checked with Helm Cabs. They've nothing booked this afternoon except a couple of school runs and a patient transfer to Netherdale General.'

'So he's vanished into thin air, has he? Clara, you've read the file. I don't remember seeing a note about any family or friends, do you?'

Mironova shook her head. 'Vickers was an only child. There were no other family members listed. What do we do now?'

'There's no point all of us kicking our heels here.' Nash glanced at his watch. 'It's almost six o'clock. I might as well take up my shift. I can take care of the house even though I've nobody to protect. Go back to the station. Tell the uniforms to keep searching. Send our colleague back to Bishopton. I'll ring him if he's needed tomorrow. If Vickers doesn't turn up there's no point.'

Once they'd gone Nash wandered from room to room. The house seemed oddly silent. Outside there was plenty of activity as neighbours arrived home from work. He could hear the sound of children laughing and running up and down the pavement. Why had Vickers' departure been so sudden? Or was it planned? Nash was beginning to believe Vickers had every move worked out in advance.

His wandering took him to the first floor. He looked in the front bedroom. It was large and well appointed, with fitted wardrobes and a comfortable double bed. A door led to an en-suite shower room. It was better than the room Vickers had slept in. Nash opened the wardrobe doors to find men's clothing on hangers, mostly shirts, slacks and jeans. They looked expensive, but dated. The rest of the wardrobe was empty, although there were several hangers suspended from the rail. Some of these were skirt hangers. Probably they'd held Gemma's clothing before she moved out. It was a similar story with the drawers: men's underwear and socks but no feminine clothing.

Nash sat on the bed. Something was puzzling here. Why had Vickers opted to sleep in the smaller, less comfortable room? What was it he'd said? 'That room is the only place in this house where I can be certain of a good night's sleep.' Why would he feel more comfortable in the room of his victim than the one he'd shared with his lover?

Nash added this to the growing list of questions he wanted to ask Vickers. The need to find him was doubly urgent. Nash hoped it wouldn't be too late.

chapter fourteen

Nash's concern was mounting. Despite constant patrols through the town there were no reported sightings. It was with a mixture of anger and relief that he heard the front door open shortly after 7 p.m. Nash went from the kitchen, where he'd been nursing a mug of coffee, his pace almost a run. He stopped dead in the doorway. Vickers was standing in the hall. His face, hands and clothing were stained with what looked like soil and grass. And something else perhaps. 'Where the hell have you been?' Nash demanded.

Vickers looked vaguely shamefaced. 'I've been looking for something.' As an explanation, it was way short of detail.

'Why did you run away?'

'I wasn't running away. I came back, didn't I? I needed to go alone. I'm not under arrest. I've done my time. What's the problem?'

'That depends. The officer was here for your protection. What do you think would have happened if you'd been recognized by someone like Jake Fletcher?'

'I wasn't. Relax, everything's alright. I'm going to get cleaned up and change my clothes.' He started to walk towards the stairs.

'Aren't you going to tell me what you've been up to?'

Vickers turned, one hand on the banister rail. He gave Nash a long, curious look before replying. 'No, I don't think so.'

Nash stared at the retreating figure in exasperation. Maybe he'd get more from him later.

After they'd dined, Nash began questioning him. 'In Felling, you promised you'd tell me more about what happened once you were back here. I want to know your version. All I've had so far is the official report and a few vague hints from you.'

'I don't know where to begin.'

'Tell me how it all started?'

'With Gemma, you mean?'

Nash nodded.

'I'd been alone too long. My parents died when I was fourteen. They were on their way to see me at boarding school. Their car was cleaned up by a drunk driver. They were killed instantaneously. He got off with a few scratches, a three-year sentence and a ten-year driving ban.'

'It still hurts?'

'Of course it bloody does. Anyway, I was twenty-one when I met Gemma. I'd had little or nothing to do with girls. I was at Netherdale College, just finished a three-year arts course. It was the day of the graduation ceremony. Gemma was there making notes for an advertising feature. We got talking and I was fascinated by her. OK, she was a lot older than me. Thirteen years to be precise. It didn't seem to matter. I still don't know how I plucked up courage to ask her out, but I did. She seemed so sophisticated; I was astonished when she said yes. I think she was flattered she could attract someone that much younger. One thing led to another and we became lovers. I asked her to move in with me. To begin with it was terrific.' Vickers grinned. 'Exhausting but fun. However, that was at the start and it didn't take long for us to realize we'd made a mistake. Once the passion was gone we'd little in common. Gemma didn't want love. Not the love of someone like me at any rate. She did want sex. She was too overpowering.'

Vickers paused. 'I wanted to end it but couldn't pluck up courage. Believe it or not, I was scared of her. I hadn't enough experience to deal with a woman like Gemma. She moved out of my room to the one at the back of the house.'

'When did you meet Stacey?'

'That came later. I didn't even know Gemma had a daughter. Apparently Stacey was the result of a one-night stand when Gemma was sixteen. Stacey told me that. Told me her mother used to throw it at her, like an accusation. Stacey had been away on a gap year before going to university. She'd been working in Malaysia. It came as quite a shock when Gemma got a phone call one day. She'd been living here nine months or so when Stacey arrived home. I took one look at her and fell head over heels in love.'

'Did Gemma know?'

Vickers shuddered. 'I don't think so. I'm not sure, in view of what happened later. I certainly wouldn't have dared tell her.'

'What about Stacey? She must have known how things were between you and her mother. Or how they had been?'

Vickers smiled and Nash realized it was the first time he'd shown anything like pleasure. 'I didn't know for a while, but apparently she felt the same about me.'

'It sounds like a highly explosive situation.'

'You're not kidding. Gemma has a ferocious temper. If she'd even caught a whiff of how Stacey and I felt, she'd have gone berserk.'

'Even though she no longer wanted you?'

'That's how Gemma is. By then I was sure she was involved with someone else. She'd come back sometimes with a sort of glow about her. I recognized that look. It meant she'd been making love. She thought she had to keep it from me, in case I chucked her out, I guess. She didn't know it suited me fine. I could be close to Stacey.' Vickers saw the question forming and shook his head. 'No, I've no idea who her new lover was. I was so taken up with Stacey, nothing and nobody else mattered. It served one useful purpose. It blinded Gemma from what was going on.'

'You became lovers whilst her mother was living in the same house?'

'Dead right; we'd wait until Gemma went to work and within five minutes we'd be in bed. We nearly got caught a couple of times. It used to bother us that we couldn't hold hands or kiss one another when we wanted.'

Nash studied him for a moment. 'OK, you've nothing to gain by lying. You've done your time. The law can't touch you. So answer me this. Did you kill Stacey?'

Vickers looked at him for a long time, then sighed. 'No, I loved her too much to hurt her. I neither raped nor killed her. We'd been so bloody careful; I still don't believe anyone knew about us. The fact that we were sleeping together, I mean. When all that forensic evidence came out at my trial, it must have seemed like manna from heaven for the prosecution. I was in the classic position for a fall guy, wasn't I? Left alone for long periods with a beautiful young girl; unable to control my desire. Well, that was true enough, but not the way they made it sound.

'The fact was, Stacey's feelings for me were just as strong, just as physical, as mine were for her; more so at times. But the prosecution made it all sound so dirty, so sordid. As if I was some kind of pervert; peeping through the keyhole whilst she got her kit off, then bursting in and raping her. It just didn't happen that way. They suggested I raped her repeatedly then got scared of the consequences. Scared she'd tell her mother. Scared of what Jake and Ronnie would do. The last thing Stacey was going to do was tell her mother about us. But to the prosecution and the jury, it must have seemed the only logical explanation.

'Even though the jury didn't know what a fearsome reputation Jake and Ronnie Fletcher had, they'd seen them in court, and drawn their own conclusions. It's hardly surprising the police and CPS didn't bother looking any further, is it?'

Nash studied him again. 'If what you told me about your affair is true, it would certainly explain that damaging forensic evidence. If you didn't kill her, who did? And, if you didn't kill her, why keep quiet about it at your trial? Why didn't you ask for the evidence to be re-examined? You certainly made a nuisance of yourself in other ways, so why no appeal? It seemed to me when I read your file that you might have been protecting someone. Who was it, Gary? Who do you believe murdered Stacey?'

Vickers remained silent for so long, Nash thought he wasn't going to answer. Then he shuffled uncomfortably in his chair. 'You're the first person to ask that. The only one who's seen beyond the evidence. The reason I insisted on coming here was to find out the truth about who killed Stacey.'

'But you suspect someone, don't you?'

There was another pause. 'Yes and no. I thought at the time that Gemma killed her. But I wasn't thinking straight. I was grieving and felt guilty; guilty that I hadn't been able to protect Stacey. Don't ask me why I believed it was Gemma. I tried to find out who was behind the attempts to kill me in prison, but I couldn't make any headway. All I was able to do was send a message that if they wanted me to keep quiet, they'd lay off. The fact that the attacks ceased convinced me I was right. I say I suspected Gemma, but I've no real proof. Don't think I haven't asked myself the question a hundred, a thousand times. I always come up against the same stumbling block. What motive would Gemma have for killing her daughter? At one time it could have been jealousy, but Gemma had long given up on me. And if it was because she found out I'd deflowered her daughter, to use a quaint old-fashioned phrase, why kill Stacey? Why not come after the man who'd done it? Why not set Jake and Ronnie on me? They'd have done a far more thorough job. Jake, in particular, he doted on Stacey.'

'You say you've no proof. But that's what you've been looking for, isn't it? You believe there is some.'

'I'm not sure. I think there was something. I don't know what it was, or if it's been destroyed.' Vickers sighed. 'Look, can we finish this? I'm tired and I want to go to bed.' Nash glanced at the clock and was surprised to find it was almost midnight.

Alone in the kitchen, Nash mulled over what Vickers had told him. As an explanation it was convincing, as far as it went. But he was certain there was more; sure Vickers hadn't told him everything. Things Nash was determined to find out.

He was halfway to believing Vickers' version of events. Which was all very well, but proving him innocent would be quite another matter. Keeping him alive until the question of guilt could be resolved was going to be challenge enough.

The night proved uneventful. Nash left the chastened Bishopton officer in charge of their subject and headed home. After a long shower he felt more refreshed. By 9 a.m. he was in the CID suite. Apart from post-mortem findings on the knife victim, there was little to engage his attention. As Mironova was likewise less than stretched, Nash decided he could afford a break. 'I'm going to clear off early,' he told her as they sat with their sandwiches at lunchtime. 'Viv will be in later this afternoon. I'm going to get my head down for a few hours. I'm getting too old for long stints without sleep.'

Clara grinned. 'I thought with your social life you'd be used to sleepless nights.'

'That's totally different. Anyway, there's no chance of that at present.'

'Don't tell me you're actually reduced to celibacy?'

'Clara!' Nash scowled. 'Go do some work. I'll see you tomorrow.' He yawned. 'I'm going to bed. Alone,' he added hastily.

Although Nash was weary he didn't manage much sleep. By 7 p.m. he was up and about, wondering if he could summon the energy to make himself a meal or whether to opt for a takeaway. In the end he decided on the bold option and set off for La Giaconda.

He'd finished his meal and was chatting to Gino when his mobile rang. He glanced at the screen. 'Yes, Clara, what is it?' He listened for a moment. 'Can you pick me up? I'll be outside La Giaconda. I've had a couple of glasses of wine and I'm on foot. OK?'

He disconnected before Clara could indulge in any sarcastic comments.

*

They were strolling along the river bank hand in hand, pausing regularly to exchange kisses that grew more intense, more passionate with each one. The evening was warm. The sun had been shining all day. Now it was getting towards sunset, but the rays still shone through the tall trees, dappling the grass. It formed the perfect backdrop for what he'd planned. He was almost eighteen. She was a couple of years younger. He was fairly sure she was over the age of consent. Reasonably sure she was still a virgin. Neither fact worried him too much. He hoped to change the latter within the next couple of hours. Not that he thought of her in those terms. Well, not completely. She meant more to him than that alone. Much more than the other girls he'd been with.

They'd almost reached the place he had in mind, a clearing in the woods. There they'd be able to settle down in some comfort and complete privacy. His thoughts were rudely interrupted by a tug on his hand as she stumbled. She twisted to see what had tripped her. He too glanced down. In a split second, all passion fled. Horror replaced lust. Then she screamed. He pulled her close, shielding her trembling body with his arms. Shielding her from what lay behind them. Unaware that he too was trembling. That he was also on the verge of screaming.

They looked at one another briefly. Then he grabbed her hand, and without a word they began to run. In blind panic, they stumbled over tree roots and tussocks of grass. Oblivious to everything except their mutual, burning desire: desire to escape. To put as much distance as they could from what they'd seen, and to do it as fast as possible.

It was nearly dusk when Clara pulled up. As Nash was fastening his seatbelt, she asked, 'Still friends?'

'How do you mean?' Nash was defensive, suspicious.

'It's not every bloke who takes kindly to someone who's been shagging his sister. Italians take a particularly dim view of that, I'm told. Aren't you afraid of the Cosa Nostra?'

'Gino's perfectly aware of the relationship. He was sympathetic because Leonie's gone to New York. Anyway, what's happened?'

'Couple of teenagers found a body near a clearing in Helm Woods.'

'What were they doing there?'

'Dunno, haven't spoken to them yet. From what the uniform who rang me said, I'd guess they were courting.'

Nash frowned. 'Clara, how come whenever anybody else does it, you refer to it as courting? When you're talking about me, it's always shagging. Where's the difference?'

Clara repressed a smile. 'The difference is, you rarely go courting. You're always too busy shagging.'

'What do we know about the body?'

'Just that. That it's a body. The kids were so scared they ran all the way back to Helmsdale nick. Both of them had mobiles in their pockets. Neither of them thought to use them.'

'Kids today – it's surprising they didn't take photos and post them on YouTube. Man or woman?'

'No idea. Uniform sent a solitary PC with the boy, for him to show him the spot. He radioed confirmation in. They called me, I called you. Oh, I called Mexican Pete as well. He was sarcastic.'

'He would be. He's either making snide remarks about me or trying to make a pass at you. You must be losing your charm.'

'You know what, Mike, you're really gallant sometimes. How do you get to be such a smoothie?'

'Must be all the shagging.'

The car park appeared full when they pulled in. Nash recognized one of the cars. 'Mexican Pete's here before us.'

A bored-looking constable hovered at the entrance to the woods. He nodded to the detectives. 'Follow the path,' he told them. 'Where it splits, follow the sign for Kirk Bolton. Have you got a torch?'

Mironova held up her hand. The beam from her torch lit the path more than adequately. As they approached the site, a series of flood-lights was switched on. 'Somebody's been doing some thinking,' Nash approved. 'Bringing a generator with them,' he added in answer to Mironova's querying glance.

They ducked under the incident tape and approached a group of officers who were standing about. Nash recognized the sergeant in charge. 'Jack Binns,' he pointed out to Clara. 'That explains the gener-ator. Evening, Jack.'

Binns looked across. 'Evening, Mike, Clara.'

'What's matter, Jack, life in Netherdale too quiet? After a slice of Helmsdale action?'

'They call it the short straw. You know how it is. Anything happens out of hours, there's never enough personnel in Helmsdale to handle an incident, so they have to pull in reinforcements.' He paused and added slyly, 'Despite what Creepy and DCC King think.'

Nash winced and changed the subject. 'What have we got?'

'Unidentified male, late forties I'd estimate. Wound to the throat, looks like it was slit; blood everywhere. Body was found by a young couple. Reckon they were going shagging, until she tripped over the corpse. That cooled their ardour.'

'Tut-tut, Jack. You mustn't refer to it as shagging. It's only shagging when I do it. Anyone else, it's courting.'

'Well, his plans to give her a good courting took a bit of a blow.'

'I'll speak to him later. Let's see what Mexican Pete has to tell us.' Nash paused. 'When you say unidentified, does that mean you've not checked the body?'

Binns shook his head. 'More than my life's worth. Daren't even fart near a body until forensics have finished.'

'That must be a problem for you,' Nash agreed.

Ramirez looked up as they approached. 'I wondered how long it would be before you appeared,' he told Nash. 'What kept you? You're usually first on the scene, sniffing around like a half-starved vulture. You must be losing your touch. It's certainly not for lack of practice.'

'Maybe I'm getting old,' Nash commented. 'What can you tell us?'

'Male, mid to late forties. Overweight and out of condition. Sedentary job at a guess, certainly not a manual worker. Dead twenty-four to thirty-six hours. I'll tell you more when I've done the calculations.'

'Cause of death?'

'Asphyxiation caused by strangulation. Not manual, though. I'll need to examine the corpse more closely.'

'What about the blood?' Nash gestured to the grass surrounding the victim's head that was stained dark. Clara followed his gaze. She could see movement. Hundreds of ants were scurrying to and fro in the patch of dried blood. The first of a queue of diners, waiting to feast on the body. She shuddered and turned away. 'Binns reckoned he'd been knifed?'

'Sergeant Binns should come on one of my pathology courses. There's no single entry point as you'd find from a knife wound. At a guess I'd say he was garrotted. But I'll know better after I've examined the corpse under a decent light.'

'Any ID?'

'I've checked the pockets I can reach – nothing in them. The others will have to wait until the forensic work's been done.'

Nash studied the body. 'Pity he's laid face down. No chance of recognition. Thanks, Professor. I'll keep in touch.'

'I feared you'd say that,' Ramirez mocked him. 'You could always get Mironova to do the liaison work.'

'I would do,' Nash told him gravely, 'but she gets overcome by your hot-blooded Latin ardour and she's frightened she'd betray her latent passion.'

Nash signalled to Mironova to follow him and detailed Binns to ensure the frightened teenager was taken back to Helmsdale station. They paused for a quick word with him. 'Sergeant Mironova will take statements from you and your girlfriend there.' Nash smiled and added, 'After that you can go home. This evening's been a bit of an ordeal for you. Not quite what you were hoping for.' The youngster blushed.

'We can't do much more here,' Nash told Binns, 'not until daylight anyway. Leave somebody to make sure the site's secure. In the morning we'll organize a fingertip search of the area. By then we might have a clue as to the weapon.'

When they reached the car park, Nash paused. 'What is it, Mike?' Clara knew from experience his thoughts were elsewhere.

'How did he get here?'

'The dead man?'

Nash nodded. 'Mexican Pete said he wasn't the type to take much exercise. Besides which he wasn't dressed for walking. His shoes were certainly unsuitable. That means he was given a lift, or there's a vehicle parked somewhere.'

'And that would give us his identity.'

'If he had a vehicle, why isn't it here?' Nash gestured round the car park. 'This place rarely gets crowded except at weekends. Why not use the car park?'

'Maybe he did get a lift, which would mean he knew his killer.'

Nash sighed. 'We don't have sufficient facts to work with. All we can do is speculate. We'll have to leave it until morning. I'll let Tom know what's happened, you get those statements done. We'll make a start as soon as it gets light. I'll ask Tom for extra bodies to help with the area search.' He paused and thought for a moment. 'On second thoughts, it would be a waste both of us being tied up supervising. I'll come here; you stay in the office and try to get some more info out of Mexican Pete. Do me a favour, though. On your way in tomorrow, call and get me a coffee from Ready Breaks in the Market Place. Drop it off as you're passing.'

'I thought you didn't like their coffee. Last one you had you complained it was too bitter.'

'Yes, I reckon they got the recipe from you. Put an extra sugar in it and give it a good stir. I'll try and put up with it.'

chapter fifteen

Nash marshalled the officers for the search. They'd been working almost an hour when Mironova arrived. 'How are they getting on?' She gestured to the team.

'A collection of sweet wrappers and assorted junk. It's all been bagged but I doubt it'll throw up anything useful.'

'OK, I'll chase up the perverted pathologist.'

'Making a pass at you isn't perverted. It shows good taste.'

'I call it perverted when somebody makes a pass at you whilst they're holding a human thigh bone in one hand.'

Nash smiled. 'You might have a point. When did that happen?'

'When I was on the forensics refresher course.'

Nash shook his head and laughed. 'I'd like you to pop back at lunchtime with fresh supplies for the troops.' Nash scrabbled in his pocket. 'I've got a list of what everyone wants.' He pulled out a piece of paper. 'Add a sandwich for me, and more coffee, please.'

The morning's search brought nothing, and Nash was beginning to think there would be little point continuing through the afternoon. Mironova returned shortly before 1 p.m. bearing two large carriers. Nash called a halt and the officers crowded round to collect their food. As Nash ate his sandwich, Clara relayed her conversation with Ramirez. 'Mexican Pete said there was nothing in the victim's pockets. I asked him about the weapon. He's confirmed the man was garrotted. He suggests the weapon was some form of thin wire. Thin and flexible, but extremely strong.'

'Piano wire,' Nash suggested.

'What made you think of that?'

'I don't rightly know. Maybe the fact I've just reread the file on the Stacey Fletcher murder. Remember, she was garrotted with piano wire. The difference is the wire was left by her body. This time the killer took the weapon with him. Or so we believe. Unless our men find something.'

'Trying to find a short length of fine wire in these woods?' Mironova gestured at the high banks of bramble and briar. 'A needle in a haystack would be easier.'

'Maybe, but if the wire's stained with the victim's blood we might have a chance. I'll get the dogs in. See if they can find anything. But that'll have to wait until the forensics boys are finished.'

Mironova was about to depart when a constable came panting towards them, his face pink with exertion. He looked too young to be in uniform. 'What's matter?' Nash asked, checking himself from adding 'son'.

'I've found a car, sir.'

'Whereabouts?'

'It was parked along a farm track at the edge of the wood. I saw it through a gap in the trees.'

'You'd better show us.' Nash gestured to Mironova.

'I think it's been here a while,' the constable offered as they walked along the track.

'What makes you say that?' The question was delivered in a mildly enquiring tone.

'There are pine needles all over the roof,' the constable stammered nervously.

'It's been a bit breezy. Couldn't they have dropped off this morning?'

'I don't think so. There's quite a lot. Also, I felt the bonnet and the radiator grille. They're both cold.'

'That's observant,' Nash approved.

They surveyed the vehicle. The car would have been all but invisible from the road. Was that deliberate? Had the owner parked here to avoid detection? Was it the killer's car, or the victim's? Perhaps a stolen car that had been dumped? Or was there a perfectly innocent explanation? Nash couldn't think of one. 'Check the number plate with DVLA,' he told Clara.

She had the answer within five minutes. 'The car's registered to a John Thomas Tucker, a local man.' She glanced at Nash; saw the surprise on his face. 'You know him?'

'Yes, and so do you.' Nash waited for comprehension to dawn. 'JT Tucker?' he prompted. 'Reporter for the *Netherdale Gazette*.'

'Good Lord, yes. What's his car doing here?'

'At a guess I'd say Tucker's a prime candidate for our victim. Unfortunately, he was laid face down. If I'd got a look at him, I'd have identified him. Get onto our randy pathologist. Ask him to send a picture message of the victim's face.'

They waited quarter of an hour for it to come through. Nash needed only one glance. 'That's Tucker,' he confirmed.

'Are you sure?'

'Yes, I saw him last Sunday, when I collected Vickers. He was trying to get an interview. Vickers told him he'd talk to him once he got back to Helmsdale.'

Clara thought for a moment. 'Mexican Pete said Tucker had been dead twenty-four to thirty-six hours. That would make time of death sometime on Tuesday. Wasn't that when Vickers went walkabout?'

Nash nodded.

'And,' Clara continued, 'you said when Vickers returned he was dishevelled and his clothing was stained and muddy. Just like you'd be if you'd been in woodland like this. What were the stains? Blood? Tucker was killed the same way as Stacey Fletcher. If we find the weapon it might even prove to be piano wire, just the same as Stacey's. Bit of a coincidence, don't you think?'

'It may be. I hope it is coincidence. But it's certainly worth asking Vickers for a detailed explanation of his movements on Tuesday. It won't do any harm to have forensics check the clothing he was wearing either.'

'Let's just hope Vickers isn't too domesticated. It won't help if he stuck them straight into the washing machine.'

Nash winced. 'Don't even think about it. In fact ...' Nash was about to continue, but tailed off into silence. Clara glanced at her boss. He was wearing the faraway expression she knew well: 'thinking, do not disturb'. She waited patiently.

Nash looked round. 'Follow me,' he told Clara. 'You stay here,' he instructed the constable. As they walked back along the path leading to the clearing he said, 'I should have realized earlier.' They emerged from the shadow of the trees, blinking for a second in the sunshine. 'Tell me what you see.'

Clara frowned. 'I don't understand.'

'Doesn't anything strike you about this place?'

She looked again. 'Sorry, Mike. What am I supposed to be looking for?'

'Doesn't this bit of woodland seem familiar? Doesn't it remind you of anything?'

She obviously hadn't made the connection. 'Think back to the photos in the Stacey Fletcher file. This is the same place. Add fifteen years' growth to the trees but it's definitely where the girl was murdered.'

'Good God, Mike! That means ...'

'It means we're going to have to stretch coincidence a long way. Two murders in the same spot, using possibly identical weapons and both victims connected to Gary Vickers. A man who hasn't got an alibi for either crime. That might be one coincidence too many. But let's not jump the gun.'

'We ought to question Vickers straightaway.'

'Hold your horses. We'll get round to him in a while. Remember I've got grave doubts about his conviction for Stacey Fletcher's murder anyway.'

'So if Vickers didn't kill Stacey?'

'Then it's highly unlikely that he killed Tucker.'

'So what do we do now?'

'I want to look inside that car.' They retraced their steps to the edge of the wood. 'Do we have anyone in the search party who'll be able to get in it easily?'

The young constable was listening. 'There's one of the guys from traffic. He's a dab hand at that sort of thing.' They looked at him enquiringly. He blushed slightly. 'He helped me when I'd locked myself out of my car.'

'I'd better not ask where he acquired that know-how. Fetch him, will you.' Nash watched the officer walk back along the track. 'Bright young man,' he observed quietly. 'Might be worth making a note of his name.'

Clara nodded agreement. 'Will it be in order to search the car? Wouldn't we be better waiting on the SOCOs to finish with it?'

'I'll take the risk. From what I can see there's not much danger of contaminating evidence.'

Mironova peered through the car window. The interior was a mess. Used sandwich cartons, empty crisp packets and chocolate wrappers jostled against water and Coke bottles and old copies of newspapers. 'I guess you're right. He'd hardly win awards for tidiness. What are we looking for?'

Nash shrugged. 'Anything relevant.'

The constable returned with another officer who was carrying what looked like a tyre lever. 'Can you open the driver's door?' Nash asked.

The officer glanced at the car. 'Dead easy. Give me a minute.'

When the door swung open, the wail of the car alarm echoed from the surrounding trees. The officer reached inside and fiddled below the dashboard. The alarm fell silent. He nodded to Nash. 'All clear now,' he confirmed. 'The boot release is down there.' He pointed to a lever alongside the driver's seat.

'Thanks.' Nash pulled a pair of latex gloves from his pocket. 'Tell your boss we'll have the car ready for them in quarter of an hour.'

'Do you want me to help?' Clara asked.

'I want you to go to the other side of the car and watch. I want a witness that I'm doing everything by the book.' Nash looked at the mess. 'Although I doubt we'll find anything in here that'll point to the killer.'

He reached in and flipped open the centre console. 'Aha!' he exclaimed. Clara watched him remove a keyring containing a bunch of house keys. 'That's what I was looking for. You realize what this means?'

Clara shook her head.

'It means we can search Tucker's home.'

Next, Nash flipped the lever and the boot sprang open. Inside was a further collection of waste paper. 'Doesn't spend much time recycling,' Clara muttered.

Nash moved a pile of paper. Jammed against the rear of the back seat was a small bag. Nash lifted it out. 'Camera bag?' Clara guessed.

Nash nodded. The bag was empty. 'At a guess I'd say he had the camera with him. Which means either the killer took it, or it's been hidden. We'd better ask them to go over the area again. There's an outside chance they might have missed it.'

The oversight was understandable. The crime scene was pock-marked with rabbit burrows. Some of the holes were quite large and it was pure chance that the camera had landed in one of them. It was only when a manual search of each burrow was conducted that it was discovered.

'Pure fluke,' the SOCO chief said defensively. 'We covered the surface thoroughly. Nobody gave the warren a thought.'

'Not to worry,' Nash pacified him. 'You'd better check the rest of the burrows.' He watched as the camera was sealed inside an evidence bag. 'Let me have that as soon as you've finished with it. I'm anxious to see what's on the film.' He glanced at his watch. 'I'm going to knock off now. I've got work to do tonight. I've removed a set of house keys from Tucker's car. The rest is as we found it. I'll leave you to organize removal.'

Nash and Mironova walked back to the car park. 'Do you want me to come along to Tucker's flat?'

'It won't take two of us. You keep on with the paperwork. Tell Viv I'm putting him on Vickers watch again tonight. I'm going to Tucker's place. After that I'll drop in on Vickers. I want to hear what he's got to say about Tuesday.'

Earlier that afternoon Becky Pollard had chance to think about Tucker's continued lack of contact. She buzzed down to reception. 'Has JT been in touch?'

The receptionist was emphatic. 'He hasn't rung, or been here. Still hasn't collected that parcel.'

'I've never known JT so inaccessible and his copy's due in. I just hope the story's worth it. But I'm getting a bit concerned. His mobile constantly goes onto voicemail. I must have left half a dozen messages. There's no reply from his landline either. I hope he's not ill.'

Nash parked opposite Tucker's flat, which occupied half the ground floor of a detached house dating from the early twentieth century. The front garden had been transformed into a hard standing for cars. There were no lights on, and the car park was empty. That suited Nash perfectly. He didn't want a zealous neighbour reporting him as an intruder.

The outer door was unlocked. Nash stepped into the hall and found a light switch. He looked at the bunch of keys and tried two before the flat door swung open. Undecided, he stood in the inner hall. He reached for the light switch, then reconsidered and flicked his torch on. The short corridor contained five doors. Nash opened the first, the bathroom. The door opposite led into the kitchen. The third was a bedroom, the double bed unmade. A duvet lay crumpled on the bed.

At the end of the corridor was a sitting room. Next to it, a second bedroom had been adapted as an office. Nash looked at the desk, its surface strewn with papers. His gaze transferred to a bookcase that stretched the length of one wall. This was occupied for the most part by a collection of box files, all neatly tabulated. The first sign of organization Nash had seen. He was about to begin searching when he heard a sound. He paused, immobile, and listened.

After a second he heard it again. The creak of a dry hinge. Somewhere, a door was being opened. Cautiously? Or furtively? Nash peered down the hall. There was no one in sight. Then he heard movement: footsteps. Someone was inside the flat.

The footsteps ceased. Silence. Turning off his torch, Nash slid noiselessly into the corridor. He advanced slowly, one step at a time, each movement taking an age. As he neared the kitchen, there was a sudden flurry of movement. A solid object cannoned into him. He grappled with the intruder and they fell to the floor. Nash wrapped his arms round his assailant. He felt the soft curves. At the same instant he caught the whiff of a light, fragrant perfume. His captive squirmed and wriggled. Nash freed one hand and switched on his torch. 'It's OK. I'm not going to hurt you.'

'Who the hell are you? What are you doing here?' The voice conveyed anger and fear.

Nash scrambled to his feet. 'I was going to ask you that.' Nash's mind raced over the possibilities. Tucker's girlfriend? Neighbour? He switched the light on. The woman was young, in her early thirties he guessed. She was pretty, or would be if her features weren't contorted by fear. He reached for his warrant card. 'Police,' he told her. 'Detective Inspector Nash. Helmsdale CID. Now, who are you?'

She took the card and inspected it, even checking his likeness against the photo. She ignored his question. 'What are you here for? Where's Tucker?'

'I'll tell you, if you'll give me some answers.' He helped her to her feet.

'I came to check up on Tucker. He hasn't been in contact for a couple of days. I work with him.'

'You're with the *Gazette*?' She nodded. 'And your name is?'

'Becky Pollard. Now, please tell me why you're here.'

'I'm sorry, Miss Pollard. I'm afraid I've some bad news. Tucker's dead.'

'Dead? How? I mean, was there an accident?'

'Not exactly. His body has been found in suspicious circumstances. Let's go through to the lounge and sit down. I'll tell you what I can. In return, I need information about Tucker. What stories he was working on, that sort of thing.'

She went to move and swayed slightly, dizzy with the shock. Nash put out a hand to steady her. He turned the lounge light on and guided her to the sofa. 'Tucker's body was discovered in Helm Woods yesterday evening. The pathologist estimated he'd been dead since Tuesday. I haven't got the post-mortem results yet, but we're treating the death as suspicious.'

'I can't believe it. JT was our top reporter. He provided us with lots of great stories; some of them terrific exclusives. You're saying he was murdered, aren't you?'

'It seems highly likely, I'm afraid. Can you tell me what he was working on?'

'I don't know.' Becky's thoughts were a disjointed jumble. How was she going to break this to the *Gazette*? What was the reason for JT's murder? Should she tell this policeman what she knew? Which wasn't much.

'Very well.' Nash didn't believe she was as ignorant of Tucker's activities as she professed, but was prepared to wait. 'Tell me how he operated.'

'He was allowed to do his own thing. He was more like a freelance than a staffer, even though he was on the payroll. That was because he was so good.' Her head came up as she added with a touch of pride, 'My family has owned the *Gazette* for three generations. Part of the reason for our success is we've always been independent, with no political allegiances. That makes it easy to go in for the sort of investigative journalism JT was good at.'

Nash studied the girl as she was speaking. Attractive, intelligent and articulate were his initial impressions. 'And what's your role in the *Gazette*?'

'We tend to double up. I'm IT manager, deputy features editor, staff photographer and relief reporter all in one.'

Nash kept it light. 'That's quite a package,' he commented. 'Attractively wrapped too.'

Becky blushed slightly.

'Tell me,' Nash continued conversationally, 'in which role was it that you were working with JT? I mean, why did you come to find him, if you didn't know what he was working on?'

Becky's colour faded as quickly as it had come. 'I ... er ... he asked me to get him some equipment. It arrived and I left messages for him, but he didn't collect it.'

'What sort of equipment? Was it computer stuff or photographic?'

'Neither. It was ...' Becky hesitated, aware of the illicit nature of the listening equipment. 'It was electronic equipment.'

'We recovered a camera near the body. I'm waiting for forensics to finish with it before I check what photos are in it. Was that Tucker's camera?'

'I expect it was one JT borrowed from me. Was it analogue or digital?'

'I think it was analogue.'

'I'm fairly sure that belongs to the *Gazette*. JT wasn't much good with high-tech equipment, so the old-fashioned film-bearing camera was enough for him to cope with.'

'If he wasn't technically minded, how do you think he'd have coped with surveillance equipment?'

The question was delivered so casually, it took Becky a second to realize what Nash had said. She gasped and said weakly, 'I never said it was surveillance equipment.'

Nash laughed. 'What else could it be? You told me Tucker wasn't technical, yet he borrowed a camera rather than taking you along. You said he was an investigative journalist. Stands to reason he'd want to find out what someone was up to without being rumbled. What was it? Listening and recording gear?'

Becky nodded. 'Don't tell anyone,' she pleaded. 'I'll get in awful trouble if they find out. I was just doing him a favour. It was nothing to do with the paper.'

'I'll keep it to myself, on one condition.'

Becky eyed him with suspicion.

'Tell me what you know about the story Tucker was working on.'

'I don't know much. It had something to do with Carlton Rathmell.'

'The MEP? The one who's been making the headlines?'

Becky nodded. 'JT borrowed the camera for that story.' She was about to add more when she stopped. Her head lifted. She sniffed. 'What's that smell?'

Nash turned and inhaled. As he did so he heard a click. A letterbox? Then he caught the scent. 'Petrol!'

He jumped to his feet. Then they heard a gentle sigh of wind.

Nash took three quick strides to the lounge door, Becky alongside him. He glanced down the corridor. A tongue of flame shot upwards and began to spread. He slammed the door shut and glanced round. 'Window!'

As they stumbled around the furniture, Becky looked back. The door frame was etched in a faint orange glow. The fire was spreading. The window was their only way out. And it didn't look as if they'd much time. 'Hurry!' she urged him.

Nash stared at the frame. It was double glazed and the window locks were on. There was no key in sight. Then the room was plunged into darkness. Becky screamed and clutched his arm. 'Electrics are shot,' Nash said. His voice was calm. He didn't feel calm. 'Fire's probably burnt through the cable. I can't open these windows. They're locked and there's no key. We'll have to break them.'

Becky fought against the rising tide of panic. 'But they're double glazed.'

Nash shone his torch on the corner of the glass. There was a kitemark. 'Damn! Toughened glass; shatterproof.' Bad had just become a whole lot worse.

chapter sixteen

'Hold the torch.' Nash handed it to Becky.

'What are you going to do?' The tide of panic was rising.

'Figure out how to open this window.'

Becky looked back. The glow round the door edges was brighter. She swung the torch towards it. Along the base of the door she saw a wispy grey tendril, curling with the sinuous grace of a snake and just as deadly: smoke. She caught the first whiff in her throat and coughed.

'Bring that light back!' Nash ordered.

'There's smoke coming into the room,' Becky spluttered.

Nash glanced back. 'More reason to hurry. Shine the beam on the window.'

'Won't someone notice? Raise the alarm?'

'Not fast enough. If we're going to escape we've to do it ourselves.' There was a way. It might work, but Nash was reluctant to try it. He had his pistol; he could shoot at the pane. There was no guarantee it would break, even with the impact of a bullet. No guarantee where the bullet would ricochet. He'd have to be desperate to try. He wasn't that desperate. Not quite. Not yet.

The window wasn't new. The double glazing was from the early days. The age gave him hope. Not much, but a little. He took out a multi-bladed penknife. 'Keep the beam on the edge of the glass.' He stretched to the top corner and felt for the joint. There it was. A narrow slit between the horizontal and vertical pieces of the frame. Concealed on the outside, exposed on the interior. Nobody expected burglars to break out of a building. Hope increased; marginally.

He selected a short, stubby blade. After a few false starts, he worked it into the slit and began to lever the blade to and fro. There was a sudden cracking sound. For a second Nash thought the blade had broken. Becky swung the beam away. She gasped. Nash looked over his shoulder. The upper panel of the door had split. A tongue of flame reached round the broken timber, licking greedily at the blistering paint. The heat intensified. Instantly. 'Come on,' he urged.

She fought the desire to glance back. Better not look. Better not know. Nash inserted the blade again. There was another sharp crack. Something flew past, at eye level. She blinked.

'Got it.' Nash levered the top part of the frame away. 'Now for the others.' His voice was calm. She felt soothed by his refusal to panic. She struggled for breath, as a choking cloud of smoke billowed. The dragon hadn't given up on its victims.

Nash's hand touched her shoulder. 'Get down low, the air will be clearer. Keep the torch shining up.' She crouched down.

Nash was coughing as he set to work on the side of the frame. She watched. Watched and prayed. Within seconds both vertical strips were off. He knelt and took a long shuddering breath, then levered the bottom of the frame clear. 'Move back out of the way,' Nash ordered.

Becky felt trapped. If she moved she'd be nearer the fire. Devil or deep blue sea? She opted for the devil and shuffled backwards. The heat was on her back. The torch beam reflected curls of smoke throughout the room. Now Nash had the bottom piece of the frame in his hand. He threw it to one side and reached for the exposed edge of the pane. Becky saw him change for a longer blade and slide it under the glass. He levered it and the pane fell inwards. Nash pushed it to one side. It landed with a soft thud.

'Come forward.'

Becky needed no second invitation. She crawled alongside the detective. 'What now?' she gasped. Two words, long enough when you're choking.

'On your back. Feet against the window.'

'What?'

'We've got to try … push … the outer pane out.' Nash was gasping for breath. 'Try with … our feet … Ready?'

They lay side by side, feet against the glass. They pushed. Nothing. 'Again.' They pushed again. Still nothing.

'Kick … at the corner,' Nash coughed.

Becky's throat was tight. Her lungs felt as if they were bursting. 'Again.' His hand gripped hers. She kicked out. Feebly. Strength fading. 'Harder!'

She kicked again. Then again. She swung her foot once more. Her foot met no resistance; at the same instant a cool current of air washed over her. Momentary relief. There was a huge roaring sound behind: the dragon reached out for them. Nash dragged her half upright, then pushed her over the ledge and out through the window. He dived after her. They landed in a tangled heap, scrabbling about as if on ice. They'd fallen on the glass. Nash rolled, hauling Becky to one side, and they lay on the tarmac, gasping in huge draughts of the cool night air. Behind them the thwarted dragon roared and belched flames and smoke.

'Come on. We're not safe yet.' Nash reached down and pulled Becky to her feet. 'Falling masonry, roof tiles,' he explained succinctly. They staggered across the car park until they were clear of anything the burning building could throw at them.

Nash pulled his mobile out and dialled 999 as they slumped to the ground, exhausted, still gulping at the night air. Becky waited until he'd finished the call and tugged at his sleeve. 'Mr Nash.'

He looked at her.

'Thank you. If I'd been alone, I'd be dead now.'

Nash would have none of it. 'If I hadn't been there, you wouldn't have got inside.'

Becky hadn't the energy to argue. The adrenalin of fear had gone. Shock and reaction were setting in.

There was little hope of saving the building. The fire service deployed all their equipment and managed to check the other flats were empty, but the flames had got too strong a hold. Nash and Becky sheltered in the back of an ambulance, receiving oxygen. The paramedics tried to persuade them to go to Netherdale Hospital but they refused. The doctor who arrived shortly afterwards checked them over and reluctantly agreed to their release.

'How did you get here?' Nash's voice sounded hoarse.

'Walked. I left my car at home.' She whispered her reply, aware that her voice too was husky.

'I'll take you home.'

'Thanks.'

Nash spoke to the chief fire officer. 'Where's Doug?'

'Off duty. He'll be sorry he missed this one. Not every day we get a DI involved. You take care. Plenty of fluids, and gargle as often as possible. Smoke can do no end of damage.'

'Will do, but let me have a report in the morning.' Nash took Becky's arm. 'Let's get out of here.'

*

Vickers and Pearce had discovered a mutual liking for Indian cuisine. They studied a menu from the local takeaway. The restaurant had recently introduced a home delivery service. 'Cash and Curry,' Viv explained.

Vickers groaned. 'I hope the food's better than your jokes.'

There would be a forty-minute wait, Pearce was told. 'I'll check the front and back whilst we're waiting. Don't do a runner. Nash would have my bollocks on a platter if we lost you again.'

Vickers smiled. 'You don't think I'm going to disappear having ordered that food, do you? You like Nash, don't you?' he asked as an afterthought. 'Is he a decent bloke to work for?'

'The best,' Viv told him. 'We had a couple of wasters before him. Mike's a top man. He's got his failings, but they don't intrude on work.'

'What failings?'

'One, to be exact.' Pearce made a gesture with one hand on the other forearm, his fist clenched.

'Women?'

Viv nodded. 'You've heard the expression "sexoholic"?'

'Nash is one?'

'Pretty much. He loves women and they adore him. I can think of more than a handful he's slept with since I've known him. All stunners too.'

'Lucky bastard.'

'That's as maybe. We reckon they're substitutes for the one he lost.'

Vickers lifted an enquiring eyebrow. 'His girlfriend was killed a while back. Mike put the murderer away, but I don't think he's ever got over it.'

'Cancel "lucky bastard" then. Seems Nash and I have more in common than I thought.'

Pearce stared at him.

'Forget what you've been told.' Vickers' voice took on a harsher note. 'Stacey and I were lovers. Somebody robbed me twice. They took Stacey from me and they took fifteen years of my life.'

'You didn't kill her? But all the forensic evidence …'

'Points to the fact I'd had sex with her? Well, of course I had. Every chance we could get. But there's no evidence that shows I raped her.' Vickers' voice lowered. It was almost as if he was speaking to someone else; to the ghost of a long-dead girl perhaps? 'I didn't need to rape her, did I? She was there for me whenever I wanted her, as I was there for her when she needed me. Until that last time, the time she needed me most; the time when she was in danger. Then she was alone. And one day I'll find her killer. I'll not rest until the bastard who took Stacey's life pays. With theirs.'

Viv continued his inspection of the exterior, which took only minutes. 'All secure,' he reported as he re-entered the kitchen. 'I've left the front door on the latch for when the delivery arrives.' He was about to slide the bolt on the back door shut when the doorbell rang.

'I'll get it.' Vickers was out of the room before Pearce could object. He heard the sound of voices from the hall. One at least sounded angry. He took a few cautious steps into the dining room. The hall door was open. He looked through the slit, between door and frame. His view was obstructed by a man's shoulder. Not Vickers. Pearce moved slightly, changed the angle of vision. He was only able to see part of another man's face in the gap; enough to recognize him. It wasn't a takeaway delivery. Not unless Ronnie Fletcher had a new job.

Nash and Becky had reached the Market Place when his phone rang. He pulled off the road onto the cobbles. 'Sorry, won't take a minute.'

He glanced at the screen. 'Yes, Viv?' he croaked.

Becky saw his expression change. The tension was back; in full. He gestured to Becky. She didn't understand at first. He signalled again, a driving motion. It was only when he got out of the car that she got the message. He was still clutching the mobile to his ear as he opened the passenger door. She slid across to the driving seat, adjusted the seat and mirror, fumbling with the unfamiliar controls. Nash began to speak. Not to her but to the caller, his voice barely above a whisper. 'I'll be there as fast as I can. Keep out of sight. Don't try anything. Don't provoke them. I'll come to the back. Five minutes.'

Becky engaged first gear and waited. Nash pointed ahead. She let the clutch out slowly. The car moved off easily. Nash was still listening. Then he lowered the phone and looked at the screen.

'Where am I going?'

'Grove Road. I'll direct you.'

'What's happened?'

'Potential hostage situation,' Nash pressed a button on the phone and waited.

'Clara? Get to Vickers' ASAP. Bring as many uniforms as you can. Better request an ARU from Netherdale too. Ronnie Fletcher's turned up. He and one of the Floyd brothers have got hold of Vickers. Viv rang me. He was out of the room when they arrived. As I was talking to him the phone went dead. I'm on my way there now.'

'Direct me where to go.' The tension had got to Becky.

'Turn right in about a hundred yards.' Nash pointed. 'Just past where that van's parked. Keep moving. Drive slowly to the end of the street, then turn right at the junction. There's a back lane runs parallel – turn into it. I'll tell you when to stop.'

Nash kept one eye on his mobile. Willing it to ring again, hoping Viv had cut him off to avoid discovery. Praying he wasn't a hostage; fearing the worst.

'What are you going to do? I assume Pearce is one of your men, but who are the others?'

'DC Pearce is one of my officers and the home owner is under our protection. I can't explain why. The others are the ones we're protecting him from.'

'What will you do?' Becky was persistent.

'I've no idea till I get there.' Nash was coughing from speaking so much.

As they turned into Grove Road, Nash shuffled sideways. He leaned as far across her as was safe. He could smell the mixture of her perfume, smoke from the fire and perspiration from their ordeal. He found it mildly erotic and distracting. 'Slow right down,' he said. 'That's thirty-two, the one with the bay.'

Becky took her eyes from the road for a second. Subconsciously her foot eased off the accelerator. 'Not too slow,' Nash warned. 'We don't want to stall it.'

Becky glimpsed a figure standing inside the bay. They were alongside now. She dare not risk another look. The space between parked cars was too narrow for one thing. Nor did she want to risk discovery. 'Who's that?'

Nash had time for a longer look. Too tall for Vickers, not broad enough for Pearce. 'That's Ronnie Fletcher.' His tone was grim.

'You know him?'

'Too well.' Nash was busy with his phone. 'Clara, go round to the back. Fletcher's looking out of the front.' He glanced sideways. 'Look for my car. There'll be a young woman waiting, name of Becky Pollard. I'll explain later. I'm going to try and get in.'

Becky followed Nash's directions, still driving slowly. 'I thought it better not to speed up after we passed the house,' she explained. 'That would look suspicious.'

Nash eyed her approvingly. 'Good thinking. We need to go ten houses up.'

The lane was little wider than an alley, certainly not broad enough to allow cars to pass. Becky pulled up opposite the rear of number thirty-two. 'What now?'

'Wait here until my sergeant arrives. Her name's Mironova, Clara Mironova. Get her to follow me in with the uniforms. Whatever happens, you stay here. Clear?'

Becky watched Nash walk into the back yard but couldn't see what he was doing for the boundary wall. There was a sudden blaze of reflected light. The door had been opened. By Nash?

The car felt too confined. She got out and leaned against the door. Where was this sergeant? What was her name? Mironova, that was it. Clara would be easier to remember. Why hadn't she arrived? Helmsdale wasn't that big. What was keeping her? Nash was up against two dangerous men, without backup.

She paced to and fro. Her journalist's instinct took over. She walked slowly towards the gate. If she opened the back door, she might be able to hear what was happening.

Nash tiptoed across the kitchen, careful not to ground his heels. There was no sound. The dining room door was ajar. Nash eased it wider. The room was empty. Nash gambled everyone was in the lounge.

Pistol in hand, he gently opened the hall door. Prayed it wouldn't squeak. No guard in sight. He heard a noise, the low sound of a voice from the lounge. He crossed the hall and had almost reached the lounge door when he heard the squeak of a trainer on the polished floor. He turned as a shape flung itself at him. Nash was never sure if he fired the gun, or it simply went off. His assailant crashed into him and Nash felt a sharp pain in his left arm. He was thrust violently back. He hit the doorknob, painfully. The door burst open under their combined weight. Nash squirmed to disentangle himself from his attacker. He had a fleeting vision of Pearce and Vickers on the sofa, linked by Pearce's handcuffs. As Nash fell, the side of his head struck the door knob. Then everything went dark.

*

The first thing Nash felt was pain. Pain in his head, his arm, his back. He struggled to remember. Memory brought anxiety. Grove Road. What had happened? He opened his eyes. Wished he hadn't and closed them. He tried again, marginally better. He waited for focus. He was staring at a white ceiling and saw why his eyes hurt. He was looking straight into a bank of lights and turned his head away. 'Hello.' A whisper. 'Where am I?'

Clara looked relieved. 'Netherdale General, A & E department, Cubicle 3.'

'What happened? How's Viv?'

'He's alright. Pride's hurt, that's all. He's still at Grove Road with Vickers.'

'I was attacked. Then something hit my head. That's all I remember.'

'You were in the hall. The man who was with Fletcher went for you with a knife, nicked your arm. We think you must have turned aside otherwise he might have done more damage. Apparently it's only a flesh wound, couple of stitches, that's all. Your gun went off.' Clara grinned. 'You'll have some forms to fill in.'

Nash winced at the prospect.

'You must have hit him. There's a trail of blood. He got away, cannoned into Miss Pollard on the way out. Viv saw the rest. He said you were flat out. Ronnie Fletcher was about to hit you with a crowbar when Miss Pollard intervened.'

'I told her to wait in the car.'

'As well she didn't. You'd be dead if she had. Viv said Fletcher had lost it completely. He'd swung his arm right back. Then Miss Pollard felled him.'

'She did what?'

'She followed you inside and was in the dining room when she heard the gunshot, then this guy came rushing past. She saw a poker in the companion set. Picked it up and got to the lounge in time to clobber Fletcher. Not once but twice. He's in the next cubicle with head injuries.' Clara jerked her thumb over her shoulder.

Nash closed his eyes again. 'What do the medics say about him?'

'They're waiting to do a brain scan on Fletcher. I told them that'd be a waste of time.' Nash opened his eyes. Clara was grinning again. 'Then they said you might have concussion. I asked them how we'd know.'

'Thank you, Sergeant.' Nash frowned. 'What kept you? I mean, where were you when all this went down?'

Clara's smile vanished. 'Still en route. Tom was off duty. All Netherdale CID calls were being re-routed to King. He wasted ten minutes asking bloody stupid questions before he'd let me have a two-man ARU team. Started out making a lot of snide comments about our inability to deal with things. I reckon I'd still be arguing the toss with him if I hadn't threatened to go over his head and phone the chief.'

'You'll be off his Christmas card list.'

'That's not going to keep me awake. They'll want to examine you, now you're conscious. And you've a visitor. I'll go deal with the paperwork. From what I hear and the look of you, you've had quite a night of it. May be better if they keep you in.'

'Not ruddy likely. Who's my visitor?' Nash's voice was almost non-existent by now. But Clara had gone. She was replaced by a couple of stern-faced medics. Despite their reluctance, they could find no reason to detain Nash. Their efforts to dissuade him took over fifteen minutes. Eventually they departed and Nash closed his eyes in relief. When he reopened them, a familiar face hovered over him, watching anxiously. He smiled. 'Hello, Becky.'

She smiled back, a little weakly. Nash held out a hand. 'Do you know that's the first time I've seen you smile? I understand I owe you a vote of thanks. They tell me you're a dab hand with a poker.'

'I didn't know what else to do. It was awful. I just hit him.'

'Don't feel sorry for him. He was about to crush my skull. Anyway, thank you.'

'I hope you don't mind. I used your car to get here.'

'Good. Then you can drive me home.'

'You're not leaving? Surely they'll want to keep you in?'

'No way. I hate these places. Just give me chance to get dressed.'

The cubicle curtain was thrust back. DCC King marched in. 'What the hell's going on, Nash? There's going to be trouble over tonight's fiasco. You've shot one man and beaten another to pulp. A block of flats has been razed to the ground and you've called on reserves I said you weren't allowed. You'd better start talking fast. I'll see you carpeted for this.'

Nash squeezed Becky's hand. 'Clear off.'

He said it so quietly, his tone so matter of fact, that it failed to register with either of his listeners for a few seconds. King went red, then apoplectic purple. 'What did you say?'

'I said, clear off! Is that plain enough? You've been nothing but a nuisance ever since you came here. Tonight you endangered the lives of three men, two of them your own officers. All because of your dilatory actions.'

'You'll face a disciplinary hearing for this, Nash. I'll call this doctor as witness to your insubordination. Kindly remember every word, miss.'

Nash squeezed Becky's hand again. 'Did you hear me say anything?'

She shook her head. King's colour darkened further, if that was possible. 'I see.' His tone was icy. 'This isn't a doctor. Just another of the cheap tarts you keep round you. Well, don't imagine the fact that you're screwing this floozy will prevent me calling her as a witness.' He turned and barked at Becky, 'I'll need your name.'

Nash leaned back. This could be entertaining.

'You'd better tell me yours first.' Becky's tone was also ice-cold.

'I am Deputy Chief Constable King.' It was less of an introduction, more of an announcement.

Becky removed a small notebook and pen from her pocket and scribbled the name down.

'What are you doing?'

'I just want to get my facts straight. My name's Pollard, by the way. Rebecca Pollard.'

The name obviously meant nothing to King, who managed to get a sneer of contempt into his voice. 'Well, Miss Pollard, I should warn you that despite your association with Nash, any attempt to pervert the course of justice and commit perjury will land you facing criminal charges.'

'Really? Is this part of standard procedures or a new direction in local policing policy?'

'What do you mean?' King's confidence had ebbed slightly.

'You know very well a disciplinary hearing has no legal status. So you can't threaten anyone with perjury. Not only that, but there won't be a disciplinary hearing. Not over Detective Inspector Nash anyway. Not after what he's done tonight.'

'Oh yes there will. I intend to see him removed from the force. He's not fit to represent the police under my command.'

'Can I quote you on that?'

There was a long silence, painful for King as realization of Becky's short sentence struck home. Hugely enjoyable for Nash. Becky waited impassively.

'Quote? What do you mean, quote? Who did you say you are?' King blustered.

'Rebecca Pollard, *Netherdale Gazette*.'

King decided attack was the best form of defence. 'You trapped me.' His tone was accusatory. He jabbed a finger in her direction. 'If you print a word of this private conversation, I shall complain to your employers.'

Go on, Nash thought. Keep digging.

Becky smiled sweetly. 'You're new round here, aren't you?'

'What of it?'

'If you knew the area better, you'd be aware the Pollard family have owned the *Gazette* for three generations.'

'Irrelevant! I still intend to see Nash before a tribunal over this.'

Becky's smile broadened. 'Don't count on it. My godmother won't like it.'

Even Nash did a double take at that.

'Your godmother!' King spluttered.

'Aunt Gloria has been Mother's best friend since they were at school. You'll know her better as Chief Constable O'Donnell. I spoke to her a few minutes ago. I told her Detective Inspector Nash saved my life tonight. She's more likely to recommend him for a medal than discipline him.'

They watched King blunder from the cubicle. Nash realized Becky was still holding his hand. 'So Gloria's your godmother, is she?'

'You bet.'

Nash's eyes appeared to be closed, but he watched her under the lids. 'Did she say anything else about me?'

'Oh, lots and lots.' He saw her grin widen. 'Tell me something. If your name's Michael, why does she call you Dick?' Her expression was guileless, innocent. Far too innocent.

chapter seventeen

Nash woke late. He remembered little, beyond Becky driving him home. He sat up; painfully. His back felt tender, he'd a pounding headache, a sore throat and his arm itched. The bedroom door opened. Becky Pollard smiled. 'How do you feel?'

'Bloody awful,' Nash croaked. 'What time is it?'

'Just gone eleven o'clock. I've brought you a drink. The tea bags are out of date, so I presume you're a coffee drinker.'

'Thank you, but how did you get in?'

She smiled. 'I never left. I'd to help you; you were out on your feet. It was three o'clock by then. I didn't fancy walking through town, so I curled up on your sofa. I hope you don't mind?'

'Why should I?' The conversation was stilted. Nash couldn't work out why.

'Drink your coffee. Then I suggest you take a hot bath. It might ease the aches.'

'What about you?'

'I'll shower when I get home. I've got the day off. I phoned the *Gazette*. Told them about JT and what happened at the flat, and at Grove Road.' She looked suddenly anxious. 'I hope that was alright?'

Nash shrugged, painfully. 'It's going to be public knowledge soon.'

'I had to use your phone. I think I lost my mobile.'

'Feel free. Anybody rung?'

'You've had three calls. One from your sergeant – she didn't seem surprised to find me here. One from some guy called Ramirez. He called me "The Bride of Dracula", whatever that means.'

'That's his idea of a joke. He thinks I've a morbid attraction for corpses. You said there were three?'

'The other was from Aunt Gloria.'

'Oh no,' Nash groaned. 'What did she say?'

Becky smiled. 'She demanded to know what I was doing here. Said

132

she'd be having words with you. I told her it was OK, that you were in bed. She said that's where you're most dangerous. I told her you were asleep. She said maybe, but who knows what you were dreaming about.'

'I'm really looking forward to talking to her.' Nash's sarcasm wasn't lost on Becky. 'I wonder what Mexican Pete wanted?'

'Is that what you call Mr Ramirez?' Nash nodded. 'Why do you call him … Oh, *Eskimo Nell*, I see.'

'I'll stick some clothes on. I'll bathe later. I don't remember getting undressed.'

'That's because you were unconscious. I had to undress you.'

Nash stared at the closing door. He shook his head; a bad mistake.

As they drank another coffee, Becky asked Nash to explain the significance of what had happened at Grove Road. 'Sergeant Mironova told me one or two bits,' she prompted him, 'but I think she was being careful. She knows where I work.'

'As long as you understand this is completely off the record?'

'I wouldn't upset Aunt Gloria,' Becky laughed.

Nash told her a little of Vickers' history, and the relationship with Fletcher. There must have been something in his tone that conveyed his doubt. 'You don't think Vickers was guilty?' Becky suggested.

'On the surface, the evidence looks cast iron. When you look deeper, things don't add up.'

'What about JT's murder? Do you think that's connected?'

'I don't believe in coincidence,' Nash stared into his mug. 'Tucker was killed close to where Stacey Fletcher's body was found, and in a similar fashion. And Vickers' movements are unaccounted for.' Nash fell silent, his eyes reflective, his thoughts far away.

'I've some photos Tucker shot,' Becky volunteered.

Nash looked at her, all attention now.

'He brought some films for me to develop. I sent him the prints, but I kept the negatives.'

'Can you remember what was on them?'

'Some of Rathmell meeting Councillor Appleyard. Others were of Rathmell and a woman. They were … well, you know.'

Nash grinned. 'Really? Did you recognize her?'

'No. I think Tucker knew, but he didn't say.'

'I want to see them.'

'I can let you have them tomorrow.'

'I'd better go to work. I dread to think what's waiting,' Nash sighed.

'I'm going home. I've to write an obit on JT. First, though, I must take a shower.' She glanced down. 'I stink.'

Nash stood up, slowly. 'Thanks for everything, Becky. For saving my life, and for taking care of me.'

Becky grinned. 'We're quits now; you saved me from the fire.'

After she left, Nash walked stiffly to the bathroom. As he filled the bath he thought about Becky. She didn't lack resourcefulness, or courage. She was intelligent and certainly good-looking. Nash thought about her godmother. He winced at what she'd have to say.

He reached the CID suite shortly before 1 p.m. Clara looked harassed. 'Glad you could tear yourself away from your girlfriend,' she greeted him tartly. 'There's a string of phone calls waiting. The list's on your desk. I've enough to do, without acting as your secretary.'

'Sorry to have deserted you,' Nash replied, so quietly Clara hardly managed to catch what he said.

She looked at him closely. 'Are you alright? The hospital said your injuries were nothing to worry about, but you don't look well. And what's happened to your voice?'

'Smoke damage. I've a stinking headache, my back aches and my arm's sore.'

'I know about the fire, but nobody gave me details. What happened?'

Nash explained. 'The firemen reckoned another five minutes and we'd not have got out.'

'I'm sorry, Mike, I didn't realize it was that bad. Sounds like you had two lucky escapes.'

'I've Becky to thank for one.'

'How long have you been seeing her?'

'I'm not seeing her. I only met her last night.'

'But she stayed at your place, so I thought you and she were ...'

Nash shook his head. 'She drove me home. She didn't want to walk through town in the early hours, so she dossed down on my sofa. I didn't know she was there until this morning.'

Clara smiled. 'Bit of a new experience.'

'Better not make any snide remarks about her. She's the chief's goddaughter.'

'Blimey! You know how to pick them. No wonder God's been on the phone three times. If she thinks you're sniffing around her goddaughter, you could be in big trouble.'

'Not half as much as King.' Nash related the encounter at the hospital. 'That reminds me. When you get a free moment, I want you to give Jack Binns a call. I need some information from him about the fire at the Hassan flat.' Nash explained what he needed. 'I'd better start dealing with the phone calls – if anyone can hear me.'

'Oh, I forgot. There's a parcel on your desk, from forensics. It's the camera retrieved from near Tucker's body. They've found two sets of prints on it – Tucker's and an unidentified set.'

'Probably Becky's. She lent Tucker the camera. I'll call her later; I want to see what photos he took.'

Nash sat down wearily at his desk and looked at the list. The chief constable, Superintendent Pratt, Professor Ramirez and the doctor in charge of A & E at Netherdale General. Alongside the last name Clara had scribbled, 're Ronnie Fletcher'. Nash decided to get the worst over with.

Contrary to his fears, the chief constable was concerned with his health. She barely referred to his overnight visitor until she informed him, 'I had a long talk with Becky this morning. I understand you've been having some problems with DCC King. I've spoken to him on the matter. Let me know if there's any more trouble. Now tell me what went on last night.'

Nash described the chain of events. The chief listened without comment, right to the end. 'Have you the personnel to cope?'

'At the moment, yes, but if another major incident blows up we'll have problems.'

'I'll talk to Pratt and Crawley. If you holler, they've to come running. With every man they can spare. And I want you to stop playing the hero. Don't you put yourself in danger again. Understood?'

'Yes, ma'am,' Nash croaked.

'I'm not going to insult you by warning you off Becky. She's old enough to take care of herself. Just be careful not to hurt her. Understood?'

'Loud and clear, ma'am.'

Pratt's call was a repeat of the chief's in many ways. Nash finished with him and rang the pathologist.

'I understand you nearly finished up in one of my drawers?' Ramirez began. 'Well, don't say I haven't warned you.'

'What did you want me for? Not just to enquire about my well-being?'

'I found some bruising around Tucker's mouth and nose. I ran a toxicology test. He was put to sleep before he was garrotted.'

'Chloroform?'

'Yes. That means the killer need not be someone of great strength.'

'Could it have been a woman?'

'I see no reason why not.'

'Thanks, Professor. I'm not sure whether that makes things better or worse.'

Nash was about to ring Netherdale General when Clara came in. 'Jake and Gemma Fletcher are downstairs kicking up a fuss. They want Ronnie released from hospital, and they're getting very aggressive. Do you want me to deal with it?'

'No, I'll talk to them. Do me a favour. Ring that doctor at the hospital and ask what the state of play is. Find out when Ronnie will be fit to be brought here.'

Nash had seen photos of Gemma Fletcher in the Vickers case file. The woman standing by the reception desk was fifteen years older, but it didn't show. Although she'd be over fifty she looked a good deal younger. She was slim, which helped, with fine features and high cheekbones. 'I understand you're asking about Ronnie Fletcher?'

Gemma and Jake swung round. 'Who are you?' Gemma demanded.

'Detective Inspector Nash. Your brother's in Netherdale Hospital under police guard. When he's fit to leave, he'll be brought here. He's facing charges of assault and attempted murder.'

'Attempted murder! Killing that bastard shouldn't be a crime. He should get a medal,' Jake spluttered.

'Possibly,' Nash replied calmly. 'However, I'm not referring to Vickers. Your brother will be charged with assaulting a detective constable and attempting to murder me.'

'You're making this up.'

'He tried to hit me with an iron bar. If he hadn't been stopped, the charge would have been murder. If you want to see him, I'll allow one of you to visit, once he's in custody. But I warn you, the visit will be recorded. Now, unless you've any questions, I'd like you to leave peacefully, and in future please refrain from intimidating my receptionist.'

*

Clara reported that Fletcher would be fit for release next morning.

'Make arrangements to have him brought here. I'll complete my report then I'm going home. My head's pounding.'

He reached the flat, having called at the chemists. He'd barely got inside when the doorbell rang. He found Becky Pollard outside, clutching a carrier bag. 'I came to see how you are. I thought if you weren't feeling up to it, I'd cook you a meal.' She proffered the bag.

'I've a rotten head,' Nash admitted, 'and my voice has gone. Throat feels as if it's on fire. How about you? You must be feeling rough, not that it shows.'

'I'm much better. I got some sleep when I got home. Bit of a sore throat, that's all. But I didn't get knocked out. Are you brave enough to risk my cooking?'

'Anything's better than having to cook for myself.'

Becky handed Nash an envelope. 'These are the photos JT took. I had the negatives brought from the office and developed them at home.' They spread the photos on the kitchen worktop. 'I wonder who she is?'

Nash didn't respond. Becky glanced at him. He was staring at the photos. His mouth worked a couple of times before he spoke. 'I was talking to her an hour ago.'

'Who is she?'

'Gemma Fletcher.'

'Gemma Fletcher? Is she related to the man who attacked you?'

'His sister. Gary Vickers' ex-lover. The woman whose daughter Vickers allegedly raped and murdered. And here she is, enjoying a passionate encounter with a prominent politician.' Nash bent to examine the photos. 'In what looks very much like the place where her daughter's and Tucker's bodies were found. There may be more photos; I've got the camera back from forensics. The report says there were two sets of fingerprints on it – Tucker's and another, probably yours. They didn't think to develop the film. Could I ask a favour? Would you do it?'

'Sure. When are you thinking of?'

'Tomorrow morning?'

'I'm not working. There's no sporting fixtures to cover, so I'm all yours.'

'That sounds promising. Before you handle the camera, I'll need a set of your prints. I'll bring the kit with me. I'm not sure what time it'll be.'

'No problem. Now, sit down and I'll start cooking.'

*

Next morning, Nash's head felt clearer and his throat less sore. When he arrived at the station, Fletcher was already in a holding cell. Clara walked in quarter of an hour later.

'You do the interview,' Nash told her. 'Get someone over from Netherdale to take in with you. Better if I'm not involved. I'm going to get the film from that camera developed. You sort out Fletcher and charge him. I'll ask Becky to make a statement.'

The flat Becky ushered him into was light and spacious, the furnishings modern, with light wood and bright colours tastefully blended. 'Coffee's on,' she said. 'Kitchen's this way.'

After Nash had taken her fingerprints he took the camera out of the evidence bag, handling it with latex gloves. He gave Becky a pair.

'I'll take this through to the darkroom when we've had our coffee.'

The darkroom was little more than a store cupboard. 'It used to be a pantry, but being on my own, I've no use for that much storage,' she said as they crammed into the tight space.

'No boyfriend then?' he asked lightly.

'Not at present.' She was concentrating on the camera as she spoke.

In the confined space, he could smell her perfume. His pulse quickened slightly. Careful, he thought. Don't go there.

She began the developing process. 'Give it a few minutes. There look to be only half a dozen exposures.'

The prints showed the time and date they were taken. Nash stared at the results. The first ones were of Vickers and Nash outside Felling Prison. He glanced at the others.

'Is that who I think it is?' Becky asked.

Nash's face was bleak, an expression she'd not seen before. 'It is,' he told her. 'Look at the date and time – 5 p.m. on Tuesday. Tucker must have taken these just before he was killed. Probably dropped the camera in the struggle, which would explain how it fell into the rabbit hole. The killer can't have known Tucker took them.'

'You don't think there's any doubt?'

'I don't see how there can be. Tucker was killed in the same place as Stacey Fletcher. The weapon and method were the same. And here's evidence of Vickers walking towards Tucker just before the murder.'

chapter eighteen

Nash dialled Helmsdale station. DS Mironova was still interviewing Fletcher. He was put through to Pearce. 'Viv, get Clara to ring me back immediately she's finished, will you?'

'Right you are, Mike. Oh, hang on, she's here.'

'How did you get on?'

'Fletcher didn't say a word.'

'Don't worry about him. I want you to get a warrant and go to Grove Road.'

'What for?'

'To bring in Gary Vickers' – Nash paused – 'on suspicion of the murder of John Thomas Tucker.'

'You're not serious?'

'Too right I am. I've just seen the film from Tucker's camera. There are four shots of Vickers walking towards the camera. The time and date match.'

'Hell's bells!' Clara paused for a moment. 'There'll be a right hullabaloo when Fletcher finds he's in the next cell to the man who killed his niece.'

'That's his problem. Get on it straightaway. I don't want Vickers doing another disappearing act. Whilst you're at it, get a search warrant for the house as well.' Nash ended the call and stood for a moment, phone in hand.

'I suppose you'll want to dash straight off?' Becky asked.

Nash looked at her. Or at least he looked in her direction, but she realized his thoughts were far away, in deep concentration. Despite her godmother's warning, she couldn't help but wonder about him. What was it Aunt Gloria had said? 'Better keep your hand on your ha'penny if he's anywhere near you. They don't call him Dead Eyed Dick for nothing. He's had more women than I've had hot dinners.' Should she take the warning seriously? He was certainly attractive.

Not handsome, but pleasant enough. So what was it that women found irresistible?

His gaze returned from the middle distance. At the same time he smiled. 'Can I be cheeky, and impose on you for another coffee?'

'That isn't an imposition. When I've had enough of you, I can always throw you out.'

'I need a moment or two to think.'

She set the steaming mug in front of him. 'I'll leave you to it, if you want.'

He caught hold of her hand. 'No, stay, I want to bounce some ideas off you. I might have jumped the gun. Listen, and tell me what you think.' He collected his thoughts. 'Last Sunday I went to Felling, to collect Vickers. Tucker was waiting in the car park.' He told her what had happened. 'Vickers wanted to do some food shopping. Made some crack, about the milk he'd left in the fridge being off after fifteen years.' He related the conversation between Vickers and the till operator. 'I was sure that was the reason Vickers went into the shop. He'd a maintenance company looking after his house and contents. Why not ask them to buy food? I believe Vickers engineered the conversation round so he could make that statement.'

'Why do that? I'd have thought he'd want to keep a low profile. He must have realized the news would get round faster than if we'd splashed it all over the front page?'

'Exactly, and if he'd killed Stacey, keeping his head down would have been a natural course of action. But suppose he didn't kill her, suppose his story's true. That he and Stacey were lovers, and far from raping her, he merely made love to her. That someone else actually murdered her. If that's so, his actions become logical.'

'You mean like a gunfighter walking into town in one of those old westerns? Challenging the killers, seeking revenge, that sort of thing?'

'Couldn't have put it better. The last thing Vickers said to Tucker on Sunday was "Come round on Wednesday". As far as we're aware, the two never communicated again. Vickers didn't have any incoming phone calls or letters. He doesn't own a mobile so Tucker couldn't have sent him a text.'

Becky laughed. 'JT wouldn't have known how. Barely knew how to switch his phone on and off.'

'Then how did Vickers know where Tucker would be on Tuesday afternoon?'

'What if Tucker was following him?'

'Why would he? They'd a meeting set up for the next day. Besides, he wasn't to know Vickers would be leaving the house. Not when he was supposedly being protected by us. Anything he wanted to find out, he could ask on Wednesday.'

'I accept that, but it's still a bit theoretical.'

'Hang on, there's more. One of the first queries I had about Vickers' conviction was to do with his arrest. The police went through that house with a fine toothcomb. There was no evidence of piano wire in the house. What's more, they failed to find any evidence of Vickers buying any. So, where did he get the wire used to kill Tucker between Sunday and Tuesday?'

'He could have bought some on his way there, couldn't he?'

'Tuesday's half-day closing in Helmsdale. The only place that stocks anything like piano wire is the music shop in the arcade. And I know for a fact they're closed on Tuesday afternoon.'

'What else is making you have doubts?'

Nash stared at her. 'What makes you think there's anything else?'

Becky shrugged. 'Don't know, just a feeling.'

'You're right. The other big question is, why? I've spent time with Vickers. He's an intelligent man. He's not one to act on the spur of the moment. Given that he's not an impulse killer, and that he's not a psychopath, what motive would he have for killing Tucker? Tucker's the last person Vickers would want dead, especially before their interview. I know a lot of people want to murder journalists *after* they've written something.' Nash grinned ruefully. 'Me included from time to time, but never beforehand.'

'I can see your logic. It boils down to why Tucker wanted to interview Vickers, and why Vickers was keen to talk to him,' Becky suggested.

Nash thought about this. 'You've got a point there, Becks,' he said absentmindedly.

She smiled. In his abstraction he'd used her pet name. She didn't mind. In fact, she rather liked it.

He moved restlessly. 'Yes, that's a really good point. Why were they both so keen?'

'Maybe he wanted to announce his return, and make some sort of a statement.'

'On the lines of, "I'm coming to get you"?'

'Something of the sort.'

'And whoever felt threatened decided to silence Tucker?'

'It makes sense.'

'There are three components to murder: motive, means and opportunity. Vickers had the opportunity. But unless he knew Tucker was going to be in Helm Woods, the opportunity aspect is suspect. We can't find any way of Vickers taking possession of the murder weapon, so the means part is also weak. And we can't find any motive whatsoever.'

'Does that mean you're not going to arrest Vickers?'

'Let me think about it for a few minutes.'

Becky regarded him with mock severity. 'I suppose that means you'll want yet another coffee?'

'Yes please, Becks.' His voice was absentminded, his eyes far away again.

Becky grinned and collected the mugs. When she handed him a replacement, his attention was back. 'Go on,' she encouraged him.

'Yes, I will hold him.'

'But you said—'

'I know. But if everyone thinks Vickers is in the frame for Tucker's murder, I can dig about without putting them on guard. And it'll keep Vickers safe. I can hold him for forty-eight hours before charging him.'

'If Vickers didn't kill JT, who did?'

'I was going to say I've no idea, but that wouldn't be accurate. I've a couple of suspects in mind. The problem is I've no proof. I need to find evidence linking the murderer to both victims.'

'Both victims?' Becky echoed.

'That's what this is all about. Ever since Vickers came back, he's been looking for something. He's done everything but tear the floorboards up. He doesn't know what, but he'd been told of it, and what it represents. He said it was proof, but of what he didn't know. Still doesn't. All he is sure of is that it exists.'

'How can he be sure?'

'There've been several break-ins at Grove Road, plus an arson attack. Vickers thinks someone's trying to destroy it.' He paused, realizing he'd said too much. 'Can I trust you to keep everything we've talked about confidential? When the time's right I promise you'll have first access to any information.'

Suddenly, it was important to reassure him. 'I promise I won't send anything through until I've cleared it with you.'

'That's as much as I could ask.' He sighed. 'Not that there is anything printable yet. Not by a long way.'

'You're going to have your work cut out.'

'True, and I suppose I ought to make a start.' Before he could stop himself he added, 'Care for dinner tonight? To repay you for last night.'

'Aunt Gloria told me a lot about you,' she said, in a tone devoid of expression. 'I think she was trying to warn me you were dangerous to know.'

'She tried to scare me off too,' he admitted ruefully. 'It was a thinly veiled threat that if I didn't treat you right, I'd be in trouble.'

Becky smiled. 'Just dinner then.'

His face was an expressionless mask. 'Of course. Just dinner.'

Billy was frustrated. He'd failed; big style. The gippovan had been great, and the knifing. But that was way back. Since then things had gone bad. The pervert's house at Grove Road had been the first. Worse had followed; that family at the shop, they should have gone up. The building had, but they'd all got out. Not what Billy had in mind; not what he'd been told to do. Wipe them out, they'd said. Well, that hadn't happened. Bloody firemen got there too quick.

Then the other flat. What was it they'd called the bloke? A snooper; that was it. A dirty, stinking snooper. He'd to be stopped. He'd got something bad, bad for Danny, bad for Billy, bad for their friends. It had to be destroyed. He'd done that alright. The flat had been gutted. Everything inside went up a treat. At least he thought so. Until he watched, Billy hadn't known there was anyone inside. That'd have made it better, knowing. Then he'd seen them. He nearly screamed at the sight. At the window, desperate faces. The excitement mounted. Was that the snooper? Billy felt that thrill again as he watched them. Watched them trying to get free from the monster; his monster. The one he'd created. Then, as his excitement became close to uncontrollable, when he was on the very edge of success, they'd escaped.

That was his worst moment. Or so he thought. Then he went straight to Grove Road with Mister Ronnie. But he'd failed again. He'd failed and got shot. Just a graze, but it scared the shit out of him. He'd failed, and Mister Ronnie failed, and Mister Ronnie got done over. Would he blame Billy? Billy was scared of Mister Ronnie. More scared of Mister Jake. Mister Jake had come to the house yesterday. Billy hid under the stairs. He thought Mister Jake had come for him, because he'd let Mister Ronnie down. Turned out he'd only come to talk to Danny. But Billy'd nearly messed his pants with fright.

Billy was desperate. He needed to do something good. Something big; something dramatic. Something to prove his worth. Danny had told him so. And Danny was right. Danny was always right in Billy's book. It had to be something to hurt *them*. He couldn't do all their houses. He couldn't burn the fields where they worked. Then he remembered. Some of them worked on the industrial estate. Billy knew it because he'd seen them when he was nicking stuff.

He told Danny. And Danny told Mister Jake. And the message came back. 'Burn down the places where they work,' Danny said. 'If there's no jobs for them, they'll have to fuck off, back where they came from.' That was it. Billy had a new purpose. His mood lifted. He had a target. More than that, he had a mission.

'They put Vickers at the murder scene at the right time. But there are plenty of things don't add up.' After she'd looked at the photos, Nash told Clara his reservations.

'I see what you mean. Is that why you want the search warrant? To look for something to connect Vickers to the murder? Something more than just being in the wrong place at the wrong time?'

'Not exactly. As you know I've had my doubts all along. Now we're talking murders, not murder.'

'What? Have I missed something?'

'Not that I'm aware. But I think we should be reinvestigating the death of Stacey Fletcher, as well as the murder of Tucker.'

'Do you think there's a chance, after all this time? Accepting that Vickers didn't kill the girl, how difficult is it going to be to find the killer now?'

'Very,' Nash agreed. 'But we start with several advantages.'

Clara frowned. 'Such as?'

'They were so convinced they had the right man, the police didn't look for anyone else. And they didn't know about Gemma's relationship with Rathmell.'

'You think that's relevant?'

'It might be. If that affair was going on at the time, it might be more than relevant. Look at it this way. Tucker wanted to interview Vickers as soon as he was released; presumably because he had doubts about the conviction. So, what made Tucker suspicious? Then we find out that Tucker had been following Rathmell. And in the process took those photos. Before Tucker can talk to Vickers, he's murdered. How convenient, if someone didn't want them to meet.'

'We'd have a job proving it.'

'Maybe, but we'll have to try, and I think I know how. Bring Vickers from the cells.'

The interview was short, the outcome less than satisfactory. 'I intend searching your house at Grove Road tomorrow. We've applied for a search warrant. We'll be examining the clothing you were wearing on Tuesday. Just pray there's nothing on it to connect you to Tucker's murder.'

Vickers shrugged. 'I didn't kill him. Why would I? But I didn't kill Stacey either, and it didn't stop them then. So, do your worst.'

When Vickers was back in his cell, Clara pulled out a slip of paper from her pocket. 'I've just remembered this. It's that information from Jack Binns.'

Nash read it. 'Right, I'm just going to have a word with Doug Curran.'

Clara stared after him in surprise as he walked down the corridor. She thought she knew her boss better than most people. But there were times when she was miles away from fathoming out how his mind worked. Fifteen minutes later he was back. He signalled to Mironova to follow him into his office. Inside, he picked the phone up and dialled Netherdale.

'Jack, it's Mike Nash. I need a favour. I want you to photocopy the original of that stuff you gave Clara. Let me have it, will you? And Jack, keep it quiet. I don't want anybody to know. Not yet.' He put the phone down; his expression was grim, grimmer than Clara had seen it for a long time.

'What is it, Mike?' she asked quietly.

He laid two sheets of paper on the desk. 'That's the info Jack gave you about the Hassan flat fire.' Then he pointed to the other one. 'And that's what I've just got from Curran about the same incident. Look at them carefully.'

Clara read them twice before she realized the significance. 'That's impossible.'

'No, it isn't. Not in certain circumstances.'

Clara caught on. 'Good God! What are you going to do?'

'Nothing, for the time being.' Nash smiled with neither warmth nor humour. 'I need more than this.' He tapped the paperwork. 'For the moment, these stay locked in my desk. I'll be looking for something as backup though. And when I'm ready ...'

Clara had seen that look before. It was the look of Nash the hunter,

Nash the shark. She almost felt sorry for his prey. Almost, but not quite.

Rathmell felt a slight tremor of apprehension when he saw the man at the door. He recognized Nash. Then he remembered what he'd been told about him, and relaxed. If rumour was to be believed there was little to fear. 'Can I help you?'

Nash showed his warrant card. 'I'm sorry to disturb you, sir. I appreciate how busy you must be. I wonder if I could take up five minutes of your time? I've a couple of questions regarding a matter we're investigating. Purely routine, of course.' Nash smiled, wondering if he could have crammed any more clichés into so few sentences.

'As long as it doesn't take longer than that, Inspector, er?'

'Nash, sir.'

'As you said, I'm particularly busy at the moment. Do come in.'

Nash followed the MEP across the hall and glanced to the right, where the lounge door was open. He took a second look, grateful that Rathmell was in front, that the politician couldn't see his expression.

'It's to do with the murder of a journalist, JT Tucker, sir. We examined his mobile phone and found your number listed in the memory. I wondered if he'd been in contact. And if so what he wanted from you?'

'I certainly haven't spoken to him that I'm aware of. But you must understand this last week I've had hordes of journalists and other media people buzzing around. It's because of the new political initiative we've laid out.' Rathmell smiled. 'No doubt you're aware of it, Inspector Nash? I can only assume that was why he had my number. No doubt he was going to call me, had this terrible event not happened.'

'Quite so, sir. And that's all? You can't think of any other possible reason Tucker might have wanted to speak to you?'

'Absolutely not,' Rathmell assured him.

He escorted the detective out and watched as Nash's car drove slowly down the drive. He turned and walked back into his study. The apprehension he'd felt at the beginning of the interview was compounded now. Rathmell felt threatened. He picked up the phone. 'I've just had a visit, one that's rather concerned me. I think we need to take some, shall I say, radical steps.'

146

A few minutes later, he dialled another number and waited. 'Frank, it's Carl. Can you get hold of Jake? I'd like you both to come up to the house as soon as you can. Yes, this afternoon if possible. There are things to sort out; urgently.'

His third call took even less time. 'It's me. I've visitors coming. It'd be better if they don't see you here. Who? Martin, Frank, and your brother.'

Once he'd reached the main road, Nash stopped the car and reached for his mobile. 'Clara, I won't be back until late. No, I'm starting a surveillance job. I need Viv to take over from me as soon as he can get here.'

He reversed into a farm gateway and parked. It was almost half an hour before there was any activity. The first car contained two people. Nash recognized them as Councillor Appleyard and Jake Fletcher, too deep in conversation to notice either Nash or his car. He watched them turn into Houlston Grange and then saw another vehicle approaching. At first he thought it was Pearce. As it got nearer he realized his mistake. A DC's salary doesn't run to a Range Rover. Nash bent down to avoid being seen. Despite his crouched position he managed to get a good view of the driver. He stared in disbelief as he watched the vehicle pull into Rathmell's drive. He was still recovering from the shock when Pearce drew alongside him. 'Keep a note of arrivals and departures,' Nash instructed him. 'But whatever you do, avoid being seen. That's absolutely crucial, OK?'

Nash set off for Helmsdale and called Mironova again. 'I'll be half an hour or so. I've just got to do a bit of shopping.' Clara would have been astonished had she seen the shop he went into.

Appleyard was getting twitchy. It was one thing to pontificate on the perceived wrongs of the nation; direct action was quite another matter. When he'd learned that the supposed protests at the Residents' Association meeting had been carefully orchestrated, that hadn't seemed too bad. It was when the violence spiralled that Appleyard became scared. Scared of the monster he'd helped to create and scared for his own well-being. The presence of Jake Fletcher in the car didn't help.

Later, as they drove away from the meeting, Appleyard was unaware that his own position was being debated. It was a strictly private meeting. No sooner had the second car left the Grange than Pearce observed the arrival of Gemma Fletcher's sports car.

She'd only been inside the building five minutes when Rathmell hauled her upstairs. Their first encounter took only a short time. As they lay recovering from their exertions, she asked how the meeting had gone. 'We've got a potential problem,' Rathmell said.

'What's that?'

'One of our number is less keen than I'd hoped.'

'That'll be the officer of the law, I assume?'

'You're wrong.'

Gemma turned and supported her head with her hand. 'Really? I thought if anyone was going to backslide, he'd be the one.'

'No, he's as keen as ever – keener in fact. No, it's our worthy councillor whose feet are getting cold.'

'How much does he know?'

'Too much. He could cause a lot of bother if he decided to turn on us.'

'He'd be dropping himself in it.'

'True, my darling, but we can't afford to take the chance.' Rathmell began to caress her. Her response aroused him again.

'What have you in mind? Apart from what you're doing with your hand.'

'In the history of politics, every great cause had at least one martyr. I believe the time is right for us to create ours.'

'You mean?'

'With careful stage management, the deed can be ascribed to our enemies. Frank will become the victim of those who are afraid of his philosophy. In his death, he'll do our cause the world of good. Whilst mourning our brave colleague, we'll point out that it was his courage in speaking out that was responsible for his callous assassination. It will be up to us to carry on the struggle in his memory. There, what do you reckon?'

'That's genius, Carl; fucking genius.'

'No.' He rolled over until he was on top of her. 'This is fucking genius.'

Much later, as they ate a leisurely meal, she asked, 'How will you arrange it?'

'A shooting, I think. It's traditional, particularly in America. Who are we to fail to uphold a noble tradition?'

The cold-blooded cynicism with which Rathmell was discussing a man's murder would have appalled many. Gemma found it overwhelmingly sensual. But then she'd already lost everything to him, given him all she had. Many years ago, she'd stepped across that divide and entered his dark world. There was no way back, even if she'd wanted to return: which she didn't.

'Is that all you've got planned?'

'Not quite. This lawless element in our midst will stop at nothing. When our colleague's brutal murder is being investigated, the officer in charge of the investigation will get too close to the perpetrators. These scoundrels will stop at nothing to avoid being brought to book. Even to the extent of killing a high-ranking police officer. A detective inspector, no less.'

'Nash? Are you really worried by him?'

'I wasn't, until he turned up here this afternoon. He asked me a couple of banal questions.'

'So what's to worry about?'

'He was asking about Tucker. Said he'd found my number in Tucker's mobile. That was when I realized how dangerous Nash is. And how much he might have found out.'

'I don't understand.'

'The reason I think Nash is dangerous' – Rathmell reached into his pocket – 'is because this is Tucker's phone.'

chapter nineteen

When Nash returned, Mironova was filling in forms. She glanced up. Nash looked brighter than she'd seen him for a while. 'You look as if you've had a good afternoon.'

'I have, and I'm looking forward to an enjoyable evening.'

'Oh yes, what's her name?'

Nash smiled. 'I'm taking Becky Pollard to dinner.'

Clara whistled. 'You'd better be careful, or you'll feel the wrath of God.'

'I said I was taking her to dinner, not to bed.'

'With you, there never seems to be much difference.'

'If you'll stop making offensive comments about my personal life, I'll tell you what happened this afternoon.'

'They may be offensive but they're accurate.'

'Do you want to hear or not?'

'Go on.'

'I went to see Rathmell. I made up some lame tale about finding his number on Tucker's mobile. I asked a couple of meaningless questions and left.'

'What was the point?'

'I wanted to see if Rathmell would get rattled. He's intelligent enough to know there had to be more to my visit. And if he was involved in Tucker's murder, he'd know we hadn't recovered his mobile. So I parked down the lane and waited. Within half an hour he'd called a meeting. And very interesting personnel attended it too.'

'Such as?'

Nash told her.

'That confirms your suspicions.'

'That's not all. When Viv took over, I went shopping like I said.'

'What did you buy?'

'Nothing, but I got some very interesting information.' Nash related his experience.

'What made you think of that?'

'Something I saw at Rathmell's house.'

'That's proof, surely?'

'No, it isn't. Not in itself. It might prove useful as circumstantial evidence, but no more. We need to find something else. That's why I want that search warrant.'

'It'll be here in the morning. Do you want Vickers present?'

'I think so. We can't leave anything to chance. We still don't know what we're looking for.'

When Becky returned from work, she found a message from Nash on her voicemail explaining he was running late. She decided to phone her godmother. 'Aunt Gloria, I want to ask you about Mike. You said he was looking for a substitute. What did you mean?'

'Tell me why you're asking.'

'He's invited me for dinner.'

'Oh, I hoped this wouldn't happen. Mike Nash is one of the nicest, most charming people you're likely to meet. Unfortunately, a lot of women have fallen for that charm. I'm not saying he's the sort to go in for one-night stands and I think when he enters a relationship he intends it to last. That never seems to happen. I believe that's because he's constantly searching for a replacement.'

'What do you mean?'

'Part of my job is to know all about my officers. Nash is an exceptional detective. He met a girl during the course of an investigation soon after he came here. She got badly injured, ended up in a wheelchair. Later, by tragic coincidence, she was attacked and died. You remember that big human trafficking case?'

'Yes, now you mention it.'

'Anyway, Mike took it very badly.'

'You're saying he's more sinned against than sinning?'

Her aunt laughed. 'I'd hardly put it that way. What I'm trying to say is, don't get too involved. Nash may start out with all the right intentions, but it's highly likely to turn sour. Anyone who gets entangled with him will have to fight against ghosts. The ghosts of his failed relationships.'

'Thanks for the warning, Aunt Gloria. I'll be careful.'

'Of course, if all you're looking for is companionship, to put it politely, that's an altogether different matter.'

'I don't think I'm looking for anything in particular.'

'In that case I don't see the point in this call.'

Becky put the phone down and went for a shower. As she was dressing, she found herself humming a tune. It was a few moments before she realized it was the theme from *Ghostbusters*.

When Nash arrived, Becky opened her door and peered out, looking for his car. He interpreted her glance. 'I hope you don't mind walking? That way I can have a drink. I'll get you a taxi later.'

'Don't mind a bit, as long as it stays fine.'

'Where would you like to go? The choice is between Italy, India, China or Mexico.'

'Mexico, I think.'

'Very well, the Aztlan restaurant it shall be.'

'Do you know where the name comes from?'

Nash explained.

'How do you know all that?'

Nash smiled. 'I asked Chico, the owner.'

'Is he Mexican?'

'Not unless Barnsley is an outpost of the Aztec empire. He researched it on the internet. If he comes to talk to us, don't laugh.'

'Why would I?'

'He's got the worst Mexican accent imaginable. He sounds like a cross between Speedy Gonzales and Manuel the waiter.'

'You seem cheerful tonight. I take it you've had a good day?'

'Partly that' – Nash turned to smile at her – 'but mainly the company.'

The meal was good, better than she'd expected. As Nash put it, 'More spice than fire,' which suited her perfectly. They talked little until their dessert, when Becky confessed she was being pressured into providing copy for the *Gazette* about the Tucker killing and the arrests made by Helmsdale CID. 'I'm in a bit of a bind. I promised not to write anything until you gave me clearance. But I'm not sure how long my editor's going to remain patient. He's already threatening to put someone else on the story.'

'Tell him to be patient – the story will be an exclusive, and it'll be the best scoop the paper's ever had.' Nash thought for a moment before adding, 'Tell him it'll be a fitting memorial to Tucker.'

'Can you say anything more? Off the record, of course.'

'I'm going to Grove Road tomorrow. I must find that missing

evidence, if it exists. I've got a theory as to who killed Tucker and why. But all the evidence is circumstantial. If I can't get enough to make a murder charge stick, the whole thing could become very messy.'

'What do you mean by circumstantial evidence?'

'I can't tell you that. Not yet anyway. Put it this way, what I've found out points away from Vickers. But it's more complicated than I thought. Far more complicated.'

The evening light had faded during their dinner. They emerged from the Aztlan into a fine, warm, starlit night. Despite her protests Nash insisted on walking her home. 'This town is far too dangerous at present for a woman to walk around in darkness alone.'

Becky gave in. Her protests had only been half-hearted anyway. As they walked, Nash held her hand. She was mildly surprised but certainly not unhappy with this arrangement. They walked slowly, but all too soon for Nash's liking they were outside her door.

'Do you want to come in for coffee?'

Nash hesitated. He thought of her godmother. He thought of all the reasons he shouldn't. 'Just coffee,' he said.

'Just coffee,' she repeated, as firmly as she'd said 'just dinner'.

She was waiting for the kettle to boil when Nash slipped his arms round her from behind. She turned to face him. He kissed her, gently at first then with increasing fervour. After a moment she pulled away, put a restraining hand on his chest. 'No, Mike. Not yet.'

'Sorry. I didn't mean that. You look so lovely, I just couldn't resist. I realize it's too sudden.'

'It's not that. Well, not exactly. I want to be sure it's me you're kissing.'

'I don't understand.'

'I need to be certain you're not kissing me and thinking of someone else. I won't be anybody's substitute. Not even for you.'

'Ouch. I suppose I deserved that. Who's been talking? Your godmother?'

Becky nodded. 'Come to me when you've got rid of the ghosts. When you've got your lost loves out of your system. Then we'll see.'

'When I was little, if I asked for something and my mother said "we'll see", I always used to get it.'

'Your mother was obviously a very nice woman.' Becky leaned forward. 'And here's a little incentive for you.'

*

Mironova had just taken her coat off when Nash entered the CID suite the following morning.

'Morning, Clara.' He waved a sheet of paper. 'The warrant's arrived. As soon as Viv gets in we'll head off for Grove Road.'

'I thought you had Viv on surveillance at Rathmell's place?'

'I phoned him first thing. This is more important.'

'You're looking very sprightly. How did last night go?'

'We had a very pleasant evening. And a very nice meal.'

'Where did you go? Not La Giaconda, I'll bet.'

'No, we went to the Aztlan.'

'And that was it? No afters? I mean, when you go out with a girl, next day you usually look like something the cat dragged in. Don't tell me you failed? No leg over for dessert then?'

'I told you – just dinner.'

'You're not chicken, are you? Afraid of what'll happen when God finds out?'

'Nothing of the sort. And stop taking the piss – it's insubordinate.'

'Bollocks! I don't believe it. She turned you down, didn't she?'

'Clara!'

'She did! She actually turned you down! You must be getting old, or losing your touch. Poor thing! It's all downhill from now. Before long you'll have to rely on the little blue pills.'

'When you've quite finished, DS Mironova! Now, bugger off and fetch Vickers.'

They arrived at Grove Road shortly after 9 a.m. As soon as they were inside, Nash signalled to Pearce to release his prisoner. 'Clara, make sure the doors are locked and bolted. Gary, before we start I think it's time you told us what we're looking for.'

'I told you, I don't know.'

'Who told you about it? Was it Stacey?'

Vickers looked down. 'Yes,' he admitted.

'I know it's hard to talk about her, but I need you to think.'

There was a long silence.

'Gary, this is the only thing Stacey can do for you now. Do you understand? I want you to think very carefully. What did she actually say when she told you about this thing? What were her exact words?'

'As far as I remember, she said it was something to use if her mother found out about us. Later on, she said she was sure her mother was on to us and that she was going to have to use it.'

Nash shrugged. 'OK, we'll do the ground floor first.'

Pearce turned to Vickers. 'That doesn't give you the right to put that bloody CD player on, right?' He saw Clara's enquiring glance. 'He plays ruddy Beatles albums back-to-back non-stop. Nearly drove me crazy.'

'I like The Beatles,' Vickers muttered.

'That's no reason to play them all day and all night. And, as if that's not bad enough,' Pearce turned to Nash, 'he adds insult to injury by whistling the melody.' He paused and added, 'Very badly and very out of tune.'

'It's got to be better than that crap music you play,' Nash told him.

'The expression's rap music, Mike.' Clara paused. 'No, on second thoughts, maybe you were right.'

It was almost 1 p.m. before they were ready to tackle the first floor. Even with four of them, Nash's insistence that they take up the carpets made the task wearisome. 'I propose we have a break. Viv, you go get some sandwiches.'

The food and rest gave them renewed energy. By 5 p.m. they'd searched the upper floor. Nash and Vickers had even entered the roof void. They stopped for a drink. Their lack of success had dampened their enthusiasm.

Nash paced up and down the hall, deep in thought. He turned to Vickers. 'This is just a wild idea, so bear with me, but I'm going to call in somebody to help.'

Nash got on the phone. 'Can you pop round to Grove Road? We need your help. I'll explain when you get here.'

It was no more than twenty minutes later when a yellow Mini Cooper drew up outside and the doorbell rang. 'Answer that, will you, Viv? It'll be Becky. Clara, go with him, be on the safe side.'

They returned in a matter of seconds. 'Gary, you've met Becky Pollard before.' Vickers nodded to the newcomer.

'Becky, the reason I asked you to come round is we've searched everywhere, without success. I want you to walk through the house and look again for us.'

'What makes you think Becky will have any more luck than we've had?'

'Good question, Clara. I said it was a wild idea. But Stacey was studying photography. Maybe another photographer will spot something we've missed.'

Becky walked slowly from room to room, looking at the photographs, followed by her interested entourage. Eventually she returned to the lounge. Over the fireplace was a large photograph. 'Did Stacey take this?' she asked.

Vickers nodded. 'It was her entry for a photographic competition. Stacey won second prize.'

They stared at the picture. It was of a vixen suckling her cubs. 'She must have been proud of it.' Becky thought for a moment. 'But why are there three copies?'

They stared at her in silence.

She turned to Nash. 'There's an identical photograph in two of the bedrooms. Different sizes, but the same subject.'

'I didn't notice,' Nash confessed.

'The ones upstairs are spare prints. After she won the prize she had this enlarged and framed. She said she'd done it just for me. That I had to keep it, always.' Vickers turned away so the others couldn't see the tears in his eyes.

'I see.' Becky stepped forward and examined the photo closely. 'The frame's a bit heavy for the subject matter, don't you think? Let's take a closer look.'

They lifted the picture from the wall, carried it through to the kitchen and laid it face down on the table. 'Pass me a sharp knife, would you?' Becky slid her fingers round the back of the frame. 'I'm going to loosen the tape,' she told Vickers. 'I promise not to damage the picture.'

Her actions were quick and neat. Within minutes she lifted the back-plate clear. 'Bingo!'

They crowded round. Inside was a second plate. Neatly fixed to it with photo mounts was a collection of smaller photos. Each was inscribed with a date, a time and a location. The couple in the shots, admittedly much younger, were instantly recognizable to everyone except Vickers. 'That's Gemma, but who's that?' Vickers pointed to the man.

'No idea,' Nash said quickly, his glance warning the others.

Vickers continued to stare at the photos. 'What's so special about these? Apart from the fact that they prove Gemma was having it off with someone? Why did Stacey bother to take them and why hide them so carefully?'

'We'll borrow these. In the meantime, Viv, take Gary back to the station whilst we secure the house.'

When Viv had left with Vickers, Clara said, 'That's Carlton Rathmell. Why deny you knew him?'

'If Vickers found out who it was, I dread to think what he'd do. But I know why Stacey hid these. Rathmell entered politics on the back of his wife's money. He was a fledgling MP in those days, certainly unable to withstand the scandal of a juicy divorce. Mrs Rathmell's family are staunch Catholics. If this' – Nash flicked a hand over the photos – 'had come to light, his funding would have dried up overnight.'

'That was then. What about now?'

'The situation's not a lot different. Rathmell's just begun this new political initiative. Split right away from mainstream politics. If anything, he's more vulnerable now than he was then. And in consequence even more reliant on his wife's money. These photos were dynamite then. They're more like Semtex now. And their existence, coupled with the ones Tucker shot, provide a very strong motive for murder. Or murders.'

'You think Rathmell killed Stacey? And Tucker?' Clara asked.

'I don't know. Not for sure,' Nash admitted. 'But I'm convinced one of the people in these photos committed both murders.'

Becky stared at Nash in horror. 'You can't believe Gemma Fletcher murdered her own daughter? Just because she'd found out about this affair?'

'You haven't met her,' Nash replied grimly. 'If her affair with Rathmell has lasted all this time, that shows a passion I wouldn't have suspected Gemma was capable of. I honestly believe Gemma Fletcher would have gone to any lengths to protect Rathmell. Still would to this day. A small matter like the murder of a journalist would be something she'd not think twice about. Nor do I believe she'd flinch from disposing of her own daughter if she felt threatened. Gary told me Stacey was the result of Gemma's one-night stand. In her file the birth certificate reads "father unknown". I'm not sure there was ever such a thing as a normal maternal relationship between Gemma and Stacey.'

'You reckon it was Gemma, rather than Rathmell?' Becky persisted.

'On balance, I think Rathmell's favourite. In my opinion he's a cold, calculating, evil bastard. He's prepared to use any means to get what he wants. Look at this political campaign he's launched; a lethal mixture of xenophobia and racism. I don't think it's a coincidence that the racially motivated attacks have taken place just as Rathmell's starting this "new political initiative". He's charismatic, gives the impression of latent power, and that attracts those weak enough to believe in him. They mistake ruthlessness for strength. You take a man like that, put him in a relationship with a woman like Gemma Fletcher, give him chance to wield some authority, and the mixture is like an unexploded bomb. The violence we've seen could only be the prelude to far worse, unless we nip it in the bud. As for poor Stacey, I'm afraid that coming between those two, she didn't stand a chance. I certainly wasn't going to give Vickers any hint as to who might be responsible.'

Nash didn't have any difficulty getting to sleep; the events of the day ensured that. At one point, he half stirred at the sound of a distant siren. A while later he heard it again, closer this time. Then closer still. After some confusion he realized it was his mobile. 'Nash.'

Seconds later he was wide awake. His contribution to the conversation was mostly monosyllabic. 'What? Where? When?'

He switched the light on and pressed a number on his phone. 'Clara, we've got a problem.'

Nash surveyed the scene from a safe distance. Two fire engines had been deployed. Their hoses were trained on the source of the blaze. It was part of a terrace comprising shop units, with flats above. Nash was struck by the familiarity, but it was a few seconds before he placed it. This parade of shops was identical to the one on the other end of the estate, where the Hassan family had narrowly escaped death. Here and there were small groups of residents forced from their homes by the blaze, the danger, the insistent firemen or just plain curiosity. Those living closest to the fire were clad in a variety of nightwear hardly suitable for outdoors in Britain. Fortunately it was a warm night. The heat from the fire helped. Doug Curran approached. 'Evening, or should I say morning, Mike. Another bad one, I'm afraid.'

'Any casualties?'

'Not that we're aware of. We got everyone out of the flats. The shops were all closed, even the off licence. We managed to get into all the other units bar that one.' He pointed to the shop that was burning fiercest. He pushed his helmet back wearily. His face was stained with sooty black residue, down which rivulets of sweat formed clean trails.

'Was it deliberate?'

'Definitely. Some form of accelerant; probably petrol.'

'What was the shop?'

'It wasn't a shop. Not anymore. It was Councillor Appleyard's constituency office.'

'Really? That's interesting. Anybody contacted him yet?'

'One of my chaps was phoning his home when you arrived.'

'Excuse me, Doug.' They swung round as a fireman approached. 'I've just spoken to Mrs Appleyard. Her husband isn't home. She said he was working late.' The fireman jerked his thumb towards the inferno. 'In there.'

'If he was in there, he wouldn't stand a chance. And we'll not be able to find out either. Not for the best part of twenty-four hours.'

They glanced up at the sound of screeching brakes. Tension eased when they saw it was Mironova. 'The Belle from Belarus,' Curran exclaimed.

'I didn't realize you were an admirer.'

'I am, just don't tell the wife. Anyway, I wouldn't stand a chance. Whenever she's free from obeying your every whim, she's off gallivanting with the gallant major.'

'Now, now, Doug. You mustn't let jealousy embitter you.' Nash inspected the fire officer. 'I'm sure you look very handsome in your uniform. When it's been to the cleaners.'

'At least you can tell I've been working,' Curran retorted.

'What's going on?' Clara joined them.

Nash and Curran began to explain, issuing fragments of disjointed sentences between them.

'Hang on, hang on. One at a time.'

Nash completed the briefing, 'If Appleyard was inside, and Doug's suspicions about arson are proved right, it's murder. If he's dead, there'll be trouble when word gets out. If it's foul play, there could be mayhem. If the xenophobes turn on the asylum seekers and migrant workers, there could be wholesale slaughter.'

There seemed little the CID officers could do. 'Go get your beauty sleep,' he told Clara. He watched her car disappear through the clouds of smoke and steam. Curran had returned to directing his men. Nash took his mobile out. 'Becks, it's Mike. Would you like to come and sit by a nice warm fire?'

He laughed at the expletives coming down the phone. 'That's not very nice. I'm in the middle of the Westlea. Someone's torched a terrace of shops. I thought you might like some exclusive shots. You can chalk this up as a first. I don't usually drag women *out* of bed.'

Nash sought out Curran. 'I don't think there's much I can do.' He eyed the small knots of people staring at the burning building. 'I'll get hold of uniform and ask them to send some men to keep the onlookers at a safe distance.'

Curran snorted. 'Those aren't onlookers. They're looters, waiting for the heat to die down and they'll be in there, faster than a seagull on its way to the council tip.' He gestured at the assembly. 'I'll bet every last one has a carrier bag in their pockets. I'm astonished none of them has turned up with a supermarket trolley. Carrion, that's what they are. Speaking of which, will you inform Mexican Pete? He should be on hand when we go into the building tomorrow. We've got to assume Appleyard's in there.'

'I'll leave that until morning.' Nash glanced at his watch. 'What I will do is go talk to Mrs Appleyard.'

'That might help,' Curran admitted. 'Hello, who do we have here?'

Nash looked up and saw the Mini Cooper. 'That's Becks, Becky Pollard, photographer from the *Gazette*. I phoned her. Didn't think you'd want to miss the chance of some action photos. Our firemen heroes! That sort of thing.'

'Mike, you're a lying pillock. You're not even a convincing liar.' Curran eyed the approaching girl. 'I must say you know how to pick 'em. Are you er…?'

'Not yet, and probably not at all. She's the chief's goddaughter.'

'Christ, Mike! I thought I was the one who plays with fire.'

Becky had already taken shots of the building, the appliances and the fire crews before she joined them. Nash introduced Curran. The fire chief held out his hand hesitantly. Becky glanced down and saw the grime. She shook his hand vigorously. 'Can I take your photo?'

'I was just suggesting that as you arrived,' Nash said with a grin.

Becky took more shots. 'I had an idea on the way over,' she told Nash. 'I thought if I rush these through to Netherdale I can write up some copy whilst I'm in the office. That way, I can go back to bed later and catch up on some sleep.'

Nash thought for a moment. 'If you drop your car off, I'll give you a lift. I've a call to make, and I can tell you what we know for your article on the way.'

*

Nash pulled up outside the Appleyard residence. All the downstairs lights were on. He'd been silent since they left Helmsdale. Now Becky saw the look of increased tension on his face. 'Who are you going to see?'

'I'll tell you when I get back. Just sit tight.'

The girl who answered the door would be eighteen, no more, he guessed. She'd been crying. Nash showed his warrant card and was shown into the lounge. He introduced himself to the family; another daughter, a few years younger, and a son who Nash guessed would be in his early twenties.

'I'm sorry to intrude,' damn silly thing to say, but Nash was no good at this sort of situation. He suspected nobody did it well. 'I assume you've not heard from your husband?'

Mrs Appleyard choked on a sob. 'No.' The answer was little more than a whisper.

'And there's nowhere else he might be?'

It was the son who replied. 'Father rarely went to the pub. Certainly not until this time of night. He had no other interests. He was only concerned with politics and his family.'

'Does he often go to his office on Sundays?'

'Father's a very busy man, Inspector. He takes his responsibilities to his constituents seriously. He goes most days, regularly staying late.'

'Then all we can do is hope there's been some mistake. We won't be able to find out for sure until the fire's been brought under control.'

'How long will that take?' the older girl asked.

'The fire brigade reckon it'll be later tomorrow before it's safe to enter the building. After that, it'll be up to the forensic experts to determine if anyone was inside. In the meantime' – Nash offered his card – 'if there's anything you need, call me. My mobile number's on there.'

He got back in the car with a sigh of relief. 'I hate that job,' he admitted.

'Tell me about it?' Becky asked as he set off towards Netherdale.

Nash explained as much as he dared. 'We believe it was arson. The source was Appleyard's office. Appleyard's missing. I don't want this printing, by the way.'

Becky thought for a moment. 'How about police and fire brigade officials are treating the blaze as suspicious. One man remains unaccounted for, something on those lines?'

'That'd be alright.'

'What do you think about it?'

'I don't know. Could be connected with Appleyard's politics.'

'I went to that meeting he held for Westlea residents.'

'You mean the one where he was heckled for his "Britain for the British" ideas.'

'Heckled, my arse.'

Nash blinked in surprise. 'You've an extremely pretty arse, but why do you say that?'

She told him what she'd seen. 'After they were ejected they all went off together. Hecklers and bouncers, I mean. Matey as could be. It was all rigged. I tell you, the whole evening was scary. Do you know what it reminded me of?'

'No idea.'

'Those old black and white newsreel clips of the rallies in Germany before the war. It was just like Nuremberg, on a much smaller scale. The way everything was stage managed, the message itself and the air of menace.'

There was a long silence. Becky looked across at him. Nash appeared lost in thought. She hoped he was paying attention to the road.

'Good God.' Nash took his foot off the accelerator abruptly.

'What is it?'

He put his foot down again. 'Nothing. Just a crazy notion.'

'Tell me?'

'Later.'

Nash wandered around the *Gazette* offices whilst Becky finished her piece. 'Come on, Mike. Take me home. I'll make coffee. You can tell me your crazy notion.'

They sat in Becky's lounge. Dawn was already breaking. 'It was when you mentioned Nuremberg, I thought of The Reichstag.'

Becky looked baffled. 'Explain,' she demanded.

'I can't remember the exact dates,' Nash admitted. 'I think it was in the early 1930s. The Reichstag was the German parliament building or something like that. Anyway it burned down. The Nazis blamed Communists for it. That was how they tricked their way into power. Later it was proved that the Nazis had done it to discredit the Communists.'

'Right, I understand that. But I still don't see the connection.'

'Suppose Appleyard was in that office. I think we've got to assume he died in the blaze. If he died as a result of an arson attack, who's most likely to get the blame? His opponents, those who disagree with his politics. People would come flocking to the cause in droves. So what if it was his people who were behind it?'

'That's one gigantic leap of logic. Aunt Gloria said you were dangerous. Is that part of what she meant? She said you were a brilliant detective. Is that how you do it?'

'By thinking the crime through? I guess all detectives do that. I remember as a kid reading a lot of Edgar Wallace books. One of his detectives' favourite sayings was, "I have a criminal mind." I reckon you have to think like a criminal to catch them.'

'That's all very well, but how do you prove it?'

'Even supposing my crazy notion's true, finding out who actually ordered the fire is going to be well nigh impossible.' Nash stood up and stretched. 'I'd better go, let you get some sleep.'

'What will you do?'

'Go to the office, I suppose. There doesn't seem much point in going home.'

'You can stay here if you want.'

Nash looked at her. His pulse raced. 'You mean that? But earlier you said …'

'My couch is just as comfortable as yours,' Becky smiled.

Despite his weariness Nash was awake again in what seemed like minutes. He glanced at his watch and saw that he'd actually managed almost two hours' sleep. The early morning sun was streaming through the window, but that wasn't what had woken him. He sat up, stiff from the unaccustomed posture. He was troubled by a stray thought, an elusive memory; something that had happened the previous day.

He began pacing the floor in an effort to remember. It was after almost ten minutes of fruitless exercise that he made the connection. The realization caused him to sit down abruptly. He puzzled it over, then stood up and marched over to Becky's bedroom door. He knocked and waited. Getting no reply, he knocked again. 'What is it?' Her voice was heavy, drugged with sleep.

'Becky, get up. I need to talk to you.'

'Alright, alright.' There was a world of reluctance in her tone. 'Put the kettle on. I'll be out in a minute.'

She joined him in the kitchen. Her hair was tousled and her eyes half closed against the bright morning sun. She was wearing a towelling robe that appeared comfortable but was hardly the height of fashion. Nash thought she looked lovely. 'I'm regretting allowing you to stay,' she grumbled. 'What's the fuss about?'

'Sorry to be a nuisance but this can't wait. I was going over what happened at Grove Road yesterday. I want a woman's perspective on it. Let me explain.' He did so, in a few concise sentences.

'I see where you're coming from,' she agreed after thinking it through. 'And I believe you're right. But why the urgency?'

'Because the way fires are being started round here, I don't want to arrive and find the place a smouldering ruin.'

chapter twenty

Becky reappeared, dressed in jeans and T-shirt. 'We'll go to the station first. Collect Mironova and Pearce. Vickers as well.'

'I hate to quibble, but have you noticed the time?'

Nash glanced at his watch again. It was only 6.35 a.m. 'Oh hell,' he said in exasperation. 'I'm sorry. I didn't realize.'

Becky gave him a pitying stare. 'Toast OK? Or muesli?'

'Toast, please.'

As she was waiting for the toaster to deliver, Becky asked, 'I don't want to seem ungrateful, but why are you including me? I could understand yesterday. But you seem prepared to let me in on details I thought were confidential.'

'You've been involved since the fire at Tucker's flat. It'd be ungrateful to exclude you, after you saved my life. And you're the chief's goddaughter, which makes you special.' Nash smiled warmly. 'Apart from that, I like having you around.'

'Oh. I see. Well, that's alright then.' Becky turned to take the toast out. It gave her time to recover her composure.

Clara strode into the CID suite, her mind absorbed with the text message she'd just received. 'Mike,' she exclaimed, 'I'm glad you're in early. I need a favour.'

She noticed Becky. 'Oh, sorry, I'll catch you later.'

'I asked Becky along because I've had another idea about Grove Road.'

'You never rang the poor girl at this hour because of one of your weird ideas, did you? Mike, you're impossible.' She turned to Becky. 'I'd have put the phone down.'

'Er … it wasn't like that.' Becky was scarlet.

'Oh. Oh, I see.'

'No, you don't. You've got a filthy mind, Clara. Becky was at the fire. It was late when we finished last night, so I slept on her sofa.' Nash glared at his sergeant.

'If I've got a filthy mind, it's because I've been around you too long.'

'Anyway, what's this favour you want? The one you're so tactfully leading up to?'

'If it's personal, I'll leave.' Becky stood up.

'It's not private.' Clara turned to Nash. 'David's got a few days' leave.' She squirmed as she continued. 'Could I take some holiday? I realize it's bad timing.' Her eyes pleaded with him.

'Normally I'd say yes, but it's not that easy. Let me speak to Tom.' Nash winked at Becky. 'Aunt Gloria did say she'd given orders that I'd to have backup. Now, to business. I'd like you to fetch Vickers from the cells. When Viv arrives, we're going back to Grove Road.'

'I'll nip to the loo,' Becky said. 'My system's not used to a gallon of coffee before sunrise.'

Clara watched her go. 'She's really nice. I hope you're treating her properly, Mike.'

'I daren't do any other.'

'I suppose not. Why are you letting her get so close to the investigation?'

'It just happened. And it could be a blessing in disguise.'

'How come?'

'With King desperate to have me out, an independent observer could be extremely handy. If it came to an internal enquiry, an unbiased witness would be a godsend, if you'll pardon the pun.'

'I hadn't thought of it like that.'

'The saddest thing is that it's necessary.'

'Gary, before I explain, I want to ask you a couple of questions.'

Vickers blinked at the use of his Christian name. 'OK,' he agreed cautiously.

'Stacey told you about the photos. Not specifically, but she told you of their existence.'

Vickers nodded.

'Have you remembered what she said?'

'Not really. I've been trying to recall her exact words. I thought it might give me some idea what the proof was.'

'But you knew she'd hidden it?'

'Yes. I'd been at a series of exhibitions featuring my work.' Vickers saw the puzzled expression on his listeners' faces. He explained. 'I was a freelance graphic artist. She told me when I got back.' He sighed. 'The last show was in Bristol. I got home late. Gemma was away that night, so Stacey and I had the house to ourselves. It was only two days later that ...' Vickers' voice tailed off. He was on the verge of tears.

'How was she? Did you notice anything different about her?'

'Yes, she was on edge. More than that, I'd say she was frightened. It seemed odd. I knew she was worried about her mother, but it was more than that. When she died I was too upset to think about it. By the time I did, I was stuck in a prison cell.'

'For a murder you didn't commit,' Nash said quietly.

Vickers looked up. 'You believe that?'

'Oh yes.' Nash made it sound matter of fact. 'Which makes it doubly important that you try to remember. We've a killer to bring to justice. A murderer who I believe has killed again. So think, Gary, what was it made you certain she'd hidden something?'

'Stacey cooked supper and when we went into the dining room she'd parcelled that picture up. She said ...' Vickers paused. 'She said, "It may not be valuable now, but one day it could be worth a lot." There was something else too, but I can't remember.'

'She said it might be worth a lot? Not a lot of money? Just worth a lot?'

Vickers leaned forward, a frown of concentration on his face. 'No, she definitely didn't mention money. Not exactly, but something to do with money. What was it?' He stood up and began pacing about.

He stopped suddenly. 'Insurance! That was it. She said it might be valuable as insurance. I thought she meant I might have to insure it. I said I'd put it on my contents policy. But then she said, "It's our insurance policy. Yours and mine." She wouldn't explain. I can't understand how I forgot that.'

'You were under a lot of stress. But what you've said reinforces my idea. I thought it strange that Stacey left those photos without an explanation.'

'I don't get you, Inspector.'

'I reckon we've only found half of what Stacey hid. I think we should look again. This time we should search for a note or a letter.'

When they stood up, Pearce reached for his handcuffs. Nash shook his head. 'Gary's no longer under arrest. Tell the custody officer he's being released without charge.' He turned to Vickers. 'You're free to go, but I'd like you to consider staying here under protective custody. With all that's going on, you'll be much safer.'

'No, thanks, I've had enough of prison cells.'

Nash was relieved to see the house was intact. As they were getting out of the car his mobile rang. 'When do you think he'll be needed? Right, leave it to me. I'll get on it straightaway.'

'Doug Curran,' he explained after he ended the call. 'Go on in. I'll follow after I've spoken to Mexican Pete.'

'Professor, Nash here. There was a fire last night. CFO Curran's in charge of the scene. One man's unaccounted for. The building will be safe to enter late this afternoon. Can you be there around 4 p.m.? We'll need a forensics team too.'

'You seem to be going in for barbecues in a big way,' Ramirez told him. 'Will you bring Clara to dispense gin and tonic?'

Nash hurried inside. Clara glanced at him. 'Mexican Pete on form then?'

'As you'd expect. Talking about barbecues and G&Ts.'

'Our pathologist has a macabre sense of humour,' Clara explained to Becky.

'I know. I've spoken to him.'

'Clara, I suggest you start upstairs, along with Gary and Viv. Becky and I'll start on the ground floor.'

Nash and Becky spent most of the first hour re-examining ornaments and more photo frames. Nash went into the cabinet that housed Vickers' music centre. He hauled the collection of CDs and albums out. 'I don't think anything's been touched since Vickers went inside.'

'He's certainly a Beatles fan,' Becky commented as she looked at a pile of LPs.

'Pearce reckons that's the opposite of cool.'

The trio returned from the upper floor. Clara shrugged her shoulders. 'Nothing.'

Nash shook his head stubbornly. 'There's got to be something. Stacey wouldn't have gone to all that trouble without some sort of pointer.'

He saw Clara was far from convinced. 'Forget all you've read in the file. We know different. We have to work on Gary's version. That means there's something more than the photos.'

Becky said slowly, 'It would have to be somewhere Gary would go regularly, but somewhere no one else would find it, even by accident.'

'That makes sense,' Clara agreed. 'She'd have to hide it from casual discovery, especially if it was a smoking gun.'

'That's it!' Vickers yelped. 'That's what she said! She said it was a smoking gun. I couldn't understand it. Then she started laughing. I couldn't understand what she thought was funny.'

'What was her sense of humour like?' Nash asked. As he spoke he began sorting through the LPs.

'She loved subtle, double-meaning jokes. Why?'

'I wonder if this was an example of her sense of humour.' Nash looked around, his expression brooding. 'I wonder ...' he murmured.

'What are you on about?' Mironova asked.

Nash ignored her. 'Did Gemma share your taste in music?'

'No, she was into punk and heavy metal. If I put a Beatles album on she'd walk out of the room.'

'Did you have all your LPs transferred to CD?'

'No. I never got round to it.'

Eventually Nash reached the one he was after. He removed the record from the sleeve and laid it aside, slid his fingers inside the LP cover and removed a sheet of paper. He turned the cover over. 'There's your smoking gun.' It was The Beatles' *Revolver* album.

'It seems so obvious afterwards,' Vickers muttered.

Clara laughed. 'Well, it isn't, unless you've got a devious, twisted mind like Mike.'

Nash spread the letter on the table. 'This is addressed to you, Gary. Do you want to read it or do you want me to?'

'I should do it. I owe Stacey that.'

My dearest, darling Gary,
I hope you never have to read this. I'm afraid, desperately afraid. Afraid for us, and for the future. I've done something that's put us in danger. I did it because I couldn't see any other way for us to be together, and free. Free from her. I hate her. I didn't realize it until now. I hate and fear her. That's a terrible thing to say about your own mother. Not that I think of her like that. That's because she's never treated me like a daughter. To her I was merely an expensive encumbrance.

And now I know she hates me. How do I know? Because she told me so, when I confronted her. It took ages to pluck up enough courage, but in the end it was the only option. I haven't told her about us though. Not yet. If she found out that we're lovers, I dread to think what would happen. Not that she cares about you; she's got other fish to fry. But she'd use our love as a weapon. My greatest fear is for you, my darling, because of her, and my uncles. I couldn't put you in that sort of danger.

I told her I knew what she was doing, and who with. I told her I had proof. I said I was quite prepared to take that proof to his wife. If that happened he'd be ruined. And that would end their sordid little affair. It was then I found out what she's capable of. It was then I began to be afraid. She heard me out. Then she calmly got to her feet, and before I knew what she was going to do, she had her hands round my neck, choking me. Her language was vile. She called me all the filthy names you could think of. She told me if I valued my skin, I'd to hand over the proof and forget the whole thing. I hadn't realized until then how unutterably evil she is. I truly believe she would carry out the threats she made.

I feel so lonely now. I need you here. I need your strong arms around me. To love, and protect me, and to reassure me. Without that I'm terrified of what will happen. So I've made a decision. I'll go to her lover and tell him what I told her. Perhaps that will stop her. It's my only remaining choice.

I've concealed the proof of what they've been up to. That's how afraid I am. It's hidden inside your present. Whatever happens, my darling, I will love you forever.

Stacey

Vickers looked up. Nash almost shuddered at the venom in his expression. 'Who is he? You know, don't you?' he demanded. 'One of them killed Stacey. I don't know which, and I don't much care. It's irrelevant. But I'll tell you this, Mr Nash, I'll find out, and if you don't make them pay for what they did, I will.'

Nash tried to placate him. 'I understand your anger, Gary, but issuing threats like that isn't going to help anyone. Least of all you. And don't forget the purpose of this letter. Stacey wrote it to protect you. She wouldn't want you endangering yourself, or doing something you'd suffer for afterwards.'

'Does that mean they'll get off?'

'I didn't say that. Up to now we haven't a grain of evidence against them. I admit it won't be easy. They've had fifteen years to cover their tracks. All we can do is start working on the case as of now.' Nash pointed to the letter. 'We'll use this as a starting point.'

Vickers went to pick the letter up but Nash placed his hand on it. 'No, Gary, reading that over and over isn't going to do you any good. Besides, that letter is evidence.'

He turned to Mironova. 'Clara, go back to the office, take this with you. Make out a new file on the unlawful killing of Stacey Fletcher. Put the letter in it, together with the photos we found yesterday. I also want copies of all the statements taken at the time, together with the post-mortem results. Scan those into the computer and e-mail them to Mexican Pete. I'm going to Westlea to meet him, along with Curran and the forensics guys. I'll tell Ramirez to expect your e-mail. I want him to review the original pathologist's findings. He may spot something that was missed in the first instance. Then I'll have a word with Tom and see if he can give me cover for the next five days, so you can meet up with the galloping major. Will that do you?'

'Thanks, Mike.'

'What do you want me to do?'

Nash looked at Viv. 'You're back on protection duty. We know Gary's innocent, but there are plenty who still believe he's guilty. And I reckon the violence has been stirred to conceal the real target.' Nash turned to Vickers. 'You understand that? No more swanning off on your own. DC Pearce will stay with you for the time being. Later, I'm going to try for extra backup.'

'I understand.'

'Right, I'm off to the Westlea.'

'Mind if I tag along, Mike?'

Nash turned to Becky. 'Yes, if you want to. It may be boring and tedious though.'

'It'll save them having to send someone else to cover the story.'

A team of forensic technicians was donning hazmat suits, supervised by Curran. He ducked under the incident tape to speak to Nash. 'There's a problem with toxic fumes and asbestos. It's going to be slower than we thought. We're waiting on Mexican Pete.'

'If you see him first, tell him I need a word.'

As Curran left, Nash was hailed. 'Ayup, Mr Nash. This another of your haireem?'

They turned. 'Hello, Jonas. No, this is Becky Pollard from the *Gazette*.'

'Watch out for this feller, he's a wicked man,' Turner told her. 'Allus got a beautiful girl hanging round 'im, he has. Don't know how he does it.'

'What are you doing here?' Nash changed the subject swiftly.

'Come to watch 'em recover t' body.' Turner surveyed the blackened shell. 'It's Appleyard you're looking for, ain't it? Bought this place for a song. Much good it did 'im.'

'Do you know something?'

'You hear things.' Turner lowered his voice. 'They all knew he was inside.'

'Who do you mean?' Becky beat Nash to the question by a short head.

'Them as lives round here.'

'What's your point?' Becky asked, but Nash had already worked it out.

'They knew cos they were told to keep clear. That's what I heard.'

'You mean they knew it was going to happen?'

Turner nodded. 'Best not say any more. Not that I know anything,' he added hastily.

They watched the old man wander off. 'So the arson theory's right,' Nash said.

Becky shuddered. 'It's the sort of thing you only see on films. You don't believe it can happen in your own town.'

'The Westlea has always been a law to itself, with the Fletcher clan as sheriffs. We're the enemy round here. By "we", I mean the police.'

'Does that worry you?'

'It never used to. But this is new. What's worse is it's organized. And the gangs running amok haven't the collective brains to realize they're being manipulated.'

Nash broke off as he saw a car pull up. 'Care to meet our tame pathologist?'

'Is that Mexican Pete?'

'It is. I must get a word with him before he gets into fancy dress.'

Nash introduced Becky.

'We've already spoken on the telephone,' she told Ramirez as they shook hands.

'Have we?'

'Yes, when you rang Mike. You referred to me as the Bride of Dracula.'

'Hardly surprising, the way Nash collects corpses.' He pointed to the building. 'Only one in there?'

172

'That's all.'

'He's losing his touch. I've known days when he's been close to double figures,' Ramirez told Becky.

'Clara's sending you some old PM documents. I'd value your opinion. Now, get your space suit on,' Nash told him.

As Ramirez turned they heard a loud crack, followed swiftly by two more. Ramirez turned back to Nash. 'What was...?'

Nash flung himself at Becky and pushed her to the ground. 'Get down!' he shouted to everyone within earshot. His voice carried, even over the sound of two more reports.

'What...?' Becky gasped.

'Gunfire! Somebody's shooting at us. From over there.' Nash waved towards a clump of trees. It was impossible to get close to the shooter without serious risk. Becky felt him move, and glanced down. Nash had pulled a pistol from his holster. The sight should have comforted her. It didn't. She looked across towards the ruined building. Firemen and forensics experts were lying prone. Wounded? Dead? Or taking cover?

Ramirez hissed, 'I thought it was too good to last. You couldn't be content with one corpse, could you?'

'I hope that's all there will be,' Nash answered grimly. He hailed Curran. 'Doug? Keep your men on the deck. I'm going to discourage our sniper friend.'

'Alright, Mike.'

'What are you going to do?' Becky whispered.

'Fire a few rounds into those trees. That should scare him off.' Nash wriggled to one side before passing Becky his mobile. 'Dial short code 1, you'll get Clara. Tell her what's going on. Ask for an ARU.'

Becky was still fumbling with the phone when a loud report sounded in her ear. She almost dropped the mobile. Nash fired three more shots at intervals of twenty seconds or so.

There was a long silence after Becky finished speaking. Nash rolled over. 'I'm going to get up. I think he's scarpered, but there's only one way to find out. Everyone, stay down!' He got cautiously to his feet. There was no reaction. The silence became oppressive. Still no movement, no fresh outburst. 'He's gone.'

Becky looked up. 'How can you be so sure?'

'If he'd been going to fire again, he'd have done so by now.'

Becky scrambled to her feet. Around them, others were following their lead. 'How do you work that out?'

'If he was still there he'd have fired at me.' Nash noticed Becky's puzzled expression. 'I was the target.'

'What makes you so sure?'

'Because I've stirred them up. And you know what that means?'

Becky shook her head.

'It means I'm getting close. If I'd any remaining doubts, they've just settled them.'

chapter twenty-one

They were sitting in the car. 'Tom, Mike Nash. Yes, I'm fine. Nobody hurt.' Nash grinned at Becky. 'A couple of the forensic lads might have to change their underpants. The gunman was in a small wood alongside the fire scene. Been watching too many films, I reckon. No way he could hit anybody at that range.

'I'm ringing because Clara wants some leave. If you could lend me DC Andrews I'd be able to manage.' Nash listened for a few moments. 'That's great. I also want an armed officer in Vickers' house. I've got evidence that he didn't kill Stacey Fletcher. Would you ask the chief to agree that?'

Nash ended the call and smiled at Becky. 'I told you this would be boring.'

'Yes, I haven't been shot at for at least quarter of an hour. A really slow day. How long do you think it'll be before forensics finds anything?'

'It might not happen today. A lot depends on where the body is. It has to be done slowly to avoid disturbing evidence.'

'I'll nip back home and e-mail my copy to the paper. Will you still be here in a couple of hours?'

'I imagine so. Why?'

'I'll bring you a flask of coffee.'

It was nearer three hours before Becky called him. 'Any luck?'

'They've located the body. Fortunately there's no debris to move. We might be clear in under an hour.'

'Does that mean you don't want the coffee?'

Was there a touch of disappointment in her voice, or was that wishful thinking? 'I'll pass on the coffee if you'll keep me company. Then we could go for a meal.'

'I'll be down in quarter of an hour.'

Nash was on the phone when she arrived. 'I see. Well, thanks for trying. No, I'll have to manage. Can't be helped.'

He lowered the phone and smiled at her. It was a feeble gesture.

'What's matter?'

'That obvious, am I?'

'You look as if the horse you bet your last fiver on fell at the first fence.'

'Nearly as bad. Pratt needs higher clearance for armed protection for Vickers. Unfortunately your godmother's away at a conference for a couple of days. She left about an hour before Tom rang her office. The request got diverted to King. He took great delight in refusing it.'

'You've never explained why he has such a down on you. Not properly.'

'You'd not believe me if I tell you.'

'Try me.'

Before Nash could begin, Ramirez appeared. 'I've supervised the removal of one body,' he told Nash. 'Badly burned, but there should be some recoverable DNA. Failing which, dental records should confirm identity.'

'Cause of death?'

Ramirez stared at him. 'Too long in the oven, I imagine. I haven't thought to look for anything else. I'll know more when I've done the PM.'

They watched the pathologist leave. 'I'm ravenous. Fancy a Chinese?' Nash suggested.

'Fine by me.'

'Let's try the Few Men Chew.'

'The what?'

'Fu Manchu. Local nickname is Few Men Chew.'

Becky groaned.

During their meal, she reminded him about King.

'He's come into the area and wants to alter the way things are done.'

'No doubt you'll tell me when you're ready or it's appropriate.'

Nash saw her sceptical look. 'That's what Clara says when she doesn't believe me.'

Becky nodded. 'As long as you know. What will you do about protecting Vickers?' she asked as he was paying the bill.

'If there's no backup, I'll have to do it.'

'You'll get no sleep. You can't do that.'

'I'm only thinking of the next couple of days. When the chief's back, I'll go over King's head.'

'I'm coming with you.'

'No way, Becks,' Nash said firmly.

'Why not?'

'I can't allow a civilian to put themselves in harm's way.'

'Suit yourself. I'll walk up and down outside Vickers' house all night.'

'That's blackmail.'

'Alright, arrest me.'

'Don't tempt me.'

'You put me in a cell for the night and I'll spend the time writing my piece for the *Gazette*.'

'More blackmail.' Nash knew he was beaten. 'Very well, but if there's trouble, you keep out of the way. Understand?'

Becky smiled. 'Of course.' When he wasn't looking, she uncrossed her fingers.

Pearce opened the door. Vickers was hovering behind him. 'I'm here to protect you overnight,' Nash told him. He jerked a thumb over his shoulder. 'And she's here to protect me.'

'Blimey, Mike! You sure that's wise?'

'No, Viv, I'm not. But I don't have much choice.'

The house was quiet after Pearce left. 'What are we going to do?' Becky asked.

'The problem I had before was keeping awake,' Nash told her.

'I could always put some music on,' Gary suggested.

'Got any Status Quo?'

'How about some Rolling Stones or Queen?' Becky joined in.

Vickers shuddered. 'No chance. I said music.'

Vickers went to bed shortly before 2.30, Nash and Becky kept awake by talking and drinking black coffee. The Bishopton officer arrived shortly after 6.30 a.m. 'Superintendent Pratt ordered me here early,' he told Nash.

'Keep your guard up. You shouldn't have any trouble from Vickers. First sign of bother, you hit the alarm button. Understood?'

Nash dropped Becky at her flat before returning home. She yawned as she asked, 'Will you manage a few hours' sleep?'

'I'll grab a couple of hours. Then I'll have another nap at teatime.'

'Come round here when you've finished work and I'll make dinner. That way you can sleep until it's time to eat. Then we can go on to Grove Road.'

Any hope Nash had that the day would bring a respite from his problems was swept aside when he entered the CID suite. 'I've had Creepy on the phone,' Pearce greeted him. 'I told him I didn't know what time you were due. Don't think that pleased him much. You've to phone him the minute you arrive.'

'You ring him. Ask him what he wants. Don't bother to be polite,' he added as he went into his office.

Pearce came in and handed Nash a mug of coffee. 'Creepy's on his way. He said you've not to go out.'

Nash glanced at his watch. The journey from Netherdale would take about half an hour. 'I'm going to phone Mexican Pete. Then I'll go for the sandwiches.'

'But you'll be out … Oh, I see.' Pearce grinned.

Nash dialled the pathologist. 'Have you done the post-mortem yet, Professor?'

'Just finished. I was about to ring you. I'm assuming the victim is Appleyard, certainly a male of about the right age. There was no carbon monoxide in his lungs.'

'That means he was dead before the fire started?'

'Absolutely.'

'Any idea how?'

'It could be down to the bullet hole in his forehead.'

'That often does it,' Nash agreed.

'I'm sending the bullet to ballistics.'

Nash hung up. 'I'm going to talk to Curran,' he told Pearce. 'I'll go straight from there for the food.'

'I've got the forensic results,' the fire officer told him. 'The fire was arson. Which makes it murder.'

'It was already murder.'

Crawley was pacing up and down Nash's office. 'Where have you been?' he demanded.

'Buying my lunch.'

'I'm here to conduct an investigation into your conduct. To be specific, the reckless discharge of your firearm into a crowd of people. That is the preliminary to a board of enquiry which will assess your fitness for duty. Pending that, you're suspended from duty. Give me your pistol and your warrant card.'

Nash rounded his desk and sat down. He took out his sandwich. 'Close the door on your way out,' he replied.

'What! Did you hear what I said?'

'Yes. I'm attempting to ignore it.' Nash lifted the sandwich to take a bite; then stopped. 'Go on, disappear.'

Crawley was speechless, rooted to the spot. His face was scarlet. Nash sighed and put the sandwich down. 'You've no jurisdiction over CID. You've no jurisdiction over me. You've no jurisdiction in Helmsdale. You've no written authority. Now clear off and let me eat my lunch.'

As Crawley was hovering indecisively, Nash added, 'And tell DCC King to do his own dirty work in future.'

The office door had been open throughout. Although Crawley had attempted to keep his voice down, Nash had spoken loud enough for Pearce to hear. As the visitor blundered out of the CID suite, Pearce came in. His eyes were wide with shock.

'Listen carefully, Viv. If things go pear-shaped, here's what I want you to do. Explain to Clara exactly what's happened and tell her to activate our plan. She'll know what you mean. And if Becky Pollard from the *Gazette* asks any questions, you answer them in full. On the record. Clear? Anything she wants to know will be for publication. Now let me explain.'

If Pearce had been surprised before, he was dumbfounded when Nash finished.

By mid afternoon Nash had made a decision. The spur was a phone call from Pratt. 'I hear you've been having words with Inspector Crawley.'

'I told him to clear off, if that's what you mean.'

'He came back with his tail between his legs. Tried to get hold of King, who's away somewhere, then he came whingeing to me. I told him he was out of line, but he said he was obeying orders.'

'King's orders?'

'That's what he said. I've countermanded the orders, so I suppose there'll be a standoff with King when he gets back.'

'Maybe not,' Nash told him. 'Leave it with me.'

'Anyway, the good news is that Lisa Andrews will be with you tomorrow.'

'Good. I've got a job for her.'

'What's that?'

'I want her with me when I pull Gemma Fletcher in.'

'About Tucker's murder?'

'Tucker's, yes. But I also want to question her about her involvement in the murder of her daughter.'

When Nash rang Becky's doorbell, he was almost out on his feet. She ordered him to go and use her bed.

It was a measure of his weariness that he didn't argue and was asleep almost instantly. His last sensation was the scent of her perfume. He seemed to have been asleep only minutes when she woke him. 'Coffee,' she called brightly. He didn't respond, so she set the mug on the bedside table and shook his shoulder gently.

Nash stirred and turned over, blinking in the light. 'What time is it?'

'Half nine. I called DC Pearce. He's gone to cover for you. That way you can have a shower to freshen up before dinner. Pearce said there was no need to rush.'

'You're an angel. I need another favour though.' He explained what he needed.

'I'll do it whilst you're showering,' she promised.

When he emerged, Becky was setting the table. 'I spoke to Aunt Gloria. She's going to deal with the problem in the morning, but she says you mustn't worry. You have her full backing. From now on, you report directly to either her, when she's back, or Superintendent Pratt.'

'Was that all?'

'Er … yes, just about.'

Nash raised an eyebrow.

'She made a couple of snide remarks about you being here, until I set the record straight.'

'I hope she believed you.'

'I told her not to worry. I can take care of myself.'

'I know that. You're also pretty good at taking care of me, for which I'm more than grateful.'

'You can show your gratitude by relaxing and eating your meal,' Becky ordered.

*

Pearce reported that everything had been quiet. 'Except that Gary's been torturing me with more of what he calls music. I'm off now. Don't rush in tomorrow, boss. If King or Crawley start shouting for you I'll put them off.'

'That isn't going to happen, but if it does, don't take any nonsense from either of them. DC Andrews will be joining us in the morning. She's seconded to Helmsdale until this case is over. I've a job lined up for her. Give her the files to read.'

Shortly after Pearce left, Vickers announced he was going to bed. From the kitchen, they heard him climb the stairs followed by the sound of the toilet flushing. As the water flow ceased, Nash thought he heard another, different noise. His head jerked up. 'Did you hear that?'

Becky nodded.

'Stay here.' He reached for his pistol as he tiptoed to the dining room door and eased it open. The room was silent, undisturbed. Through the window the street light shone brightly. He heard another sound. Of a window being opened? The direction seemed to be the lounge. Front or back? If the intruder was armed, that split second could be critical. Nash guessed the back; less chance of being disturbed.

He swung the lounge door open. He'd chosen wrong. The windows at the back were intact. He turned quickly. Not fast enough. The hall light silhouetted him. Nash saw the bulky figure in front of the window. There was a bright flash and a report. Nash felt something tug at his shirt. He raised his pistol. Knowing he'd be too late. The intruder was already taking fresh aim. Nash braced himself for the impact, even as he squeezed the trigger.

There was an enormous explosion of brilliant, blinding white light. The gunshots merged in a deafening crack. The gunman dived through the open window, scrambling to his feet in a desperate attempt to escape.

'Mike, you alright?'

Nash looked up, blinking. 'I told you to stay in the kitchen.'

Vickers ran downstairs. He was wearing only underpants and socks. 'I heard shots. What happened?'

'Somebody broke in. Took a shot at me. I fired back. There was a giant flash. Put him off his aim. What the hell it was, I've no idea.'

Becky grinned. She brought her hand from behind her back. 'The camera was mightier than the pistol; especially with the flash on.'

'That's brilliant.' Nash stared at her in awe. 'It certainly ruined his aim. I don't suppose you …'

'Of course I did.' She offered Nash the viewer. 'There's your man.'

Nash looked at the image. 'Becky, you're a marvel.' The shot contained every element they needed. The background would identify the room. The date and time would confirm the incident. And the clear, sharply focused figure at the centre of the frame would have no chance to deny the charge against him. Especially not with the raised gun in his hand.

'You know him?' Vickers was peering over Nash's shoulder.

'I certainly do. That's Danny Floyd. Jake Fletcher's right-hand man.'

Within minutes, a patrol car was outside. Nash quietened the nerves of the officers sent to investigate. Then he sent them to calm the neighbours. He rang Pearce and Tom Pratt. 'I don't see why others shouldn't have a sleepless night,' he told Becky, who was examining his shirt.

Pratt agreed to send an ARU over to guard the property overnight. 'We need a forensics man as well,' Nash told him. 'No, I'm fine; he's a lousy shot, thank God. I need a new shirt, that's all. The bullet passed straight through. There are two bullets lodged in the walls. One might have cotton fibres attached. 'When the ARU arrives I'll get off home. I'm not passing up the chance of a decent night's sleep.'

It was almost 2 a.m. before they got away. 'You want me to drive?' Becky asked. He wasn't used to this. She seemed to know what he was thinking almost before he thought it.

'Would you? Then take my car. You can bring it back tomorrow.'

'I'm going nowhere until I've seen you settled.'

She ordered him to bed the moment they arrived at his flat.

Nash yawned. 'Will you lock the door?'

'I'll see to everything.'

Ten minutes later she tiptoed into his bedroom. He was fast asleep.

Nash could tell by the position of the sun round the edges of the curtains that it was late. He felt warm and comfortable, didn't want to move. He stared at the ceiling, thinking of Becky. For a second time he owed her his life, wondered how he could hope to repay her, decided he couldn't. As if the thought disturbed him, he turned to check the time on the bedside clock. He stared in surprise. Becky was lying alongside him. She was awake, watching him. She smiled, her eyes heavy with sleep.

'Good morning, lazybones. I couldn't summon the energy to drive home. And your couch isn't the most comfortable place. I hope you don't mind.'

'Of course not.' He felt desire stirring. 'What time is it?'

'Almost noon. Does it matter?'

'I don't suppose so.' Nash reached out to caress her.

She put her hand against his chest. 'You know the rules.'

'Damn the rules.' He pulled her close and kissed her.

For a second she responded, before holding him off. 'No, Mike, that's not fair.'

He broke off. 'Sorry, it was inexcusable.'

She slid out of bed. She was wearing only bra and pants. Nash's arousal was almost painful. She smiled. 'It was excusable. Just not permitted. Why don't you shower whilst I make coffee?'

He rolled onto his back. As she reached the door, Becky looked back and noticed the bedclothes. 'Better make it a cold one.'

'Vixen,' he muttered. But she was gone.

When Nash reached his office, Andrews was studying the files. 'There's a note on your desk from ballistics,' she informed him.

He rang them. 'We recovered the two rounds fired at you last night. They match casings recovered from the shooting incident earlier. The gun was also used to shoot the man whose body was recovered from the fire. There were fibres on one; we'll need your shirt at some stage.'

'Good, and we've identified the shooter. Now we can charge him with murder.'

His next call was to Ramirez, who confirmed the body was that of Appleyard.

Nash had barely put the phone down when Becky entered. 'I printed that photo off,' she announced. 'I did half a dozen copies and e-mailed one to you as well.'

'Thanks, Becky.' He told her about the identification of Appleyard and added the news about the bullets.

'Right, I'm going home to write that up. Unless you object to us printing it?'

'No problem. At the same time, put in that "in view of new evidence, we're reopening the Stacey Fletcher murder investigation".

Quote me as saying, "We now believe the original conviction was flawed." That, and the shooting story, should stir things up.'

'That's what you enjoy, isn't it? Stirring people up?'

'It often gets results.' Nash would reflect on that later. But even he couldn't anticipate the reaction to the statement. 'Before you dash off, I need a favour.'

'I'll help if I can.'

'Lisa!' Nash shouted through the open door.

DC Andrews appeared. 'Lisa, this is Becky Pollard from the *Netherdale Gazette*. Becky, I know this is asking a lot, but do you have a spare camera with a telephoto lens? If so, will you lend Lisa it and show her how to use it?'

'I've got my own digital. It's not as powerful as the one from work, but it's more than adequate. And it's virtually idiot proof.' Becky winked at Lisa. 'So even you could use it.'

Lisa stared at the building. There'd been no movement since she'd arrived. She guessed Gemma Fletcher was in her office. Her red sports car was in the car park. Lisa was wondering whether to risk going for a sandwich when Nash pulled up. 'Anything happening?' he asked.

Lisa shook her head. 'Are you going straight in? I could do with something to eat. And I need to take a leak.'

Nash looked over at the public toilets. 'I wouldn't risk going in there. If you can hang on, we'll get Gemma and take her to the station. How did you get on with Becky?'

'The camera's easy, as she promised. Anything going on? She's a really nice girl.'

'She's also the chief's goddaughter.'

Lisa whistled. 'That might cramp your style. Mind you, nothing else has.'

'You're getting as bad as Mironova for snide remarks. Anyway, after we've done with Gemma, I want you to head out to Houlston Grange. I need photos of everyone leaving and arriving. If you can't get a facial, make sure you get the number plate.'

'What makes you think there'll be any action?'

'I'm sure our chat with Gemma will stir things up. If it doesn't, I'll be disappointed.'

Nash was surprised that Gemma didn't put up any resistance. It was only when he started to interview her that the reason for her acceptance became plain.

'This isn't a formal interrogation,' he began. 'Nevertheless it's being recorded for everyone's protection. If you feel you need someone else present, just say so.'

Gemma nodded to show she understood, and Nash continued. 'The first question I want to ask is about an attack on Gary Vickers. To be exact, the second in three days. His house was broken into last night by a known associate of your brothers. Do you know anything about that?'

'Was he killed?' There was no mistaking her eagerness.

'No, he wasn't harmed. But it seems everything that's happened to Vickers can be traced to you.'

'Why should I care? I wouldn't piss on him if he was on fire.'

Nash's tone was silk-like. 'I think you should care. Especially as we now know Vickers didn't kill your daughter. That's why we're reopening the case. And that's why you're here.'

The colour drained from her face. Her expression changed. The confidence vanished. It was several moments before Gemma could speak. 'How do you know?'

'I can't disclose that. But the evidence is overwhelming. So, if he didn't kill Stacey, who do you think did?'

Gemma shook her head. Nash continued. 'Can you tell me where you were on Tuesday last, between 4 p.m. and 8 p.m.?'

There was a pause, before Gemma replied, 'I was at home. Writing reports for a sales meeting.'

'Alone?'

'Of course.'

'And where were you when Stacey was murdered?'

'I don't … I can't remember. It was fifteen years ago.'

'Really, but this was your daughter, your only child. You expect me to believe you can't recall where you were when she was murdered?'

'I think I'd like my lawyer present.'

Nash looked at her. 'I'm not going to ask you any more questions.' He paused before adding, 'For the time being you've given me all the answers I need.'

When Gemma had left, he turned to Lisa. 'What did you make of that?'

'When you told her about Vickers, she was shocked that we were sure he wasn't guilty. And when you told her you were reopening Stacey's murder investigation she was terrified. But although she was afraid, she wasn't surprised. I think she knew Vickers didn't kill Stacey.'

'I agree, and there's only one reason Gemma could know Vickers wasn't guilty. Because either Gemma killed Stacey herself, or she knows who did.'

'What's next, Mike?' Pearce and Lisa were in Nash's office.

'I want a warrant out for Danny Floyd. See to that, will you, Viv? The charge is the murder of Councillor Appleyard. Throw in two counts of attempting to murder me as well. Then I want a team getting together to arrest him. If I can find the men.'

'I presume Danny must be behind the arson attacks too. Stands to reason, if he shot Appleyard, he also torched the building. That'd put him in the frame for the Druze family killings and the other fires.'

'Probably,' Nash agreed. 'But we've no evidence he was the arsonist.'

'I'd better get off on my photo shoot,' Lisa said, pocketing the borrowed camera.

Becky's copy was too late for the early editions. However, the print room held the final edition until the report on Appleyard's murder could be included. Late that afternoon Pearce brought a copy of the paper into Nash's office.

Nash looked up from the paperwork he was reading. 'What is it, Viv?'

'This item your girlfriend's written. It's dynamite.' Pearce held out the paper.

Nash skim-read the piece. The contentious bit was at the end. The writer speculated whether Appleyard's new political directive had provoked an extreme reaction. Any hope that the problematic paragraph would escape notice, was dispelled by the headline. 'Councillor Slain,' it read. 'Was Immigration Policy The Motive?'

'Oh hell!' Nash muttered. He looked up. 'That's like an invitation to declare open season on all migrants. And there's bugger all we can do about it, except ask for reinforcements.'

'At least King's not on hand to block your request,' Pearce pointed out.

'No, but neither is the chief here to override him. And we don't know where he's gone and for how long. For all we know, he might be back. Anyway, I'll soon find out. I'm going to ring Tom immediately.'

Pratt was in the midst of reading the article. 'I can guess why you've rung. I'll put as many officers as I can on standby, and do the same at Bishopton. I'll get Binns on it straightaway.'

'Isn't it Creepy's province?'

'I'm not wasting my breath on him. Just stand up for me at the tribunal. At least King isn't around to stick his oar in.'

'Where is he?'

'Gone to that conference the chief's attending. One of the delegates couldn't make it, so they asked for King. My informant reckons that shows he's in line for a chief constable post.'

'Only time will tell,' Nash said. Fortunately Pratt was unable to see the expression on his face. 'Thanks, Tom.'

'I wish I could do more.'

Lisa Andrews was uncomfortable. Not only that, her perch was precarious. She'd been sitting in the car for over an hour before there was any activity outside Houlston Grange. Then two vehicles arrived in quick succession. The first was a pick-up truck; the second a Range Rover. Lisa's position was too distant to get identifiable photos of the occupants, even using the zoom lens. But she'd got legible snaps of the number plates. She knew Nash wanted more. He needed to know who Rathmell was meeting. She'd done a swift reconnaissance and seen a spot where the wall surrounding Rathmell's estate could be scaled. Just inside the grounds was a huge copper beech, which commanded a good view of the house. The tree was in full foliage and offered excellent cover. From thirty feet up, she could see clearly across the manicured lawns into the ground-floor rooms. This was better, with the zoom lens she could bring the occupants into sharp focus. For a long while all she could see was Rathmell. He was standing in front of one of the bay windows, his back to her. It looked as if he was addressing the others.

After twenty minutes sitting astride the branch, Lisa could feel the leaves tickling her neck. Eventually her patience and discomfort were rewarded. Rathmell moved forward. The other two men moved into view. Lisa began firing shot after shot, grateful for the speed of the shutter. She recognized one of the men and all but dropped the camera. She swayed slightly and grasped the tree trunk. By the time she recovered her balance, the room was empty. The front door opened. Lisa trained her lens on it and managed a few more shots. She scrambled down the tree and was back in her car before the two vehicles left the drive. She snapped the rear number plates as they drove off.

Fifteen minutes later Gemma Fletcher's car came down the lane. Gemma was driving with more speed than skill. She slewed into the driveway, almost clipping one of the stone gateposts as she passed in a cloud of dust. Lisa lowered the camera and smiled. Nash had been right. Their revelation of Vickers' innocence had stirred up a hornet's nest.

Lisa didn't bother trying for photos of Gemma inside the house. She'd seen more than enough photos of Gemma and Rathmell. To while away the time, she switched on the radio and tuned it to Helm Radio.

Billy was angry. He'd wanted to do the fire in the office without interference. It was a good fire. One of his best, but Danny had spoilt it. Why had he shot the man first? It was no fun setting fire to a dead man. But Danny had told him to. Why not just let him burn him to death? He could have done it easily enough. And it would have taken longer. He'd told Danny this. 'With a bit of luck we'll be able to hear him screaming. It's great when they scream. Sometimes when I hear them scream I come in my pants, it's so good.'

And Danny had looked at him so oddly, as if he was seeing him for the first time. 'Fuck you, Billy,' he'd said. 'You are one sick bastard. Do you know that? No, you can't burn him to death. I've been told. He has to be shot. Get the petrol. Wait for me outside and don't start messing about until I'm well clear. Then you can do what you like. As long as you torch the place, I don't care if you stand in the middle of the Market Place stark bollock naked.'

If Billy hadn't been allowed his own way at the fire, things had changed quickly. Today, Danny had brought Mr Jake to see him. Billy was scared of the way Mr Jake looked at you. It made something inside Billy curl up with fright. He knew Danny was afraid of Mr Jake. And nothing frightened Danny. 'We want you to use your special talent, Billy,' Mr Jake had said. He put his arm around Billy's shoulders. Billy nearly wet himself with fear. 'Tonight. As soon as you can. And make it big. Make it spectacular. Got any ideas?'

So Billy had told him. 'Them units, Mr Jake. I've had my eye on them. Where the Immigrunts work. There's lots of flammables in them. They'd go up well.' And Mr Jake had laughed. Billy wasn't sure, but he didn't think he'd said anything funny.

'So that's what you call them, is it? Immigrunts. I like that. You know, Billy, I think that's just the place. Make it good, won't you. If it's really good, I'll pay for you to have free fanny for a month, how's that?'

Billy's puny chest swelled with pride. He was being paid. Not in money admittedly. Only in kind. But that was good enough. He'd never been paid before. Now he was a professional.

chapter twenty-two

Ricky Smart had been busy. Payment arrived that afternoon, courtesy of Jake Fletcher. 'I want distribution immediately. By that I mean today. You have the goods?'

'I've enough. What you've paid for anyway.'

'Just as well.'

'I can always get more.'

'You'd better, and fast. Those were the instructions.'

For a moment Ricky was tempted to argue. Two things stopped him: Jake's reputation, and the look in his eyes. 'Don't worry,' he told Fletcher. 'I can get as much as you need, within hours.'

'Do it.'

'What, now?'

'Yes, now. I want a fresh supply by ten tonight. Got that?'

Tonight was going to be immense. Ricky was tempted to ask what it was about, but better not to know. Better to remain ignorant, about this and other things. Like who was paying, was it connected to the fires, shootings and what had happened to Appleyard. Yes, definitely better not to know.

Jake was speaking to Danny, his voice low, barely above a whisper. 'Your cue is the fire. As soon as Billy gets it going, I want you to go round the estate. Tell them the immigrants killed Appleyard. Make Appleyard into a hero. Get everybody on the streets. Get them to show that ordinary folk aren't going to be bullied. If there's any doubters, deal hard. There'll be extra gear on offer if you perform well. Got that?'

Danny nodded. Slowly, skilfully, Jake fanned the flames of Danny's hatred. By the time he'd finished, the fire burning within Danny was fiercer than anything Billy could set. Fletcher had been told to achieve total breakdown of law and order on the Westlea, to organize a mass protest by the local population following the murder of their favourite leader. How had Rathmell put it? 'When the dust settles on this uprising we'll be the ones wielding power round here. We'll be the ones the locals look to for help and guidance. And you, Jake, will be second in the chain of command: second only to me.'

Fletcher found it difficult to hide his pleasure. Much as Frank Appleyard had when Rathmell had said the same thing to him. But Jake didn't know that.

Nash left the office around 6 p.m. Instead of heading home, he drove across town to Becky's flat. There was no reply when he rang her doorbell so he pressed it again. When he rang a third time without response he was beginning to get worried, until he saw movement reflected in the glass panel. She opened the door. She was wearing a towelling robe and her hair was wet.

'Sorry, I was in the shower.' She saw the look on his face. 'What's wrong?'

He pulled his copy of the *Gazette* from his pocket. 'Did you think that would help?' His voice was raised in anger.

Becky flinched. 'Let me see. I haven't read it yet. You'd better come in, as long as you stop shouting.'

'I'm not shouting,' he hissed. 'And why do you need to read it? You wrote it, for God's sake. Look! There's your name on the by-line. Becky Pollard. That is you, isn't it?'

She winced again. She wasn't sure which was worse, the shouting or the sarcasm. She took the paper and began to read. As she got towards the end her expression changed, darkened with what? Anger, embarrassment, shame? Nash couldn't be sure.

She lowered the newspaper and looked him in the eye. 'I didn't write this.' The denial was flat, emotionless, in contrast to his pent-up fury. 'None of this last bit was in the piece I sent in, and the headline isn't mine.'

'So why has it got your name on it?'

Instead of replying, she took his hand and dragged him into her study. She switched the computer on. The room was crowded, even with only two of them in it. She went into her e-mail file and selected sent items. 'There! Read that.'

Sure enough, her copy held none of the political overtones that had appeared in the paper. Nash leaned over to view the article as she'd presented it. They were standing close together. He smelt the fresh, clean scent of her. His head swam. His pulse raced. 'Becky, I'm sorry. I thought, well, I don't know what I thought. I was angry. I thought you'd done the dirty on me. It felt like a betrayal.'

She was staring straight ahead, stony-faced. He turned her towards him. 'Will you please forgive me?' He pulled her roughly to him and began to kiss her with an intensity that surprised even him. As he felt her respond, he slid his hand to the waist of her robe and undid the belt. He reached for her, to caress her, hearing her moan gently. Then she thrust him away, and turned her back on him. 'No, Mike,' she told him firmly. 'Not until I'm sure. Sure that you're free of ghosts. Two's enough in one bed.' She was glad he couldn't see the expression on her face. Glad he couldn't tell how hard she'd to fight her own desire. Knew she dare not look at him. If she saw one hint of sadness, of unhappiness in his face, the temptation to give way would be too much.

She was still trying to recover her composure when Nash's mobile rang. She turned to look at him as he answered the phone. Within a second Becky saw by his expression the news was bad. He was already halfway out of the room before he rang off.

'What's happened?'

'Trouble! On the Westlea. Two industrial units blazing and a mob stoning the fire brigade. I have to get over there.'

Becky reached her bedroom door. She left it open and picked up her bra. 'No, Mike. We have to go. Give me two minutes.' She flung the robe on the bed and Nash had a swift glimpse of her lovely figure. She emerged seconds later, fully dressed. 'By the way, I do forgive you.'

She picked up her camera on the move. 'Come on.' She held the door open for him.

Billy had made all his preparations with care. The unit contained a company making plastics. Plastic burned well. That was all he knew about plastics. He wasn't aware that if plastic caught fire, the flames would move faster than a man could run. Such technicalities were far beyond Billy.

He lined up his bottles. Wine bottles filled with petrol. The corks replaced with cotton wool. He'd seen criminals on telly picking locks to enter buildings. Billy didn't rate that much. He simply smashed the glass panel in with a lump of wood he found lying in the yard. The burglar alarm went off. It didn't bother him. In a few minutes they'd have more to worry about than a break-in.

Once he was inside, he went into the small offices huddled in the corner. There was a short corridor with toilets to one side, a small reception area, a general office and the manager's office. Billy lit one of the wicks, opened the manager's door and tossed the first of his petrol bombs inside. He repeated the process in the general office and reception. The corner containing the door he'd entered by was now effectively sealed off. Billy didn't realize, or perhaps he was beyond caring. He looked at the rows of shelves containing stacks of plastic sheeting. Then he saw a collection of bins in the opposite corner, close to the roller-shutter door. The first one he came to was half full of liquid. Billy didn't recognize the smell. He paused. Would it burn? Worth a try. He lit another wick and tossed the bomb inside.

Danny watched Billy enter the building. He was standing no more than fifty yards away, alongside Jake Fletcher. It gave them an excellent view. 'Right, go get your troops to stir the mob up. As soon as Billy's out, and the fire catches hold, I'll dial the fire brigade. They're your first target. They're bound to call the police for protection. That's when you must change your attack. The pigs are our main target. Remember they're the ones who did for Ronnie.'

Danny set off towards the garages, where the Juniors would be gathered. They'd had their gear – now they'd have to earn it. The bonus would come later. Danny had only taken a few steps when there was a terrific explosion behind him. He spun round. At first he thought somebody had shot Jake. Fletcher was lying on his back, near where Danny had left him. Then he realized the sound had been too loud for a gunshot. He turned to his right and stared in horrified disbelief.

Half of the single-skin brick wall had been blown out. Fire was already engulfing the building. 'Billy!' Danny's cry was choked as he saw his brother emerge.

Billy stood in the centre of the hole. His eyes, crazed as if by drugs, stared straight at Danny. But Danny knew Billy couldn't see him. His head flung back and he bellowed a huge shout of triumphant laughter. Laughter that turned into a scream. Billy staggered and Danny saw with fresh horror that the whole of his back was alight. Not just alight, but an inferno. His clothing had been melted to his skin. Billy was a human torch. Before Danny could move or say anything the fireball reached out and consumed its creator. Danny saw Billy disappear, engulfed by a wall of flame. He heard a long, piercing scream of pure and absolute agony. Then there was silence. Silence; broken only by the muffled ringing of the burglar alarm and the intensifying crackle of the flames.

Jake sat up. He'd been blown off his feet by the blast. He shook his head, trying to clear the ringing sound, then realized it was the alarm. He swallowed and his hearing returned. He looked round for Billy. There was no sign of the youth. Danny too had disappeared. Within minutes Fletcher heard a fresh sound: the sonorous wail of sirens. He watched the appliances screech to a halt. The unit where Billy had set the fire was beyond rescue. The firemen would have their work cut out to save the other buildings. As they were deploying, Fletcher saw a knot of spectators forming a short distance away.

He moved towards a bank of trees and scanned the crowd. He saw several faces he recognized. Young faces. Vicious faces. Danny had roused the Juniors. Now they were moving amongst the onlookers; turning a crowd into a mob. He heard a sound, the swell of discontented chatter. Soon he recognized anger in the noise. Then a man reached down and seized a piece of broken paving slab. He threw it.

It was pure luck that the stone found its target. Even luckier for the fireman, his helmet took the brunt before he pitched forward, stunned by the blow to the head. The crowd began looking for missiles. There were plenty about. Singly at first, then in a more concentrated bombardment, the stones and pieces of wood began to rain down amongst the fire crews. One of the mob sneaked up to the rearmost appliance and sliced through the hoses. Water spewed around the engine. The jet that might have saved a building died to a trickle. Fletcher heard more sirens. This time it would be the police. There weren't sufficient in Helmsdale to contain this mob, whose numbers were growing by the second, too many to count. Jake guessed there to be over eighty.

Becky pointed into the distance at the plume of smoke. 'Look at that. That's a hell of a blaze.'

Nash took his eyes off the road for a split second. 'Well organized.'

She frowned. 'What do you mean?'

'Every attack, whether it's a shooting, knifing or arson, seems carefully timed to interact with our investigation.' He glanced sideways and saw her look of surprise. 'Don't tell me you haven't noticed? It's all being carefully orchestrated.'

'What are you going to do?'

'When we get there? Not much I can do. There's Viv and me plus half a dozen uniforms until reinforcements arrive. Try and protect the fire brigade, that's about it.'

'Be careful.'

'Listen to your own advice then. Keep well back. I don't want to have to spend all the time trying to protect you.'

'I can take care of myself.'

'Not against a mob you can't. At least I'm armed.'

'You're not planning to use it, are you? Your pistol, I mean?'

'Not unless I have to. I don't like the bloody things. Using it would be the last resort.'

They were still almost a mile away from the industrial estate when Nash heard the sirens. He glanced in his rear-view mirror and saw the flashing red and blue lights. He pulled to one side and watched as the trio of vans swept past. 'Your men are quick,' Becky said.

'Aren't they just.' Nash pulled the car to a standstill. 'Except that those men aren't from Helmsdale.'

'I don't understand.'

'Helmsdale hasn't enough men to fill one of those vans. They're from Netherdale.'

'But if you've only had chance to get across town, how come they've arrived so quickly?'

'That's a very good question. An extremely good question. Not the first time I've asked myself that.'

'Care to explain?'

'Later, perhaps, when the dust settles. Anyway, I reckon those guys will sort the trouble out. No need for us to hurry. When we get there, we'll park a discreet distance from the action. I'd like you to take plenty of photos.' He reached for his phone. 'Tom, Mike Nash. Your men are here in Helmsdale.' Apart from the occasional grunt, he made almost no further contribution to the call.

They arrived at the industrial estate and Becky started to record the scene. 'Have you got the timer record facility in use?'

'I never switch it off.'

'Good. I want some close-up shots, please.'

'No problem. It'd be difficult if the mob was wearing masks or hoods.'

'I'm not interested in the mob. I want you to take photos of the police.'

Becky lowered the camera and stared at Nash. 'You're joking?' Then saw the expression on his face. 'You're not joking.'

'Never been more serious.'

Nash watched her for a few seconds. Then his mobile rang. 'Hi, Mike, it's Lisa.'

'Anything doing?'

'There was plenty of action earlier. Rathmell had a couple of visitors. You'll never guess who one of them was.'

Nash said a name.

'How did you guess?' Lisa asked. 'Oh, it wasn't a guess, was it? Anyway, they left and Gemma arrived. She's just gone. I rang you because I heard about the riot on Helm Radio. Wondered if you need help?'

'Did you really?' Nash glanced at his watch. It showed 7.15 p.m. 'Was that a newsflash or one of the regular bulletins?'

'The seven o'clock news. Why, is it important?'

'I think so. I'm interested to know how they found out about the riot five minutes before I got to know.'

Fletcher watched a flashing display of lights which signalled the arrival of three vans. These would be from Netherdale. The riot shields in front of the windscreens were taking a battering from the stone throwers, even before they reached the scene. The rear doors of the vans opened almost in unison. Helmeted officers sprang from each. Armed officers; riot shields up. They moved relentlessly forwards.

The crowd dispersed, parting briefly to allow the police passage. Then began throwing stones. There were several soft explosions and Fletcher saw what appeared to be smoke spreading among the crowd. 'Tear gas,' he muttered.

The wind took the gas and Fletcher saw it spread; heard the coughing, choking sounds. The riot police were forced to withdraw or suffer along with their attackers. The mob retreated in disarray. His attention was distracted momentarily by a car. It arrived quietly, coasting to a halt only yards from where Jake was concealed. A couple got out, unseen or unnoticed by everyone bar Fletcher. He didn't recognize the woman. The man he knew only too well. 'Nash,' he breathed. 'What the hell's he doing? Why isn't he in amongst the rest? And who's that with him?'

He saw the girl reach back in the car and remove something. He wasn't sure what, until she lifted it head high. It was a camera. He saw Nash pointing. Directed by Nash, the girl was taking photographs; recording the scene. Fletcher was in a quandary. He knew Nash was the danger, wanted him out of the equation. But Fletcher was alone. And Nash was armed. He knew that because he'd been told Nash would be carrying.

The mob hadn't dispersed. That was never the plan. The police charge had been met with only token resistance. When the officers advanced, the crowd separated into groups and moved away, down the maze of intersecting streets. There they would re-form and seek new targets. At the head of each group was a member of the Juniors. They had their plan and knew their role to perfection. Hardly surprising, as they'd been coached in it for days.

From their vantage point Nash and Becky watched the retreat. 'That was very tame,' she said.

'Too tame. I don't like the look of this. I don't like it at all.' Nash pulled out his mobile.

'Tom? Where are you?'

'Just coming into the estate. How are things looking?'

Nash gave him a quick rundown. 'It's too well organized. As if they knew what they'd be up against and how to deal with it. What concerns me is what they'll do once they're out of reach.'

'I'll be there in a few minutes. What do you suggest?'

'Who's in charge of the uniforms?'

'Jack Binns is running the guys with shields and batons. Creepy's headed up the ARU.'

'I suggest you split them. Put some of the blokes in riot gear into groups with one or two armed men. Follow the rioters. Do what they're doing. Split up and walk through the estate. I think they'll either regroup, or form small attack units. This doesn't seem like a spontaneous uprising. It all looks carefully orchestrated.'

'Any ideas as to their targets?'

'At a guess, migrant workers and their property. All done in the name of, and in memory of, Appleyard.'

'Are you out of harm's way?'

'As you ordered, Tom. For once I'm following instructions.'

'And have you any more thoughts about tonight?'

'Oh yes, Tom. As soon as this is over, I'm going to start asking questions.' Nash disconnected and stood watching.

'What was that all about?' Becky asked.

'When I spoke to the superintendent earlier, he ordered me to stay clear of trouble. He wasn't prepared to have me finish up as the victim of a mob. Not when there were reinforcements on the scene. He told me to keep a watching brief.'

'That's not all though, is it? What about your conspiracy theory? About the way the mob acted?'

'You mean the fact that they're being controlled? That the level of violence is just enough to grab newspaper headlines and be put out in radio bulletins? Or the fact that for the second time in the past few days, police from Netherdale arrived suspiciously quickly; quicker than those from Helmsdale? I can't comment yet. Not on the record.'

Nash scanned the scene in front of him. A movement in his peripheral vision caught his attention. 'Lend me your camera a sec.'

Becky passed it over. 'How do you work the telephoto?'

'Twist the barrel of the camera. When it's fully extended, that's your close-up. Turn it the other way for wide angle.'

Using the camera as a telescope, Nash concentrated on the figure he'd glimpsed on the outskirts of the mob. He kept the camera steady. 'Get my mobile out of my pocket. Press redial and hold it to my ear, will you? I don't want to lose sight of this character.'

He waited for his call to connect. 'Tom? I need a group of lads to chase someone down. Four should be enough. As long as one of them is armed.'

Danny took a swig from the flask. The neat spirit was harsh, painful almost. He didn't mind that. It was what he needed. That and the drugs he'd taken, needed, to cope. The war he was in had claimed Billy's life. Danny knew who to blame. Now it was payback time. All he needed was a target.

It didn't take long for him to find one; or rather two. Two men heading home through the estate, steering well clear of the violent mob. Men Danny recognized. Juris and another worker from the farm. He took another hefty swig from his flask. Time for action and this time there'd be no mistake. This time he wouldn't leave everything to chance. This time he'd not risk missing them. He'd walk right up to them. Stick his gun in their scrawny bellies and pull the trigger.

It took him longer to get close to them than he'd banked on. Partly because they were walking quicker than he'd expected, and partly because he didn't want to show himself until the last minute. They were within sight of their house when he reached them. He pulled the pistol from his pocket and walked up to Juris.

Danny had been so preoccupied, he'd not seen anything. Not heard anything. His finger was actually curling round the trigger when he heard a sound. In the same instant he saw a blur of movement to his right. Then a sharp pain shot through his hand. He heard the crunch of breaking bone. As he cried out, he saw what was happening clearly. Saw the baton swing back. Then down. He squealed in agony; dropped the gun. Then felt a second blow across his shoulders. Then a third at the back of his knees. Danny howled, staggered; then ran.

'Mike? Jack Binns. Danny Floyd's escaped. We caught up with him. He was about to off a couple of migrant workers. Our lads fetched him a few good whacks, but he bolted down one of the alleys. We chased him, but this place is a warren. Could be anywhere by now. One good thing though. We've recovered his gun; dropped it when he was hit.'

Bereft of their leader, the Juniors began to lose heart. The amount they'd ingested didn't help. The riot petered out; the mob disappeared. A few went home, more gathered in The Wagon and Horses. The Westlea troubles were over. Not counting Billy Floyd's death, the most serious casualties were Danny's broken fingers and a scalp wound for one of the firemen.

Nash met Pratt outside the industrial units. The fire was under control now. As they stood watching, Doug Curran joined them and said, 'We've had reports that there was someone inside when the blaze started. Probably the bloke who torched the place. You'll not need a cremation service. With this wind, he'll be all over the county by morning.'

'Doug, sometimes you're a sick bastard.'

Curran grinned cheerfully. 'I'll leave one of you to phone Mexican Pete and the forensics.' He waved farewell.

Pratt watched him depart. 'I'll see to that. What's your next move?'

'I've got to check on Vickers. Then I'm going home, hopefully to get some kip.'

'Anything you want from me?'

'There is something.' Nash told him what he wanted.

'Right, I'll fax the details in the morning. Care to explain?'

Nash shook his head. 'I'd prefer to leave it until I'm certain.'

*

Nash returned to Becky. 'Let me give you a lift home.'

'Are you going to Grove Road? That would mean doubling back. Do that first, then drop me off.'

'Right, let's go. I've had enough of the Westlea for one night.'

The armed guard reported that all was quiet, both inside and out. 'Vickers is very much on edge,' the man told him. 'I think he wants a word with you.'

'I'll see what he wants.'

Becky joined him as he went up to the door. 'You don't have to come in if you don't want.'

'You're not leaving me out.'

Nash could tell Vickers was restless. 'What's eating you?'

'Have you made any progress? Finding out who killed Stacey, I mean?'

'I'm nearly sure I know who killed her,' Nash told him quietly. 'All we need is more evidence.'

Vickers looked at him oddly. 'I'm going to bed now. One of the minders will let you out.'

When the door closed behind Vickers, Becky asked, 'Are you serious? You think it was Gemma or Carlton Rathmell, don't you? Does that mean they murdered JT as well?'

'Oh yes,' Nash said calmly. 'The problem is the only evidence I have in either case is circumstantial. Short of a confession, I can't see a hope in hell of proving it. I don't honestly think we'll ever bring the killer to trial.'

'Have you any idea which of them actually committed the murders?'

Nash's mind went back a couple of days. He was standing in a shop in the Market Place. Becky saw the distant look on his face and wondered again about Nash's thought processes. This was what her godmother had described, she guessed.

It was a shop Nash had never been in before. The owner was surrounded by stacks of CDs and assorted musical instruments. 'Do you stock piano wire?' Nash asked him.

Between listening to the man's complaint that he sold so little it wasn't worth keeping it, except as a service for a few dwindling customers, Nash gleaned the information he was seeking. The names of those who'd bought piano wire recently. There were very few, but one name stood out. A woman's name. A woman who'd bought piano wire within the last week, and also fifteen years earlier. The shopkeeper knew her well; had good reason to. A reason he explained to Nash. And when he heard that name, Nash knew the identity of the killer.

Nash returned to the present. 'Yes, I know which of them did the actual killing, the one who killed both Stacey and Tucker. But I'll never be able to prove it. How can I stand a chance of telling whether both parties knew about the murders beforehand? I suspect they did, but I'm not sure it really matters. In my eyes they're equally guilty.'

On the other side of the door Gary Vickers listened intently. Nash had grown to like Vickers. He believed the convicted killer to be a pleasant, easygoing character. As Nash was speaking, there was nothing likeable about Vickers' expression. It was neither pleasant nor easygoing.

Becky hopped out of the car when Nash pulled up. 'Go get some sleep,' she told him. 'I'm going to work on my report of tonight's fun and games. I'll bring it round to your place in the morning. I'd rather you saw it before I send it in.'

'There's no need, Becks. I trust you.'

'I know.' She smiled brightly. 'But I want to. And you should be able to get some rest, now all the trouble's died down.'

chapter twenty-three

Gemma Fletcher had always been an early riser. She was up and about by 7.15. By 8 a.m. she was showered and dressed. She sat on a bar stool in her kitchen with a mug of coffee, going through the paperwork she'd need. When the doorbell rang she glanced at the clock. Too early for the postman; it could be a parcel. But she wasn't expecting anything. She went to the door and opened it slightly. Not wide. This was the Westlea after all.

Her visitor pushed the door open. 'You!' She gasped. 'What are you doing here?' She looked down. Saw what was in her visitor's hand. Her knees trembled with fear.

Nash slept so soundly he didn't hear the bell the first time it rang. He staggered to the door and peered blearily out. 'Becks! What are you doing here? What time is it?'

'I said I'd bring that article over, remember? And it's 8.30. I take it you've just got out of bed?'

'I wouldn't have, if somebody hadn't leaned on the doorbell. Come through.'

Nash read the copy. 'That looks fine, but remember, I didn't ask for it. You can't be censored by us before you go into print.'

'Normally I'd agree. But you've made me privy to things a reporter doesn't usually hear. That means I've to be extra careful not to violate the confidence.'

'I wish all reporters were like you.' He slid a glance at her. 'In more ways than one. Before I leave, I'd better check everything's OK at Grove Road. Excuse me a minute.'

He used his mobile to ring Vickers' number. It was one of the officers who answered. 'Yes, it was quiet all night. The biggest problem was keeping awake.'

'What about Vickers?'

'Don't know. He hasn't surfaced yet.'

'And I thought I was late rising.' Nash frowned. 'He doesn't usually sleep in; fifteen years of prison routine stopped that. Go check on him. I'll hold on.' He attempted to fill the kettle, one handed. 'What! How did that happen?' Nash listened. 'Right, leave it to me. Stay there. The house still needs protecting.'

'I don't bloody believe it,' he said as he disconnected. 'Vickers has done a runner – again.'

'When?'

'By the sound of it, sometime early this morning. His bed was slept in, still warm apparently. But the back bedroom window was open. He must have climbed onto the flat roof of the kitchen. Now he's roaming about Helmsdale with Jake Fletcher and his cronies after him. Just what I need.'

But Nash was wrong. Vickers was no longer the prey. He was the hunter.

Nash was still pondering this development when his mobile rang again. He glanced at the display. 'Yes, Viv.'

'We've had a sighting of Danny Floyd on the Westlea. By all accounts stoned out of his mind; sitting in the gutter, crying his eyes out.'

'Whereabouts?'

'That's the strange part. Apparently he's outside Gemma Fletcher's place.'

'Take some uniforms. I'll meet you there.'

Nash looked round. Becky was watching him. 'Want a slice of the action?'

'Try keeping me away.'

'In that case, you drive. I might need to use the phone.'

'The downside of all this preferential treatment is I finish up as a glorified chauffeur,' Becky grumbled.

'Regard it as a public service.'

'Where are we headed?'

Nash gave her the address and explained as she drove. They arrived at the same time as Pearce. Sure enough, Floyd was half sitting, half lying at the edge of the pavement. He would have been flat out but for the road sign propping him up. Nash signalled to the others to stay back.

'Danny.' He spoke slowly and clearly, as if to a deaf man. 'Danny, can you hear me?'

Floyd squinted up at the voice. 'Nash, Nash, copper to bash,' he chanted. 'Got my orders, got my orders, bash Nash, bash Nash.'

Nash smiled grimly. 'Who else had you orders for, Danny?'

'Vickers, Vickers, frilly knickers. Seen him, seen him, tried to bean him.'

'Seen him? Seen who?'

Floyd was rambling; Nash couldn't be sure who he was talking about from one sentence to the next.

'Seen him, seen him, tried to bean him.'

'Yes, Danny, we know that. But who have you seen?'

'Vickers, frilly knickers, Vickers. Seen him, seen him.'

'You've seen Vickers, have you?'

'Seen him.'

'Where did you see him? And when?'

Two questions at once was too much. Floyd lapsed into silence.

'Where did you see Vickers, Danny?'

'Gemma Fletcher, gonna getcha, gonna getcha.'

'You saw Vickers here? With Gemma Fletcher?'

'Where's the slag, where's the slag?'

'Did you talk to Vickers? Danny, listen! Did ... you ... talk ... to Vickers?'

'Where's the slag live? Where's the slag live?'

'Vickers asked you where Gemma Fletcher lives? Is that right?'

'In the car, not too far.'

'Vickers left here with Gemma Fletcher? Is that what you're telling me, Danny? In Gemma's car?'

It was a question too much. Floyd slid sideways onto the pavement and lay staring sightlessly.

'Get an ambulance,' Nash told Pearce. 'Get him to Netherdale General as quick as you can. God knows what he's been taking. Stay with him and when he's fit enough, stick him in a cell.'

'What about Vickers?'

'I'll deal with him. I'm more concerned with Gemma Fletcher's safety. If there was any truth in Danny's ramblings, Vickers has Gemma hostage. He thinks she killed Stacey. If we don't find them quickly, I don't give much for her chances.' Nash's phone rang. He answered and listened intently. Eventually he spoke. 'Oh no! When did it happen?' He listened again. 'Where is he?' After a pause he said, 'Keep me up to date, will you? I'd come through, but I can't as things are. Thanks, Jack.'

He lowered the phone and stared blankly ahead.

'What is it?'

Nash looked at Becky as if she wasn't there. His gaze transferred to Pearce, who was in the middle of organizing the ambulance. He beckoned the DC over. 'Bad news, Viv. Tom Pratt's collapsed in his office; suspected heart attack. He's been taken to Intensive Care at Netherdale. Too early to say how bad it is. When you get there, see what you can find out? Binns promised to keep me up to date, but as you'll be in the building you might be able to learn more.'

'I'll do my best. Poor Tom.'

Pearce turned away and went to check on Floyd. Becky laid a sympathetic hand on Nash's arm. 'I'm sorry, Mike. Mr Pratt's such a nice bloke. You're pretty close to him, aren't you?'

Nash nodded. 'Tom's one of the best. Not just as a copper. And yes, we work really well together. I trust him. When Tom says he'll do something, it always gets done.'

'How will this affect what's happening?'

Nash tried to force his mind back to the situation in hand. 'It isn't going to make life any easier, that's for sure. For one thing I'll now be reporting directly to DCC King. And won't that be fun,' he added sourly.

He should be concentrating on what had happened to Gemma Fletcher. Had she been kidnapped or had she gone with Vickers of her own free will? Nash thought it unlikely. But if he'd taken her, how had he coerced her? He wasn't armed. Or at least he hadn't been. Had he collected a weapon en route? If so, how and where? And what would it be? Nash couldn't think straight. The news about Tom Pratt had knocked him sideways. 'Bloody hell! I can't concentrate,' he fumed.

'Mike, you have to,' Becky urged him. 'There's nobody else. And I'm sure Superintendent Pratt wouldn't want you worrying about him at the expense of solving this case. Or rescuing somebody from danger.'

Nash was still trying to marshal his thoughts when his mobile rang. It was the officer at Vickers' house. 'What now?'

'Sorry, sir.' Over the officer's voice, Nash could hear another.

'Who's that?'

'Next-door neighbour. Came round to complain as soon as she could. She'd have been here earlier, but she'd to take the kids to school. Apparently she saw Vickers leaving.'

'What's she complaining about?'

The officer explained. Nash was still trying to make sense of this, and to puzzle out where Vickers had gone, when his mobile rang again. Nash glanced at his watch. It was almost 10.15. If Vickers had taken Gemma out of town, they could be anywhere by now. Anywhere within a fifty-mile radius. Needles in haystacks would be easier to find. He answered the phone, dreading what this call might tell him. Becky could see the tension in his face relax as he realized who the caller was. 'Lisa. I've some bad news for you I'm afraid.'

He told her about Pratt. 'But we've still got a job to do. And what's happened this morning means it's far from over yet.'

'What do you mean, what's happened?'

'Vickers has got away from the officer protecting him and kidnapped Gemma Fletcher. Or that's what we think has happened. Unfortunately we've only Danny Floyd's word for that. And he's spaced out and not making sense. Are you at Rathmell's place?'

'Yes. Do you still need me to watch him, or have you anything else for me to do?'

'No, hang on there. There's a chance Vickers will pole up with Gemma. Give me a bell if anything happens.'

Nash began wandering aimlessly around. In the distance the high-pitched wail of an ambulance siren could be heard. Nash looked over at where Pearce and the other officers were standing round the coma-tose figure. Someone had put Floyd into the recovery position. Nash walked across. 'How is he?'

Pearce felt Danny's pulse. 'Still living,' he reported. 'Pulse is erratic, but I suppose that's to be expected.'

Nash turned to the others. 'I'm going to need you two, after you've seen to this.' He pointed to Floyd. 'So get back in the van and wait for fresh orders. Hopefully by then I'll have had a flash of inspiration.'

Nash wandered off towards the building where Gemma Fletcher lived. Becky thought she could guess what was going through his mind. Trying to puzzle out what Vickers was planning. Why had he taken Gemma? Where had he gone with her? And what was he going to do?

As he was struggling for inspiration, his mobile rang again. 'Mike, it's Lisa. Rathmell's just left the Grange in a tearing hurry. Damn near took the gatepost with him. Do you want me to stay here, or follow him?'

In an instant Nash's mind cleared. Now he knew what Vickers had in mind. 'Follow him, Lisa. And make sure you don't lose him. Rathmell's our only hope of finding Gemma.'

Nash signalled to the team. He made a wind-up motion. 'Ring me when you've some idea where he's headed, Lisa. You've got hands-free, haven't you?'

'No problem.'

'Thank God for technology.'

'Sorry, Becks, we might have to move at a moment's notice. This could get nasty, and I can't take the risk of you getting hurt.' He smiled at her. 'I'm not putting you in harm's way. We've been lucky a few times. I don't want to push our luck. You mean too much. Besides,' he added, straight-faced, 'I don't want to risk your godmother's wrath.'

'Don't worry. I can walk back to town. But let me know when it's over. And be careful, Mike. Please be careful.'

Nash watched her walk away. He didn't want her to go. He wanted to run after her and bring her back. He sighed. She'd really got to him. The fact that he was missing her when she was still within sight proved that. Now he had to do some proving of his own. He had to convince her there were no ghosts. No dead lovers or memories of other girls. But that would be for later. For the present he had a job to do. And it was the hardest part of a policeman's job. Waiting.

'We're heading towards Helmsdale,' Lisa told him. 'Just coming up to the ring road. Hang on; he's signalling to turn left.'

As Lisa spoke, Nash realized where Rathmell was going; knew where Vickers had taken Gemma, and why.

'He's heading for Helm Woods, towards the river,' Nash told her. 'That's where Vickers has gone. He's taken Gemma to the place where Stacey was killed.'

Gemma was scared. She'd never been so terrified in her life. She was used to being in control. Always got what she wanted, either by her own efforts or with the help of her brothers. She knew what she wanted and she'd have it, no matter who got in her way.

Now she was alone and terrified. She was in the hands of a man she'd used and discarded. A man who'd come seeking revenge. In the last few minutes Gemma had learnt why he needed revenge, and how terrible that revenge would be. Now she knew how, and why, she was going to die.

Her plight was desperate, her position precarious; hands tied behind her back, a noose round her neck. She was standing on the branch of a huge fir tree. On the edge of the clearing she knew so well. One slip and she'd be dead. The drop was no more than fifteen feet. Gemma was only five feet six inches tall. The noose chafed her neck. But that was the least of her worries. By a long way.

'Rathmell will probably turn into the car park next to the picnic area,' Nash told Lisa. 'Drive past slowly; you'll probably see Gemma's car there. Park further down the lane and wait for us. We'll be ten minutes or so.'

Nash hadn't reckoned on the terrain and the time of year. Narrow country lanes, a tractor and trailer loaded with round bales, the driver oblivious to the sirens and flashing lights. Nash cursed and edged out. Every time he got a straight bit of road there was a vehicle coming in the other direction. Nor did his siren help. The tractor driver had ear defenders on, attached to his iPod. With Led Zeppelin blasting through the earphones, Nash didn't stand a chance.

At last, the farmer turned off. Nash surged forward and within seconds spotted DC Andrews' car. He drove into the car park with the squad van in close attendance. Seconds later Lisa pulled in.

'The place we're heading for is the clearing where Tucker was found. The situation's delicate. Vickers has taken Gemma Fletcher hostage. I want a softly-softly approach. When we get close, I want you to spread out behind me. Understood?'

Rathmell reached the clearing. There was no sign of life. Then he heard a slight noise, like a muffled scream. Movement caught his peripheral vision. His mouth opened with shock. He sensed someone close at hand. He felt a sudden pain at the back of his head. Then everything went black. 'Hello, Carl,' a voice said in his ear. But Rathmell was beyond hearing.

Nash heard the sound first. He held up a hand, motioning them to stop. He signalled Lisa forward. 'Do you hear that?' he whispered.

Lisa strained to catch the slightest noise. Then she heard it. 'It sounds …' She stopped. It was too incongruous. 'It's somebody whistling. Isn't it?'

Nash nodded, his face grim as he edged forward cautiously. He saw something move on his left. He walked quickly round to the far side of the clearing, close to the banks of the Helm, sheltered by a bank of ancient and massive trees.

Hardened as he was, Nash almost vomited. Vickers was on his knees. The front of his jeans and T-shirt were liberally daubed with a mixture of blood, brains and cranial fluid. Nash watched in horror as Vickers wielded the 7lb lump hammer. Time and again he lifted it and brought it crashing down. As it struck, it made a soft, squelching sound. With each strike Vickers' clothing received a fresh splattering.

Vickers continued to whistle as he continued to strike. He whistled, even though his victim must have been long dead. He whistled, even though his victim was by now unrecognizable. As Nash listened he recognized the tune, recognized it, and its sick significance.

Maxwell's Silver Hammer.

'Gary,' Nash spoke gently, 'put the hammer down, please.'

Vickers looked up and gave Nash a dreamy smile. He seemed perplexed by Nash's request. 'Hello, Mr Nash,' he greeted the detective brightly. 'I've become politically active. Mr Carlton Rathmell said the ordinary people of this country need to stand up and be counted. I read it in the paper. He said they need to take direct action to get a fair deal for themselves. So that's what I've done. Such sensible advice, don't you think?'

Nash looked down at the corpse.

Vickers was calm, unnaturally calm. 'Have you met Mr Carlton Rathmell?' He gestured to the remains. His voice lowered to a reverential tone. 'He's a very important man, you know. A member of the European Parliament, no less. What do you think about that?'

'Gary.' Nash fought to keep his voice calm. He didn't feel calm. 'Where's Gemma? What have you done with Gemma?'

'Gemma?' Vickers giggled insanely. 'Oh, she's hanging around somewhere. She's always hanging around when Rathmell's about. Did you know they were lovers, Mr Nash? I didn't. I hadn't the slightest suspicion. And him a married man too. Don't you think that's naughty, Mr Nash? I do. I think they should be punished. Yes. Punished.' He lifted the hammer once more and brought it down with a sickening thud. 'I'd no idea. None at all. Not until Stacey told me, but I wish she'd told me who,' he said somewhat wistfully. 'But, yes,' he repeated, 'I do believe Gemma's hanging around somewhere.'

Vickers seemed to find this immeasurably funny. It was a few seconds before he calmed down. Then, to Nash's horror, he started whistling again. *Norwegian Wood.* What on earth did that mean in Vickers' tormented brain? Nash looked around, for clues, inspiration, anything.

A gentle breeze ruffled the trees. It was then Nash saw Gemma, and realized why Vickers had stolen his neighbour's clothes line. Gemma was beneath the branch of a large fir tree. Her face was purple, constricted by the line around her neck. As the breeze strengthened, her body swung, in time with the leaves, in time with Vickers' whistling. A stray inappropriate thought crossed Nash's mine. Was the fir tree Norwegian? Shock, he realized had almost taken control. Hysteria wasn't far away.

'Gary.' Nash again fought to keep his voice calm. 'Don't you think we should go now? We should leave this place.'

Vickers had been watching him, waiting for his reaction. Nash's suggestion seemed to shock him beyond measure. 'Leave them alone, Mr Nash? I don't think that would be right and proper. Do you think it would be wise? Heaven knows what sort of wickedness they might get up to if we leave them alone. You don't know them like I do. I know what they're capable of, you see.' He lowered his voice and continued in a confidential tone. 'I made the mistake of leaving them alone once, and they murdered Stacey. They killed her, because she threatened them, and their dirty little affair.' He began to cry.

'They can't harm anyone now, Gary,' Nash comforted him. 'You've seen to that.'

Vickers stared at the detective for a long, silent moment, then looked across at where Gemma hung from the tree. He glanced down at Rathmell's corpse and a slow smile of satisfaction spread across his face. 'I have, haven't I? Do you think Stacey will be pleased, when I tell her?'

'I'm sure she will. Now come on, let's be going.'

Nash helped Vickers to his feet. He motioned to the others to keep back. He didn't bother with handcuffs. Vickers was quiet now, a spent force. He cast a glance back as they left the clearing. Lisa ran to Gemma and checked her pulse. She turned to Nash and shook her head. The sight of Gemma's body seemed to comfort Vickers. He allowed Nash to lead him back down the path towards the car park. Nash handcuffed him and handed him over to the uniformed men. 'Take him back to Helmsdale station. Make sure he's not able to harm himself. Lisa, get onto Mexican Pete and SOCO, would you.'

Nash watched them put Vickers into the police car. For a brief moment Vickers stared out of the window towards the detective. But Nash guessed all Vickers could see was Stacey. Then, as the car pulled away, Nash heard the sound of a voice raised in song. As the words filtered through the driver's window, he recognized the melody. *Yesterday*. Nash shuddered. There was an awful, appropriate irony in the words. Yesterday was all Vickers had left.

Nash saw Lisa was busy on the phone. He walked into the shelter of the trees and leaned against a massive oak. Reaction overtook him. He began to tremble. Before he knew it, he started to cry. Not for Rathmell, and not for Gemma. He wept for Stacey, for Gary, and for all the other victims.

Eventually he recovered and glanced back at the car park. Lisa was still on the phone. He took out his mobile. 'Becks,' he said quietly, 'it's over.'

chapter twenty-four

Viv had joined them in the woods on his return from Netherdale.
'They reckon Floyd will recover, but he won't be compos mentis until
tomorrow at the earliest. By the way, you remember that rumour? The
one that said the arsonist went up in his own fire? I bumped into
Mexican Pete when I was leaving the hospital. He said they'd been
able to recover some bone fragments. They might be able to pull some
DNA from it. He was taking the sample to the lab, then he's coming
straight over.'

'I want you to pull Jake Fletcher in. Don't tell him Gemma's dead.
I want that to come as a surprise. Before you go, I want you to apply
for a search warrant. It's urgent, so don't waste any time. If possible,
I want to be able to execute it later this evening.'

Nash gave Pearce the details. Pearce wrote the address down in his
notebook. When he left the crime scene fifteen minutes later, he was
still puzzling over Nash's request.

By 6 p.m. Nash made it back to the office. The day had been wearisome. Hamstrung by the lack of available personnel, Nash had been
unable to request assistance. He could have asked, but with Pratt
unavailable, knew he'd be wasting his breath.

The news from Netherdale General was as noncommittal as
hospital bulletins usually are. 'Comfortable' and 'as well as can be
expected' were all Nash could get.

Before going to interview Jake Fletcher, Nash collected a file from his
desk. He checked the contents as he walked along the corridor. Only
when he was satisfied did he open the door.

Fletcher was sitting opposite Pearce. Of the two, he looked the
more relaxed. Probably because he'd had the less stressful day, Nash
thought. Well, he'd soon change that.

'Thank you for joining us, Jake.' Nash nodded to Pearce, who went to set up the tape machine. 'Now, we've had a bit of a day of it here, so I'd like to get on. First of all I have some bad news. Your sister was killed this morning.'

Nash saw Fletcher's face drain of colour. 'What?' Fletcher croaked.

'I'm afraid so. She was murdered in Helm Woods. Close to where your niece was killed.'

Eventually Fletcher asked, 'How was she killed?' His voice was shaky and Nash saw his hands trembling. The iron man was coming apart.

'She was strangled.' Nash was letting the information out in dribs and drabs. 'There was another body close by.'

'Whose body?' Fletcher was struggling to take all this in.

'Carlton Rathmell, the MEP,' Nash told him. 'I believe you know Rathmell?'

'Was he strangled?'

'No, his head was beaten to a pulp with a lump hammer.'

Fletcher went even paler, if that was possible. Nash waited again. 'We've arrested someone in connection with the killings. There's no doubt this time that we've got the right man.'

'Who is it? And what do you mean, "no doubt this time"? What other time do you mean?'

'The man we arrested is Gary Vickers. We know he killed Gemma and Rathmell. Just as we know for certain he didn't kill Stacey.'

Fletcher jumped to his feet, the colour back in his face in abundance. 'That bastard! Let me at him. I'll kill the—'

'Sit down!' Nash's voice was like a whiplash. 'Now!' Nash continued. 'Some might call it murder. What he did today, I mean. Others would call it justice.'

'How do you mean, justice?'

'Justice or revenge. Of course, I can't condone it. But I can understand why. Because he knew that your sister and Rathmell killed Stacey. Just as they killed the journalist, Tucker.'

'I don't believe you. This is a cover-up. What motive could Gemma have for wanting Stacey dead? You know Vickers killed her. A jury convicted him. He raped her, then strangled her.'

'No, he didn't. He didn't rape her at all. Vickers was in love with Stacey and she was in love with him. Sure, they had sex together. As often as they could, by what Vickers told me.' Nash stilled Fletcher's protest with his hand. 'And I've got proof.'

'What proof? Why hasn't there been any mention of this proof before?'

'Because we only found it a few days ago. It's a letter from Stacey to Vickers, a love letter; and a warning.'

'That still doesn't mean Gemma killed Stacey. Her own daughter.'

'By what I've been told, there was never much love lost between Stacey and her mother. Certainly not the usual mother and daughter relationship. If Gemma felt threatened by Stacey, and was protecting someone, I don't think she'd have had any compunction in disposing of that threat.'

'Who's she supposed to be protecting?'

'Her lover: Carlton Rathmell. Either she killed Stacey, or he did. I can't say for sure which of them put the wire round Stacey's neck and choked her, but they certainly killed her, just as they killed Tucker, because he was also a threat.'

'Rathmell? Gemma's lover. I don't believe you. They hardly knew one another.'

Nash spilled a selection of photos onto the table. 'For the benefit of the tape I'm showing Mr Fletcher exhibit 3C. These were taken by Tucker before he was killed.'

Fletcher glanced at the images. Nash saw doubt in his eyes. He pulled more photos from the file. 'And these were taken by Stacey, exhibit 3A.'

As the doubt grew, Nash played his trump card. 'You might care to read this, Jake. It's the letter I told you about. The letter from Stacey to Gary. We found it at Grove Road. If we'd known about this all those years ago, everything that's happened since would have been avoided.'

As Fletcher was reading, Nash continued, 'The existence of this letter and those photos explains a lot. It explains the repeated attempts on Vickers' life, both when he was inside and after his release. It explains the break-ins and arson attack at Grove Road. Because Gemma and Rathmell were determined to silence Vickers, before he discovered this.' Nash indicated the paperwork. 'And when they failed to dispose of him in prison, they tried burglary. But Stacey had hidden the evidence too well for them. So they decided to burn the place down. A pretty tale, isn't it?'

Nash waited for Fletcher to digest this, then continued. 'Some people think this case is over, but I know there's more. I know Rathmell's been behind the trouble on the Westlea. He was responsible for organizing Floyd and his gang to make trouble. He was behind the attacks on the migrants. Both to further his own racist ideals, and to mask the attacks on Vickers. And I know he ordered the shooting of Appleyard.' He paused before adding, 'We have Danny Floyd in custody.'

The implication that Floyd had confessed worked. Nash could see what was left of Fletcher's confidence ebbing away. 'All I need from you is some additional information. It won't bring Stacey back. It won't bring Gemma back. Nor will it give Gary Vickers back the life that was taken from him. But you owe it to Stacey. You owe it to her and to Gary, for the life they'd have had together. They tell me you doted on her. You loved that girl as if she was your own daughter. Probably more than Gemma loved her. So it's up you, to put everyone connected with Rathmell behind bars. Rid yourself of the association. He was evil, Jake. Totally and utterly evil. I'll tell you a story to prove how evil Carlton Rathmell was.

'When I was investigating Tucker's murder, I went into the music shop in town. I wanted to find out if anyone had bought piano wire recently. The owner said, "I only have one customer for piano wire. And she only comes in every fifteen years."

'I asked him if he knew this customer. He said, "I should do – I sat next to her for five years at junior school."

'I asked him why he was sure it was fifteen years, because I didn't believe anyone could have that good a memory. So he told me, "Because it was the day before I got married. My father-in-law ran the shop whilst we went on honeymoon. If she'd come in a day later I wouldn't have seen her." That was when he told me her name, and the date. He never forgets his wedding anniversary.'

'Was it Gemma?' Fletcher's expression was tortured.

'No, Jake. I told you Rathmell was evil. The buyer was Vanessa Rathmell. He got his wife to buy the murder weapon used to kill the girl who was threatening his affair with his mistress.'

Now Fletcher was only too keen to reveal everything he knew about Rathmell. The information only acted to confirm what Nash already knew. But for Pearce, hearing it for the first time, it was like a thunderbolt.

On the way back to the CID suite, Nash was stopped by the receptionist. 'There've been a couple of calls for you. Or rather half a dozen calls but only from two people. DCC King has been on four times. And a Miss Pollard rang twice.'

'Any messages?'

'DCC King said he was going off duty, but you should speak to Inspector Crawley immediately you're available. He was very insistent.'

'He would be. You didn't tell him who I was interviewing, I hope?'

'No, he didn't ask.'

'Good. Did Miss Pollard leave a message?'

'She asked if you'd ring her, if you weren't too busy. She'd understand if you couldn't.'

From his office he rang Becky. 'Hi, Becks, how goes it?'

'Mike, are you OK?'

'I'm alright, I suppose. The thing with Vickers knocked me sideways. And I've just interviewed a witness, which was a bit harrowing in places.'

'Are you still busy?'

'I'm just waiting for Pearce. He's getting the witness statement transcribed. Then it has to be signed. After that we've a search warrant to execute. Or at least I was going to, but I'll probably defer it until morning.'

'Have you eaten?'

'Not yet. I'll probably grab a takeaway.'

'Why not come round here? I'll do a risotto or something?'

'I bet that was how Eve tempted Adam. Risotto sounds much better than a Granny Smith.'

'Give me a call when you're leaving.'

Nash put the phone down and smiled. His expression changed swiftly as he realized he still had to phone Crawley. He dialled again. 'I had a message. What do you want?' Nash's tone was on the abrupt side of curt.

'Nash, DCC King has been trying to contact you for several hours.'

'So? What do you want?'

'I've to inform you that DCC King expects you to report to his office at 10.30 a.m. tomorrow without fail.'

'Tell him to expect away.'

'I beg your pardon?'

'I'm busy in the morning. Can't make it.'

'DCC King said you'd to be there.'

'I know; heard you first time. No can do.'

'This attitude will do you no good, Nash. I'm warning you for the last time. You are expected at 10.30 prompt, tomorrow morning.'

'Crawley, are you learning impaired? Which part of the word *no* don't you understand? For the final time, I won't be there. Is that clear enough? Tell King I should be free sometime tomorrow afternoon. I'll see him then.'

Nash put the phone down as Pearce wandered in. 'They're typing Jake Fletcher's statement. I'll get it signed as soon as it's ready.' Pearce glanced at the clock. 'Do you want to do that other job tonight?'

'No, Viv, I've had enough for one day. Is Lisa still here?'

'She went off about half an hour ago, straight after she'd been to inform Mrs Rathmell.'

'Damn. Give her a call, will you? Ask her to be here as early as she can tomorrow. Say no later than 8.30. I've a change of plan. I want her along with me to do the search.'

Pearce's face fell. 'I thought you wanted me to do that?'

'I've got another job for you. I want you to get something for me. And I want it ready by lunchtime. Then we're all going through to Netherdale.'

Nash was quiet throughout the meal. Becky watched him. He offered little in the way of conversation and seemed preoccupied. 'Are you thinking about what happened today? You couldn't have prevented it, you know. And a lot of people would say that if you couldn't get them for the murders they committed, what Vickers did was a kind of justice.'

'I realize that. It doesn't make me feel any better though. But I wasn't thinking about today, actually. I'm more concerned with tomorrow.'

'Why? What's going on tomorrow?'

Nash told her. As he spoke her eyes widened. 'There's something I want you to do for me. A couple of things actually.'

'I'll do whatever I can.'

Nash explained. 'First of all, I want you to be available tomorrow afternoon. Can you do that?'

'What time?'

'Say, around one o'clock. It may take the rest of the day though.'

'OK. What else?'

'Bring those photos you took the other night. The ones at the Westlea riot.'

'No problem, I've got them here. Is that it?'

'Er, almost. I wonder if you'd mind making a phone call for me? Here's what I want you to say.'

It was almost ten o'clock when they finished eating. 'I'd better get off,' Nash told her. 'Not that I want to seem ungrateful. It was a great risotto. Thank you, Becks, much better than a takeaway, or an apple. But if I don't go soon I'll be asleep on my feet, and I'll be good for nothing in the morning.'

She walked to the door with him and smiled. 'Go on, get yourself off and get a good night's sleep.'

'Just one thing before I go.' He reached forward and kissed her.

She felt the desire in his embrace, the longing and the passion. She knew she could respond. She pushed him away. 'Go home to bed.'

He reached for her again. 'I'd rather stay here and go to bed.'

'Maybe, but you're not. Not with what you've got to do tomorrow.'

'Spoilsport.'

'Good night, Mike.'

Nash's first impression of Vanessa Rathmell was of coldness. She was in her mid fifties, he guessed. Her hair was bleached blonde, but the effect was more mousey than striking. Her figure would be called slim by anyone with tact. Scrawny by someone striving for accuracy. Her blue eyes stared at Nash with chilling hostility.

'Why do you insist on searching my house? Isn't it enough that my husband has been murdered, without putting me through this ordeal? Why are you not concentrating on catching the perpetrators? No doubt some enemies of my husband – possibly one of those migrants.'

Generations of landowning quasi-aristocracy had left her with the undoubted notion that when she spoke, others should obey. Her nasal tones betrayed her though, the overall impression being more of whining self-pity. There was certainly little sign of grief.

Nash opted for shock tactics. 'We already have the person responsible in custody. And it wasn't a politically motivated crime. Your husband's body was discovered close to that of the woman who'd been his mistress for over fifteen years. The man who killed them did so as an act of revenge. You see, Mrs Rathmell' – Nash leaned forward slightly – 'he learned that your husband and his mistress murdered the woman's daughter to keep their affair secret. More recently they murdered a journalist for the same reason. Would you like to know what the murder weapon was?' He didn't give her time to answer. 'It was a length of piano wire. Wire bought from the music shop in town. Bought by you, Mrs Rathmell.'

Nash pressed home his advantage. 'The reason we intend to search this house is that we have evidence your husband was behind the violence that has left at least six people dead. Others were involved in the plot, but your husband was the ringleader. We're here to find proof of the involvement of others. Now, I've a busy day ahead, Mrs Rathmell, so we'll start with his study. If we find what we're looking for there, we might not need to search the rest of the house. We'll try to keep disruption to a minimum.'

Nash nodded to Lisa. 'Get the rest of the team inside, will you?' He signalled towards the room they'd just left. 'I want the forensic boys to check that piano and see if any of the strings have been replaced recently. I don't want anything left to chance. I'll be in Rathmell's study.'

When Andrews returned she brought four of the team with her. 'The others are on with the piano. Where do you want me to start?'

'The desk,' Nash said. 'I've unlocked it. I'm going to concentrate on the safe.'

Within an hour, they had what they wanted. Nash studied the documents keenly. Lisa watched his expression change to one Mironova would have recognized. Nash the hunter: remorseless and dedicated.

Nash was back at Helmsdale station before 1 p.m. Pearce was reading the early edition of the *Netherdale Gazette*. 'Tomorrow's will be even more dramatic,' Nash told him. 'Did you get what I asked for?'

'Yes, but it was a bit of a struggle. I don't think I'd have stood a chance but for the backup.'

'Right, be ready in five minutes. I've a phone call to make before we go.'

Nash got through to the *Gazette*. 'Becks, we're setting off. We'll meet you at Netherdale nick, in the car park.'

Outside, Nash tossed Pearce the keys. 'You drive. I want to collect something from home.' When they reached his flat, Nash went inside. A few minutes later Pearce stared in astonishment at the object in Nash's hand. Lisa, on the other hand, showed no surprise.

They pulled into Netherdale police station yard a few minutes before 2 p.m. Becky Pollard sauntered over. 'Everything set up?' Nash asked her.

'Just as you asked,' Becky replied. She tapped a slim document case. 'I've brought the stuff, and made the phone call.'

'Right, let's get on with it.'

Inside, Nash paused to talk to Binns. 'Everything OK, Jack?'

Binns nodded. 'I had a phone call from the ward half an hour ago. Tom's off the critical list. They reckon he should make a full recovery.'

'That's great news. And the other matter?'

'All in hand. Come with me.'

DCC King was seated at his desk, Crawley opposite him. Nash entered without knocking, leaving the door open behind him. 'Nash! How dare you burst into my office?'

'I thought you wanted to see me,' Nash spoke quietly.

'I need an explanation. You allowed Vickers to escape. He killed an innocent woman and a highly respected member of the European Parliament. A man who has served this community unstintingly for over a decade. You'll be lucky to keep your job, Nash. And I, for one, will be glad to see you go. You're a disgrace to the force.'

'You never let facts get in your way, do you?' Nash was as calm as King was heated. 'Vickers didn't escape. He was a free man. Nobody could have stopped him going to Helm Woods. I agree he killed Rathmell and Gemma Fletcher. But she certainly wasn't innocent. Nor was Rathmell the selfless public servant you make him out to be. On the other hand, they were a couple of ruthless and cold-blooded murderers, who'll be no loss to the community.'

King tried to intervene, but Nash wasn't to be denied. The adjoining office door on Nash's left opened softly. Gloria O'Donnell entered, unnoticed by everyone.

'They certainly committed two murders themselves. They killed Stacey Fletcher: the crime for which Vickers was convicted. More recently, they murdered the journalist Tucker. In addition Rathmell organized a spate of violence around Helmsdale that resulted in the deaths of at least another six people.'

'This is a catalogue of rubbish. You're just trying to protect your job. You have absolutely no proof.'

Nash allowed King to rage on. When he stopped, Nash beckoned Lisa. She handed him a slim file. 'This is Jake Fletcher's statement,' Nash said. 'In it he describes a series of meetings at which the campaign of violence was planned.'

King, from being almost purple, had gone deathly white. 'What credence can you put on the unsupported testimony of a hardened criminal?'

'Fletcher's reputation is certainly not the best,' Nash agreed, 'but to describe him as a hardened criminal isn't right. He's never been convicted of anything more serious than a series of motoring offences. But I felt sure you'd not take Fletcher's word alone, so I unearthed other supporting evidence.'

Nash held up a box. 'This is a collection of tape recordings Rathmell made. They were in his safe at Houlston Grange. Effectively, they're the minutes of those meetings I mentioned. They're all neatly labelled with times and dates. They're very enlightening to listen to. Especially when we look at other evidence connected to the violence.'

'I've had enough of this. Get out of my office. You're suspended from duty forthwith, pending an investigation into your conduct. Hand in your warrant card and pistol to Inspector Crawley and leave this rubbish here. The rest of you, clear out.'

'Nice try, King,' Nash said calmly. 'Jack, do your bit, will you?'

Binns stepped forward. 'Martin James King, I am placing you under arrest for conspiracy to commit murder, arson and foment civil disorder. You are cautioned that anything you say ...'

'I take it you can prove all this, Mike?' The interruption was spoken so quietly the other occupants in the room were shocked to see the chief constable standing in the corner.

'I can indeed, ma'am. The first incident refers to the fire at the Hassan flat. DCC King ordered a rapid response unit to Helmsdale with specific instructions to protect the fire brigade who were coming under attack from an unruly mob.'

'I don't see the significance.'

Nash fished into his file. 'This is a copy of the station log recording the request for the RRU. Attached to it is the record of the 999 call made to the fire brigade. Unless DCC King is clairvoyant, I fail to see how he ordered the unit to Helmsdale five minutes before the emergency call was made.'

'I see,' the chief breathed. 'I take it there's more?'

'Yes, ma'am. These photos were taken by DC Andrews. They clearly show Jake Fletcher and King with Rathmell in his study. You will note the date and time shown on the corner of the photo.' Nash fumbled with the box of tapes and extracted one. 'This is a tape recording of that meeting. In it, the trio are planning an arson attack and riot. Jake Fletcher's statement confirms that the incident on the industrial estate that same evening resulted from that meeting. Rathmell was meticulous to the extreme. The dates and times are written on each cassette. On another tape they are discussing the disposal of Councillor Appleyard. Appleyard was beginning to get cold feet about the violence. Rathmell decided to have him killed. He said it would do the cause good to have a martyr. You can hear the others laughing at the joke. DC Pearce and I witnessed King at Houlston Grange that afternoon.'

He slid the tape into the cassette player he'd brought and pressed play. After a few minutes he switched the machine off.

'That would seem to be conclusive.' O'Donnell looked at her deputy as if he was something unpleasant she'd just stepped in. 'Take him away, Sergeant.'

Binns led the unresisting prisoner from the room. 'Well done, Mike. I'm glad that's over.'

'But it isn't, ma'am.'

'What! Surely that's everything wrapped up?'

'Not quite. There was the incident of the arson attack on the industrial estate. Becks, the photos, please?'

Becky handed Nash a sheaf of photos. 'Again, these are dated and timed. They show the officers from Netherdale quite clearly. Those officers arrived at the scene before I did. Before the uniformed men from Helmsdale. Tom Pratt, who learned of the riot by normal means, was twenty minutes after them. The incident even got onto Helm Radio before I arrived.'

'Wasn't King responsible for that as well?'

'He couldn't have been. He was away at the same conference as you. However, King's right-hand man was here, and was on duty, and did ring Helm Radio. The station requires identification before they accept a news story like that. They confirm it was Crawley who made the call. In addition, the incident room log shows the time Crawley despatched the team to Helmsdale. Again it was before the request for assistance came in.'

Nash looked at Pearce, who stepped forward. O'Donnell nodded, and Pearce administered the caution. The chief watched Crawley being taken from the room followed by the others. She turned to look at Nash. 'I hardly dare ask …'

'That's it this time, ma'am.'

'Thank goodness for that. Better get this evidence logged safely and have transcripts of those tapes made. I want to see everything before we submit details to the CPS. I'll also have to inform HM Inspector of Constabulary and the Police Complaints Commission.

You've just dropped a whole tool box into the works, I hope you realize that. Now, as you're the most senior officer remaining ...' she corrected herself, 'The only senior officer remaining, you'll have to take immediate charge here. I'll have to see what the long-term prognosis on Superintendent Pratt is before any decisions are made for the future.'

'That's alright, ma'am, as long as I can have the rest of the day free. I'll start tomorrow.'

'Any particular reason?'

'Yes. I intend to take your goddaughter out for dinner.'

It was Nash's turn to choose. He opted for La Giaconda. 'The owner might act a bit funny, but the food's terrific.'

'Why might he be funny?'

'I, er, well, I was dating his sister.'

'I see. He won't poison the lasagne, will he?'

'No, hopefully not.'

'But he might not like it, seeing me with you?'

'I don't care what he thinks.' Nash took her hand. 'You're with me. That's all that matters.'

He felt her hand quiver slightly in his. At the time he wasn't sure why.

Over the meal they kept the conversation light. At one point, however, Becky asked, 'What will happen to Vickers? Will he go back to gaol? It doesn't seem fair if it turns out like that. Not after what they did; and what he suffered because of them.'

Nash shook his head. 'We'll prepare the paperwork and send it to CPS, but I doubt if anything will come of it. Once the doctors finish examining Vickers, I think they'll report that he's unfit to plead. Effectively, he'll be locked away in a secure mental unit for the rest of his life. A rotten end to what's been a rotten case.'

'Speaking of which, I was handed a lousy job this morning too. I had to go through JT's files and stuff, clear his desk out and everything.'

Nash sympathized. 'Not the most pleasant task.'

'One file was interesting, though.' Becky fumbled in her handbag. 'JT labelled it "to follow up". It was a collection of unsolved mysteries. This was the one that intrigued me.' She passed over a newspaper cutting.

Nash looked at it. It was the report of an inquest into the death of an unidentified woman. The findings were not so much inconclusive as non-existent. Not only had the police been unable to find any clue as to the woman's identity, but the cause of death couldn't be established because of the condition of the corpse. It was the note Tucker had made in the margin that intrigued Nash.

'Well, well, well,' he said eventually.

'You see why it interested me?'

'I do indeed. But I can't see what could be done about it after all this time.'

Becky smiled. 'You never know – something might turn up.'

It was a light-hearted comment, more of a joke than anything. Nash would have cause to remember that later.

As the evening wore on, Nash became aware that he'd had too much to drink, and that Becky was in little better condition.

'I'd better get you a taxi,' he said, when he'd paid the bill and they were heading for the door.

'It's a nice night. Let's walk.'

'Are you sure? It's a long way to your place.'

'Your flat's nearer.' Her eyes sparkled as she slid her arm through his.

Nash looked at her and smiled. He looked again and his smile broadened. 'Oh. Oh, alright, then.'

Pearce was checking the tape transcripts next morning when Mironova walked in. 'You look well. Good holiday?' he asked.

'Great. We went camping in the Lake District. No radio, no telly, no newspapers or mobile phones. I didn't want to come back.' She sat at her desk and sighed. 'Anything interesting happened while I've been away?'